HALF THE SUMMER'S NIGHT

A SLASHER ROMANCE

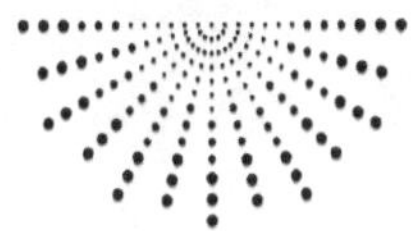

ROSE BITTERLY

A NOTE FROM THE AUTHOR

Thanks so much for picking up *Half the Summer's Night!* This is a dark horror romance featuring a murderous, morally black MMC. It also deals with themes of trauma, assault, and abuse.

As you might expect, it contains some potentially upsetting material.

Because a certain online bookseller has a history of removing books with comprehensive content warnings, I have opted to put the full, detailed list of content notes on my website, which you can access at rosebitterly.com/content-notes or via the QR code below.

Once you're on the site, just click or tap on the book's title to expand the full list of warnings.

However, there are a few triggers that I did want to list here:

- Graphic depictions of sex and violence
- Misogyny, including misogynistic slurs and misogyny-motivated murder (not by the MMC)
- The MMC's backstory involves childhood abuse from his caregivers
- The FMC's backstory involves sexual assault, which is depicted (not in graphic detail) in flashbacks

If you have any questions or would like further clarification, don't hesitate to contact me through the email on my website.

-Rose Bitterly

PROLOGUE

ROWAN

TEN YEARS EARLIER

The funeral is packed, like everyone in Rosado showed up to mourn Bobby Spencer's death, plus people from the surrounding counties, too. I don't really know why. He was an asshole in life, just like all of my uncle's various business associates.

I don't like being around so many people. They crowd into Hatch Street Funeral Parlor, the only funeral home in town, speaking in soft, hushed tones. The only reason I haven't tried to sneak out the side door is because Uncle Nash won't let me out of his sight. I guess it's kind of dangerous for me to be here, since I'm the one who killed Mr. Spencer three days ago.

"Such a tragedy, isn't it?" An older woman dabs mascara away from her eyes, leaving black marks on her handkerchief. "I suppose it's a reminder to all of us how dangerous that equipment can be."

"I know," Uncle Nash says consolingly, like he wasn't the one to send me to Mr. Spencer's ranch outside of town. *He,* of course, had been at a reception put on by the Rosado Chamber of Commerce, drinking champagne and getting his picture taken. Probably this lady had been there, too. She has the look of someone with money. "But ranching's dangerous work. Bobby knew that."

I press into the wall, wishing I could just get smaller and smaller until I disappeared entirely. Which is a stupid thing for a guy like me to think, given that I tower over most of the people here. I hate how big I am. I feel like it makes me stand out when all I want is to blend in, to go unnoticed.

The woman sniffles, although it sounds fake, and asks Uncle Nash something about how reservations are going at the Palm Breeze Hotel, which is one of the many businesses, illegal and not, that Uncle Nash operates across south Texas.

People mill around us, ebbing and flowing like the sea. A group of them drifts away, revealing the open casket at the front of the room. Uncle Nash always insists that I leave my targets recognizable. *More strategic that way,* he says. *Don't want to drag out any investigations unnecessarily.* It was tough with Mr. Spencer, though. I'd never driven a tractor before.

And then I see her. Abilene Snow.

She's standing beside the big spray of flowers displayed behind the casket, wearing a simple black dress, her dark hair swept up into a bun. She has her glasses on today, huge over-sized cat-eye frames that make her eyes seem even bigger and bluer than they do normally. She blinks out at the crowd, and I jerk my gaze away before she sees me staring.

Uncle Nash clears his throat. The rich lady is gone.

"You need to pay your respects," he says softly.

I stiffen. I understand why he's doing this. It's all a cover because Mr. Spencer is more respectable than the men I usually kill for Uncle Nash, most of whom are drug dealers and orga-nized criminals who double-cross him. Well, Mr. Spencer double-crossed him, too, I guess. Bought some property that Uncle Nash wanted.

"Go on," he says, a warning note in his voice. I don't think any of the people here would recognize it, though. To them, Uncle Nash is Nash Deegan, the richest man in Rosado. He owns half the properties on the beachfront. Mr. Spencer was trying to own the other half, which I guess is why he had to go.

I peel myself away from the wall and weave through the crowd, keeping my gaze fixed on the casket. I can feel Abilene Snow's presence, sweet and intoxicating. This is the closest I've been to her since she moved to town, trailing rumors of death.

I stop next to the casket. There's a sharp, clinical scent on the air, although Mr. Snow, the funeral director, tried to mask it with the flowers. Or maybe that's just Abilene's scent. She always smells sweet. I watch her sometimes, when she's tending to the graveyard or going for walks along the beach. Trying to work up the nerve to talk to her.

Mr. Spencer is dead. He looks better than he did when I left him, though, like a wax figure instead of a corpse. Only the top half of the casket is open, which makes sense because I completely mangled him from the waist down with one of his tractors.

The memory makes me feel hot and distracted. I enjoyed it, the way I always enjoy killing for Uncle Nash. There's something wrong with me, something so deep-rooted and choking that sometimes I feel like it might strangle me whole.

"How did you know the deceased?"

The voice is soft and musical, like church bells, but it floods me with panic because it belongs to Abilene. I jerk my head up and find her looking at me, which freezes me in place. I don't think she's ever looked at me before. When I watch her around town, I make sure she can't see me.

Well, she's seeing me now.

"I, um. Uh." I've forgotten how to talk. Abilene watches me, waiting. I have to say something. "My, um, my uncle—"

"Don't bother her, Rowan." Uncle Nash's voice is pleasant enough, but I hear the sharpness underneath it. "Ms. Snow is busy with the other guests."

"Oh, he's not being a bother." Abilene smiles up at Uncle Nash, although it's the forced smile that people use when they're at work. She flicks her eyes over to me, and my whole body shudders under her gaze. I'm not used to it, having her eyes on me. "I just want to make sure everyone's comfortable."

"We're fine. Aren't we, Rowan?" Uncle Nash puts his hand on my shoulder and squeezes.

"Yes," I say quickly, my heart thundering. She's so beautiful up close, and I want to keep staring at her, memorizing every soft line of her face and sweeping curve of her body so I can think about them later.

"Of course, sir." Abilene smiles at Uncle Nash again, thin and flimsy.

Then she smiles at me, and it's brighter. Genuine. I smell something like the wild, lemony scent of the lantana that grows around Uncle Nash's big, sprawling mansion in the center of town, and Abilene's eyes sparkle a little as she looks up at me.

Then someone calls out Abilene's name. Mr. Snow, the mortician. Abilene's uncle, who's been taking care of her ever since she moved to Rosado last year. That's one of the things we have in common, that we're both being raised by our uncles.

The other thing is that we've both killed someone.

Abilene's smile turns apologetic, and she gives us—me?—a shy little wave before ducking over to her own uncle, who's almost as tall as I am but much more gangly. He also seems kind. Kinder than Uncle Nash, anyway.

"Don't bother people," Uncle Nash says harshly, his hand still squeezing my shoulder as he pulls me away from the casket.

He's angry. I can feel his anger radiating off him like heat, and I know I fucked up.

Because he didn't know I knew about Abilene Snow, the girl who killed a football player in Magnolia, two towns over. The one girl in this world who might not think I'm a monster. Now he does.

And he's not going to let me near her ever again.

WHEN WE GET BACK HOME after the funeral, Uncle Nash throws his arm over my shoulder, stopping me from going upstairs to my bedroom. I'm still thinking about Abilene Snow, like I've been doing for the last hour, sneaking tiny little glances at her during the burial service. She hung back during most of it, waiting beneath a sprawling pecan tree beside her uncle, watching everything with a clear, pleasant expression.

"Where do you think you're going?" Uncle Nash says cheerfully, although he presses hard on the side of my neck, reminding me who's really in charge.

"Upstairs," I mutter.

"Nah." He pulls me sideways, out of the foyer and into the living room. I stumble along with him, not fighting back. Fighting back gets me punished. "Nah, you're going to have a celebratory drink with me."

He pushes me down on the sofa and ambles over to the wet bar set into the wall, glass clinking as he takes down a decanter of whiskey. "That motherfucker's finally dead," he says as he pours the drinks. I watch him and don't say anything. I know from experience that when he gets like this, it's better to just go along with him. Take the drink. Smile at his stupid jokes. He'll get bored of me eventually, and I can go hide away in my bedroom until he needs me again.

Uncle Nash turns around, holding a glass of whiskey in each

hand. I hate whiskey. Hate alcohol in general, really. "Can you mix it with a Coke?" I ask.

"*Can you mix it with a Coke?*" Uncle Nash repeats in a nasally, mocking voice. "What are you, a girl? No, you'll drink it straight."

He shoves the glass at me, and I stare down at it as he settles into his big leather armchair and kicks out the footrest. He swirls the whiskey around, gazing happily over at the never-used fireplace. "You did good with that one," he says. "Didn't hear a single whisper of foul play at the funeral."

I tilt the glass up so the whiskey presses to my lips, but I don't take a drink. Uncle Nash knocks his back, of course, smacking his lips afterward. Something about the sound makes my skin crawl with a hot, prickling anger.

That's been happening more and more lately with Uncle Nash.

"So why'd you want to go upstairs?" He looks over at me and grins. "Instead of celebrate a job well done?"

"I already celebrated that," I mutter, which is true. Whenever I kill someone particularly important for Uncle Nash, he'll arrange for a woman to spend the night with me afterward. The one he got as a thank you for Mr. Spencer had obviously been someone expensive. She was as beautiful as a movie star and smiled at me like she meant it.

But I still thought about Abilene Snow as I thrust inside her, the way I always do.

Uncle Nash chuckles. "You mean with Evelyn?" He grins. "Yeah, that one cost me a pretty penny. Was she worth it?"

I shift on the couch, the leather creaking. I don't want to talk about this. "She was nice."

I immediately know it was the wrong thing to say, because Uncle Nash howls with laughter, throwing his head back and kicking his legs against the footrest. "*Nice?*" He squawks. "You fucked a thousand-dollar whore and all you can say is that she was *nice?*"

I squeeze my whiskey glass and look down at my lap. "Can I go upstairs now?" I say darkly.

"Why? So you can jack off?"

I jerk my head up. Uncle Nash grins cruelly at me. His glass is already empty.

"No." I say it too quickly. Too defensively.

"I don't understand you, Rowan." He shakes his head and jumps out of the chair and walks back over to the wet bar. I watch him the whole time, stalking him like he's one of the many targets he's given me since my first kill when I was thirteen years old. "You know how many boys your age would kill to fuck someone like Evelyn Landry?"

I remember how Evelyn slid the straps of her dress off her shoulders in front of the open window facing the ocean. We'd been at the hotel, not here, the way it always is when Uncle Nash gets me a woman. But all I could think about as I watched her undress was Abilene. How Abilene's bare skin would look under the full moonlight, how Abilene would move through the salt-kissed air as she walked up to me, waiting for her on the bed.

"Your own personal porn star," Uncle Nash continues, walking back over to his chair with another glass of whiskey, this one much fuller than the first. "And you didn't even appreciate it."

The living room is cavernous, but it feels like the walls are squeezing in around me. Uncle Nash is too close, and I swear I can hear his body working. His blood beating, his lungs expanding. It's too much noise.

I want silence.

"What do you want from me?" he asks, settling back down in his chair. "I reward you for your work, just like I do everyone else under my employ."

He's talking about Evelyn. He's never paid me anything. I'm his personal guard dog, one he raised from a puppy to be loyal to him.

"I know." Uncle Nash snaps his fingers, like he's just had a revelation. He leans forward, his eyes boring into mine. As much as he's acting like this is some genial, friendly celebration, the menace is more than clear. "It's that girl that you want, isn't it?"

Every atom in my body lights up.

"Abilene Snow." Uncle Nash rolls her name around on his tongue, and I want to rip it out. He doesn't deserve to say her name. "Pretty enough. Too big for my tastes, though."

I stare at him, trembling. Now it's my own blood I hear rushing through my veins, boiling for a—

For a kill.

"What is it about her?" He leans forward in his chair. I'm perfectly still, clutching my undrunk whiskey in one hand, watching him like I watch a target. Uncle Nash's eyes glint with a hard, knowing cruelty. "It's because you've heard the rumors, isn't it?" He grins the way he does whenever he's watching me punish someone for him. "You think she's like you?"

My ears buzz. I squeeze the whiskey glass, targeting all my hot, concentrated rage into my fist in hopes that Uncle Nash won't see how upset I am. Because if he knows I'm upset, he'll use it against me.

"That *is* it." Uncle Nash laughs with a cruel delight. "You think because everyone says she killed that football player that she'll be okay with you? With what you are?"

I suck in my breath, all my senses zeroed in on Uncle Nash. I can see his blood pumping through his neck. A target. He's a target.

"Oh, Rowan, Rowan, Rowan." He says my name like I'm a little baby, too young to know anything. "You can't listen to rumors. That boy's death was an accident. Abilene Snow isn't going to love you." His eyes glint. "Just like your mother couldn't love you."

The whiskey glass explodes in my hand, glass and alcohol exploding outward like a star. A hunk of glass embeds in my palm, the pain electrifying me. Uncle Nash jumps.

And, just for a second, fear flickers across his face.

That fear catches on something inside me. The part of me that's broken. The part of me that isn't just a killer but *loves* killing. The part of me that, no matter how much I tell myself otherwise, would destroy Abilene Snow if I ever got too close to her.

Just like I'm going to destroy Uncle Nash.

It happens fast. Faster than it usually does. I leap to my feet and then slam into Uncle Nash, so hard that the chair tilts back and we both fly backward. At the same time, I swipe the glass still trapped in my palm across his throat, severing that vein I could feel pumping across the room.

His blood gushes out like a fountain, drenching my face in heat and life. But that's nothing compared to his confused, betrayed expression, to the satisfying way he opens and closes his mouth like a dying fish as he stares up at me.

My name. He's trying to say my name. But I think I've severed his vocal cords. I snapped something when I sliced his throat, and I can see it wriggling as he works his jaw.

I stand up and pull the glass out of my palm and toss it aside. My cock is uncomfortably hard from all the blood, and I wonder if Uncle Nash sees it, how much I like finally murdering him after ten years.

I've wanted to do this since I was eight fucking years old. Since I came to live here after my mother told me she never wanted to see me again.

Uncle Nash makes a wet rattling sound, the last of his breath escaping from his body. I'm acting on instinct now.

Instinct and training. I pick him up, so taut with adrenaline that it's like he weighs nothing.

Then I hurl him through the big picture window that looks out at his pristine swimming pool and professionally landscaped yard. Like Bobby Spencer, Uncle Nash will die from a terrible accident. He was drinking. He slipped and fell through the glass.

And now, after a decade of his abuse, I'm finally free.

1

ABI

My latest assignment arrives after lunch, right as I'm rinsing off my dishes. The chime ripples from the back of the house, soft and reassuring.

A body is here.

I got the details from the sheriff's department this morning —an accidental death at the Palm Breeze Hotel. A tourist from Oklahoma slipped in the shower and hit his head and bled out. One of the maids found him when she came in to clean. Another accidental death.

There are a lot of accidental deaths in Rosado.

The bell chimes again, and I wipe my hands and step into the funeral parlor, which takes up the entire downstairs save for the kitchen. Everything down here is tastefully decorated in sleek, midcentury furniture and muted colors. I don't hold funerals these days, not since Uncle Vic died. He loved being a mortician: meeting with the bereaved, walking them through the funeral process with his soft, even voice. Me, not so much. I'd rather work with the dead than the living, which is why I got a graduate degree in forensic science and finagled my way into the county coroner position two years ago instead.

Still, I can't bear to close up shop completely. So I keep everything how it was and do my coroner work out of the same space in the back of the house where Uncle Victor would spend hours preparing the deceased for their casket viewings.

I'm in that space now, and I heave up the big garage door that opens to the back driveway. Hector's waiting for me, leaning up against the refrigerated truck while he pulls on a silver vape pen. He lifts his hand in greeting, eyes squinted against the sun.

"You ready for him?" he asks, tilting his head toward the truck.

"Yeah, of course." I have the same anxious, prickly feeling that I've been fighting all day, ever since the call from Deputy Molinas. I held my tongue when he was going over the details, because I could tell from the clipped way he spoke that Sheriff Kaplan had told him not to entertain any of my *theories*.

Hector tucks his vape pen away and slides the body bag containing the deceased out onto a stretcher. "So what did it look like?" I say, swallowing against my dry throat. "When you picked him up?"

Hector glances at me. He knows my theories, too, and he's more willing to entertain them than Sheriff Kaplan.

"Normal," he says. "It was an accident, Abi. The tub was coated in soap scum, and the guy was older. Probably didn't have good balance."

I breathe out. I want him to be right, I do. But there have been *so* many accidental deaths in Rosado, even before I landed the role of county coroner. Uncle Vic noticed them, too. *A lot of people die badly here*, he told me once, the summer before I left for college. *I'm glad you're getting out.*

Of course, I didn't stay out. I couldn't. Not when the only other choice was to sell Hatch Street Funeral Home to one of the big funeral corporations after Uncle Vic got his cancer diagnosis. I couldn't stand to see that happen. So here I am, back in Rosado.

I follow Hector as he pushes the deceased down the hallway and into the examination room. Once everything's situated, I unzip the body bag and get my first real look at him.

Marcus Nielson. That's the name on the identification tag, scrawled out in Hector's messy hand. Mr. Nielson is older—maybe his sixties, although he looks strong for his age. The back of his head is a mess of bone fragments and brain matter, but the rest of him seems unharmed.

It does, at first glance, look like an accident.

"Thanks, Hector," I say. "I can take it from here."

He gives me a two-fingered salute. "Don't go chasing rabbits, girl," he says, heading back into the hallway. "It's just an accident. Accidents happen."

I don't say anything. *Accidents happen.* More than anyone else, I know how that isn't necessarily true.

That's an old hurt, though, one that I've managed to more or less work through, and I've got more important things to focus on today. Like Marcus Nielson.

"All right, Mr. Nielson," I tell him, snapping on my gloves. "Let's see what you can tell me."

The steps of the exam are second nature at this point. I take some photos. I record my initial observations. I tilt Mr. Nielson's head sideways to get a look at the injury site. According to the report the sheriff's office sent over, he was found slumped on the floor, the back of his head against the rim of the toilet. I click through the photos of the crime scene. Blood splatters outward around the toilet, in line with the trajectory of the fall. It does indeed look like his cause of death was blunt force trauma to the back of his head, and a slip and fall in the shower would be sufficient for that to happen.

So why do I have the distracting, persistent thought that it's more than that?

I continue my external examination, running my gloved hands over his arms, lifting his limp hands and turning them over to examine his knuckles. No bruises, no cuts. No sign of a struggle. A slip and fall, like Hector said. Or a heart attack, massive enough that he toppled through the shower curtain and hit his head before he could call for help. The internal exam will let me for sure.

But I keep looking, combing over every inch of his smooth, waxy skin. It's almost a compulsion at this point whenever an accidental death comes in. Because so many of them carry a very specific mark.

My breath tightens as I work lower down Mr. Nielson's body. I still haven't found anything. The mark, when it appears, is always small. Imperceptible. Something that could be explained away a million different ways if I didn't keep finding them in the two years that I've been back in Rosado.

I lift Mr. Nielson's leg, feeling my way down his calf with my gloved hand. There are a few cuts and scrapes, but nothing with the intentionality of what I'm looking for. What I'm certain is a sinister pattern, even if Sheriff Kaplan thinks I'm just being hysterical. His word, of course.

And then I get to Mr. Nielson's ankle.

It would be easy to miss at first—another minor cut just above the lateral malleolus on his left foot. But when I tilt his foot into the light, my breath catches in my chest.

It's a cut, very tiny and very precise. At first glance, it looks like the others I passed over. But there's something about this one that makes me reach for my big magnifying glass. And then, like that, the thick lens reveals the secret:

The letter **R**.

I stare down at it, taking deep, steady breaths even as a chill ripples down my spine.

"Who did this to you, Mr. Nielson?" I breathe out.

He doesn't answer.

I take a picture of the **R**, even though I know Sheriff Kaplan won't give a shit. He was the one person who opposed my appointment to the county coroner position, and I know damn well it's because of what happened when I was sixteen. Taking this to him will do nothing. But I'll still include it in my report, and I'll add the information to my own research.

Because I don't care if Kaplan thinks I'm some hysterical teenage girl instead of an adult woman with the training and education to do my job. It's clear to me that all these accidental deaths in Rosado aren't accidental at all. I think there's a killer stalking along our windswept beachfront.

And I think he's trying to send a message.

I STICK a red pin in my map of Rosado County, right along the beachfront where the Palm Breeze Hotel is located. It has a little flag on it, too, with the letter *R*.

Then I step back and look at everything, my arms crossed tight over my chest. There are nineteen pins total, all scattered across Rosado. Seven of them are red, each with its own letter attached. Seven bodies that came into my examination room with a tiny letter carved somewhere on them.

Right now, they spell out **YOURDAR**. And with the way they're arranged on the map, it's really more like **YOUR DAR**.

I rub my hands over my arms, chasing away the chill in the office next to my examination room, where I've set up my makeshift investigation. The air is always chilly in here, but I don't think it's just the AC that's making my skin prickle with goosebumps.

The first marked body showed up about a month after my coroner appointment. It had been a tourist death, a college student here for spring break. He'd been drinking all day and took a Jet Ski out on the water after dark. They found his body lying in the surf the next morning, cuts across his face and his lungs filled with water. An accident, obviously.

But I still found that tiny, intentional **Y**, freshly carved into the skin of his hip. After death.

Kaplan told me I was being absurd. *I don't know how they do things up in Virginia*, he said. *But you need to keep this foolishness out of your reports if you want* this *community to take you seriously*.

He stressed the word *this*, as if Rosado weren't my community, too.

The worst part was that I could tell Uncle Vic agreed with him, even if he wouldn't come out and say it. He just told me I shouldn't rock the boat, not if I wanted to hold on to my position. That people here have long memories. So I set it aside.

Until another accidental death came in, a few months later. A car collision on the beach highway. And I found a tiny carved **O** on the woman's wrist.

And they keep happening, these marked deaths. All of them get ruled as accidents. All of them *look* like accidents in every way except for those tiny letters carved into the victim's skin.

I started mapping them after Uncle Vic died. I'm sure my grief had something to do with it—I was drowning in it, and I don't have friends here in Rosado. My parents don't talk to me anymore. All I had was him, and then he was gone.

That was also around the time I started looking into strange deaths from before I came back. I found twelve that seemed similar to the ones with the carved letters—tourists, usually, or people passing through. All had been ruled accidents or suicides by the authorities. All were gruesome, though. Bloody. Disturbing.

I couldn't say it was a particularly scientific process, identifying them and throwing them up on the map. Just a hunch. A sense that they belonged with the others. I added the location of those accidents to my map, too, marking them with white pins instead of red.

I slump back against my wall, studying the map, trying to find a pattern. The red pins, with their accompanying letters, string along like Christmas lights. Or like a sentence.

YOUR DAR—

Your darling? Your darkness? Your Darwin? Possibilities buzz through my head, but none of them actually tell me anything.

I think of poor Mr. Nielson, currently resting in his cubby in the cold locker. I'm sure the sheriff's department has already told his family that there was an accident, and my report will only corroborate that. Because I *didn't* see any sign that he was killed, other than that cruel, vicious **R**. A calling card from a killer who knows how to make his deaths look unintentional.

It's not fair. Not to the victims. Not to the families. And I know I'm not really helping them, pinning these deaths to this map. I just wish I had something more, something substantial. Something that even Kaplan couldn't ignore.

I step closer to the map, sweeping my gaze over the locations of the marked deaths for the millionth time. They seem random, too, although they do run more or less parallel to the water, as if the killer is using the shoreline as a ruler. I've gone to the locations before, but they're usually isolated. An empty parking lot. A boarded-up gas station. A back road. That sort of thing.

There is one thing that's different, though. This is the first time one of the deaths has been in such a public place. A hotel is swarming with people, especially this time of year. Maybe someone saw something.

My breath quickens. Do I have the guts to investigate on my own? Kaplan will be furious if he hears I've been sniffing around during my off hours, but it's not like he can really *do* anything about it. He doesn't fucking employ me. The county does.

And I do know Palm Breeze Hotel well. It's one of the prettier ones on the beachfront, and when I walk the beach during the off-season, I usually make sure to pass it by. It was built back in the '60s, and it still has that midcentury charm, with its white stucco walls and cerulean trim. Plus, unlike most of the newer hotels, the owner is from Rosado. He still lives here, too, from what I understand. So he might be more willing to help.

I duck out of the office, my breath quickening in my chest as I close and lock up the door. Am I really going to do this?

Yes, I am. I owe it to Mr. Nielson. To all of the other victims.

Someone has to find their killer.

2

ROWAN

*R**ap rap rap.**

I look up from my computer and frown at my closed office door just in time for it to swing open. Julia, my most reliable front desk clerk, sticks her head in. "Hey, boss," she says. "There's a lady here to see you."

I blink at Julia. She has a somber look on her face, which makes me think this is about yesterday's death. Mr. Marcus Nielson, from Stillwater, Oklahoma. Room 409. Surprisingly strong for a man his age, even if I did have the element of surprise.

"Who?" I say, keeping my breath calm. "Is it the police again?"

Julia hesitates. "I don't think so," she finally says. "She just asked if she could talk with you about—" She swallows, her throat bobbing. "You know."

So I guessed right, it seems. I knew this would be a challenging one, having a death so close to my hotel. But I have a message planned, something I very much want to say, and unfortunately, the Palm Breeze Hotel was the only place I could say it.

19

A risk I was willing to take. Especially for Abilene Snow.

"Is she a reporter?" I ask.

"Maybe?" Julia shrugs. "Do you want me to ask?"

I consider it briefly. No, better to just talk to her, whoever she is, and get this over with. The sooner everyone—from the Rosado police to the insurance company to Mr. Nielson's steely-faced daughter, his only next of kin—understands that this was just a terrible, terrible accident, the sooner we can move on, and I can start planning my next kill.

"Rowan?" Julian prompts.

I blink, forcing myself to focus. "No, just send her in. I guess you didn't get her name?"

Julia shakes her head, and I wave her away and slump back in my chair, staring at my darkened computer screen and the scatter of papers across my desk. Uncle Nash left me one thing in his will: the Palm Breeze Hotel, his most profitable property, which is how I became a hotelier at the age of eighteen. All his other riches—the mansion on Aransas Street, the other hotels and restaurants along the beachfront, the millions in his bank account—were distributed among the various business partners and girlfriends he had accumulated before I threw him through that window ten years ago. I didn't mind, though. I hadn't killed him to get his money.

Another knock at the door, even though Julia had left it hanging open. I glance up, rearranging my expression to look like the hapless hotelier everyone needs to think I am.

Except I find Abilene Snow standing in the doorway.

My whole body goes rigid, and for a moment, all I can hear is the frantic pounding of my heart in my ears. *She knows it's me*, I think, and the idea terrifies me more than I expect. After all, isn't that why I started all this up two years ago? Because it was the only way I could conjure up the strength to talk to her? To get her attention?

Well, I have her attention now. Her blue eyes are fixed on

me from behind her glasses, and I think I may have forgotten how to breathe.

"You're Rowan Hanover?" she says, a hint of surprise in her voice.

I swallow because my mouth is too dry to talk. To buy myself some time, I stand up to greet her. But she keeps staring at me. I have to say something.

"Y-yes," I finally stammer out. *Get a grip*, I tell myself, in that harsh, cold voice that sounds like Uncle Nash. *Don't act suspicious*.

"I'm sorry to bother you," she says. "My name's Abi Snow—"

Abi. She goes by Abi. How did I not know that?

"—And I work as the coroner for Rosado County."

My heart is jackhammering wildly, but I somehow manage to gesture for her to come into my office. When she does, she sweeps her gaze around, her eyes lingering on the framed movie posters I have on the walls.

"How—" My voice comes out shaky and high-pitched. I force myself to focus. "How can I help you, Ms. Snow?"

"Oh, call me Abi." She turns toward me, her face lit up with a pretty smile. "I like those posters, by the way." She nods at the Italian *Blood Raiser 3* poster I bought a few years ago, a lurid painting of the movie's female killer holding a long, sharp knife. She looks a little like Abilene, with her long dark hair and high cheekbones, which is why it's my favorite of the series.

It takes me a second longer to register what the actual Abilene just said to me.

"Thank you." The words come out clearly, thank god. "I, um, I wanted to make my office feel a little more personal."

"I don't blame you." She glides up to my desk, moving with the same elegant grace I admire every time I watch her from afar. Seeing it up close, though—

I can feel myself getting hard. I also feel myself studying everything about her so I can remember it later.

She sinks into the chair across from my desk, and then I sit down, too.

"I love the Blood Raiser movies," she says lightly. "Especially the third one."

I knew this about her already. She watches it every year in the fall, around the time the first cold front blows through. The year her uncle died, she watched the whole series, all eight of them, one after another. I watched them with her, peering in from where I'd perched in the tree that lined up against her upstairs living room, shivering in my thin coat.

"The third one's my favorite, too," I say stiffly, hoping it's what a normal person would say.

Abilene—*Abi*—smiles at that, just for a second. Then it vanishes. "I'm sorry," she says. "I didn't actually come here to talk about movies. I'm just—" She stops, tucks her hair behind her ear. "I wanted to talk about the death that happened here a few days ago."

My chest tightens. With fear or excitement, I don't know. Still, I manage to find the words I know I need to say.

"I already spoke to the police."

Abi blushes, her cheeks turning a lovely shade of red, and for a second, I swear I can smell her blood. My cock strains against my pants, and I shift in my seat, trying to get more comfortable.

"I'm not with the police," she says. "I do work with the Rosado sheriff's department, but I'm not—I'm not really here in an official capacity?"

She turns the last word up like it's a question, and she gives me this kind of sheepish look like she expects me to kick her out of my office. Which of course I would *never* do. Having her so close, having her speak to me, is intoxicating. Even more so now than it was ten years ago at the funeral.

"So why *are* you here?" I say slowly, hoping I can keep the excitement out of my voice.

Abi bites her lower lip, her pretty eyes darting around. She's nervous. Scared, even, although not the kind of scared I'm used to. That's one of the things about me, one of the things that Uncle Nash was so keen to exploit. I can sense what people are feeling. I can sense when they're near, the way a dog can sniff out its quarry.

"I—Look, I don't want to alarm you, or anything." She leans forward, the chair creaking. I grip my own chair's armrests, afraid that if she gets any closer, I won't be able to control myself. "Like I said, I'm the Rosado County coroner. And I've noticed—patterns, I guess you could call them, in some of the bodies I've examined. That's what I want to talk to you about."

My heart is going to erupt out of my chest. *She knows she knows she knows.* The words circle wildly around in my head. Well, maybe she doesn't *know*, but she's seen them. The letters I chose for her and carved into the skin of my victims, small enough to go unnoticed by most. But she noticed them. Just like I hoped she would. No—like I *knew* she would.

Abi's staring at me, waiting for a response.

"Patterns?" I squeak out.

She nods. "It may be nothing, but I saw that same pattern in the most recent death, the one that occurred here at your hotel."

My thoughts are racing. This isn't how I expected this to play out. I thought I'd finish my message first, and then reveal myself to her. Not as Rowan Hanover, but as *myself*, my true self.

I never expected Abilene Snow to come to the hotel, to sit in Rowan Hanover's office, to be bathed in the sunlight from the window behind his desk. But that's what she's doing right now, and as beautiful as she is, it's all wrong.

I swallow. "What are you saying?" I finally ask. A prompt, really. I want to know more about what she's thinking.

"I'm not sure." She shakes her head, frowning a little. "I'll be perfectly transparent with you, Mr. Hanover—"

My insides twist, hearing that name. My disguise. The face I put on to hide what I am. Still, I have to play along.

"Rowan," I say. "Please."

"Rowan." Abi smiles as she says it, and it's like music or the roll of the Gulf waves over your feet or someone's final exhalation of breath. It's that pretty, the way she says my disguise. "Rowan, I really do want to be clear. I'm not here in any official capacity. The sheriff's department, the city police—they haven't taken my reports on this seriously."

It's a bit of a slap, hearing that she's reported her findings. Those words are for her, not Rosado's bumbling police officers. But I also suppose I can't fault her for it.

"I was hoping I could talk to your staff," she says, the words coming out quickly. "Not any of your guests, of course. Just staff. If they saw anything, or..."

Her voice kind of trails off, and she looks at me helplessly. My little detective, and it takes every ounce of my willpower not to come clean to her right then and there. But of course I know not to do *that*. Uncle Nash was an abusive piece of shit, but he taught me how not to get caught.

Besides, there's no fun in it. She only came to me because the kill was at the Palm Breeze Hotel, not because she actually knows it's me.

"You can talk to anyone you'd like," I say. They didn't see anything, of course. Not even Maria, who found Mr. Nielson's body. "Although I'm not sure they'll have anything for you. It does seem like it was an accident."

God, it hurts me to lie to her about that, especially when disappointment flickers darkly through her expression.

"I appreciate it," she says, squaring up her shoulders. "I really just—I mean, maybe this one was an accident, but—" She gives me a thin, trembling smile. "But if there is a killer out there, we should do something about it, shouldn't we?"

My throat is too dry to speak, so I just nod. All my emotions are twisted up strangely because Abi being here means my messages worked, and I desperately want to know what she knows. What she *thinks* she knows.

But I also don't want her solving anything too soon.

"If it's not too much trouble—" Abi prompts.

Embarrassment floods through me. I need to stay focused. "No, of course, it's not. I'll call up Maria now, and I can let the other staff know they can talk to you if they have anything."

My heart is racing at a million miles per hour, but god, it's so lovely the way Abi smiles gratefully at me. I can feel the relief rushing through her, too. I suppose she was afraid I was going to turn her down or kick her out of the hotel. As if I would *ever* do that, even though it's utterly bizarre to have her in the same room with me and have her aware of it.

I fumble for the phone on my desk and stab in the number for the housekeeping department, trying very hard not to look too closely at Abi, to play it cool so she doesn't suspect there's something wrong with me. That I'm the one she's looking for.

The phone jangles in my ear. When Darcy, the head of housekeeping, answers, I manage to say, "Could you send Maria up to my office when she gets a chance? There's someone who'd like to talk to her," and have it sound normal. Like I'm just a normal 28-year-old hotel owner and not a killer who finally impressed the woman he's been pining over for a decade.

"Thanks," Abi says when I hang up. "I really do appreciate it."

I clear my throat and pull on every ounce of training that Uncle Nash gave me in his time on this earth. He said it was for my own good, and I suppose it was, in its way. But it still hurts to have to pretend.

"Of course," I tell her. "Anything to catch a killer."

3

ABI

The owner of the Palm Breeze Hotel is not at all what I expected. He's a lot younger, for one—probably the same age as me. But he's also handsome in a way you never seen in the guys around here. Most of them are either cowboy rednecks who wandered in from the ranches to the west of town, or wannabe surfer types who drink at the bars along the beach and watch the weather report for hurricanes, since that's the only time we get waves worth surfing on.

But Rowan Hanover is different. He has this kind of nerdy awkwardness to him that I find incredibly charming, and the fact that he had a *Blood Raiser 3* poster in his office is genuinely surprising. And not even the regular poster! The Italian one! Most people, men especially, hate the third movie. But he has a framed painting of Vivienne Hartley up on his wall in all her blood-soaked glory.

I know I shouldn't be thinking about the Blood Raiser movies or about Rowan Hanover, even with his soft, curling hair and big dark eyes and a shy, infectious smile. I'm here to find out what happened to Mr. Nielson. To find anything that will get Kaplan to take me seriously instead of continuing to see

26

me as the unpopular freak who killed a football star when I was sixteen.

That was also ruled an accident. But unlike the deaths in Rosado, it *was* an accident.

Mostly.

I shove the thought aside. Rowan set me up with a table in the hotel's dining room, closed before the lunch rush. It's a nice table, too, right next to the sun-warmed window that looks out over the hotel's glittering swimming pool and then, past that, to the vine-covered dunes and the Gulf of Mexico.

He brings me over a pitcher of water, his hair falling casually into his eyes. God, he's cute.

"Just let Maddie know if you need anything else," he says, pointing to the hostess. "She can call down to my office. And I'll tell the staff they can come up here and talk to you if they have anything they want to share."

He pours the water with a practiced flourish and gives me another one of those shy, crooked smiles. My heart flutters around in my chest.

Has this guy seriously lived in Rosado this whole time? I think about all the nights I chatted with Penelope and Chloe, my two best friends who, unfortunately, live on opposite sides of the country, about my dismal dating options here. It seems I was missing at least one possibility.

"Good luck," he adds, setting the pitcher on the table. "Hope you find something out."

That just sets the butterflies to fluttering even more. Because it feels like he believes me, which is not something I can say for the other men I've told this to. Uncle Vic would probably have come around at this point, but having the confidence of a ghost doesn't really mean much.

"Thanks," I say, wrapping my fingers around the glass of water.

Rowan leaves me alone after that, and Maria, the housekeeper, comes in a few minutes later. She looks a little drawn, with a big crease down the center of her forehead. "Are you the police officer?" she asks.

"I'm not with the police." She stands next to the table while I launch into the same explanation I gave Rowan, about who I am and what I'm looking for. Maria listens carefully the whole time, the furrow in her brow deepening. When I finish, she slides into the chair across from me, although only halfway, like she doesn't expect to be here long.

"I didn't see anything strange," she says. "It was—it was awful, finding him like that. But the room was normal, you know. Not—" She swallows. "Disturbed, or anything."

It occurs to me, from the nervous way she tugs on her skirt, that I don't really know how to question people about a murder. I'm sure she's told all of this to the police, too. A dark knot of guilt tightens in my chest.

"You didn't notice anything before you went into the room?" I say, choosing my words carefully. "You know, strange people at the hotel, that sort of thing?"

Maria frowns and scrunches up her brow, like she's thinking. "No," she finally says. "No, I came in at my usual time, 4:30. It was quiet, being so early. No one was around. And I didn't hear about any—" She waves her hand around. "Weirdos, you know. We get them sometimes, and Darcy will warn me to watch out. But we didn't have any when I..." Her voice kind of trails off, and she swallows.

"Darcy?" I ask gently.

"Oh, the head of housekeeping." Maria smiles sadly. "She talks to the girls at the check-in counter to see if there's anyone we need to watch out for. But there wasn't."

I nod. "Thanks," I tell her. "That—that's good to know."

Maria smiles at me before she leaves. I settle back in my chair and look out the window at the beach below. So no one strange checked into the hotel. That doesn't necessarily mean

I'm wrong. Would they even check in as a guest? All the other deaths happened in Rosado, so it makes sense that it's someone in the area.

It could be a contractor, then. A repairman. Or even just someone who came in from the beach and made themselves look like a guest—

It could be someone who works at the hotel.

The thought hits me with a shiver of fear as sharp as an electrical current. But then, none of the other deaths had anything to do with the Palm Breeze Hotel. The locations are random, more or less. So it feels unlikely.

Whoever *did* do it had to find a way into the hotel room, though. I wonder if the police looked into that at all. I'm not surprised they interviewed Maria, since she found the body, but did they go any further than that? Talk to the clerks at the front desk?

I swivel my head around, but the hostess has vanished from her spot at the front of the restaurant. I'm alone.

I suppose I could wait for her, but there's the soft, light feeling inside me that wants an excuse to see Rowan again. So I gather up my purse and take the elevator back down to his office.

The door's hanging open, and I take a deep breath before I knock on it with the back of my knuckles.

There's an uncomfortably long pause, and then Rowan's soft voice calls out, "Julia? Is that you?"

I'm sure Julia is just someone who works at the hotel, but hearing another woman's name still makes jealousy twinge hot in my belly. "No," I say, sticking my head into the office. "No, it's me. Um, Abi."

Rowan immediately stands up when he sees me. "That was faster than I was expecting. Did Julia not come up to see you? She works the front desk, and I told her to chat with you when she had a chance."

Heat floods into my cheeks. Of course. He said he was going to send some other employees up there, didn't he?

That also answers the whole "who's Julia" question

"No, I just—" I'm fumbling over my words, my heart racing around in my chest. Why do men make me so god damned nervous? Still? After all these years, even when they're nothing like—

Nothing like *him*, the boy who attacked me when I was sixteen. Blake Fletcher.

"I had a thought," I say, taking a deep breath. "And I wanted to ask you about it. If you don't mind."

"Of course I don't mind." He walks around his desk and comes to meet me in the doorway, staring expectantly down at me through his dark, tousled hair.

"The police," I say. "How much did they really talk to your staff?"

Rowan frowns. "Not much," he admits. "They seemed to assume it was an accident."

"So they didn't ask if anyone might have asked for a room card?" I say, my cheeks still warm. Rowan's gaze is intense. Not in a bad way. Just—not in a way I'm used to. "To the room where—where Mr. Nielson was staying?"

Rowan's eyes go wide with understanding. "Oh! No, I don't think they did ask about that, now that you mention it. But I can check to see if we keyed any cards to that room."

"You can?" I'm both relieved that I don't look like a fool in front of him and also irritated that Kaplan apparently couldn't order the bare minimum of detective work.

"Yeah, of course. It's a good thought, actually." Rowan flashes me a grin. "I'm surprised the police didn't ask about it."

I'm not. I keep my mouth shut, though.

Rowan slides behind his desk and taps away on the keyboard. My heart is pounding furiously with anticipation, with the hope that this will give me something. Even if I can't investigate any further on my own, it might be enough to get Kaplan to actually listen to me—

"Ah, nope," Rowan says, blinking at the screen. "Mr. Nielson was the last one to get a key to the room. Nobody came asking for a replacement." He looks over at me. "I'm sorry. It really was a good idea."

I nod, swallowing down my disappointment. A dead end. Anytime I try to investigate these deaths, that's always where I end up. I shouldn't be surprised that this time is any different, even if I put in the effort of talking to people.

"Well, I appreciate you checking it out for me." I plaster on a smile, hoping I don't sound too fake. I do appreciate Rowan's help. I just wish I could catch a break.

Because I *know* there's something more here. Those marks on the bodies aren't some weird coincidence. Not after seven of them, for fuck's sake.

"Is there—is there anything else I could help you with?" Rowan looks up at me through a curl of hair that's fallen across his eyebrows. I want to say yes, even though I don't know what it could possibly be. "Do you want me to call Julia in? She might be busy, if that's why she didn't come up to see you—"

"It's fine." The words come out too quickly, and they taste bitter on my tongue. I doubt she'll have anything, either.

I can just hear Kaplan mocking me, asking me in that snide way he has if I really think I'm the best person for the coroner appointment.

Rowan frowns. He looks like he wants to say something, and I'm suddenly afraid he's going to mock me, too. Crack a joke at my expense.

"Thanks for your help," I say, stepping backward toward the door. "I, um, I don't want to take up any of your time, but I just thought—" I swallow, not sure what to say. "I guess I was mistaken. I hope I didn't scare any of your emp—"

"You didn't," he says, pushing his chair back so he can stand up. We stare at each other from across the office. "I was happy to help. Do you want..." His voice kind of trails off, and he looks over at the Blood Raiser poster. "I can give you my number."

My heart leaps, stupidly.

"You know, in case you think of anything else." He looks back over at me, his big brown eyes drinking me in. "And maybe... You can give me yours?"

Is he flirting with me? He can't possibly be flirting with me.

"Yeah, I can do that." My voice comes out kind of high-pitched and squeaky, and I slide my phone out of my purse, heart hammering.

"I'll give you my number," he says. "And then you can call me, okay? To make sure I have yours."

He wants to make sure he has my number.

"In case I need to follow up on anything," he adds.

Of course. He's just being helpful. I told him I thought a murder took place in his hotel. *Of course* he wants to have my phone number.

Still, I punch off the number he rattles off to me. Then I press CALL, and his phone lights up on his desk.

"There you are." He grins at me, and my heart starts fluttering stupidly again. "I'll, um—" He stops, almost like he's hesitating. "If anything comes up, I'll give you a call."

"I'd appreciate that."

We stare at each other. If Penelope were here, she'd tell me to ask him out. *Just go for it*, she'd say. *The worst he can do is say no.*

But I can't bring myself to do it, even though the question is on the tip of my tongue. A coffee date at the little shop on the beachfront. A five-minute walk from here. Nothing, really.

Rowan blinks at me.

And I just duck out the door.

4

ROWAN

Holy shit. Holy shit, holy shit, holy shit.

It's *fucking working.*

The door to my little beach bungalow slams shut behind me, and for a moment, all I can do is stare at my sparse living room. It's a far cry from Uncle Nash's mansion, but at least it's mine. I don't have to do anyone's bidding to earn my right to live here.

I throw myself down on my sofa and stare down at Abilene's phone number for what feels like the millionth time. And I know it's hers, too. Because she called me from her phone right in front of me. She *gave* her number to me. Willingly.

I've no doubt I could have scrounged up her number at some point since she came back to Rosado, but I didn't see the point. Who answers an unknown caller? I had a much easier time becoming familiar with the Hatch Street Funeral Parlor, where she lived the first time I saw her and where she still lives now. There's the big oak tree that lets me look into her living room, plus all the loose windows and wriggly little side doors that make it easy for me to find my way inside whenever I have the urge to get a closer look. Plus, it's such a big house, always creaking and groaning, that it's easy for me to lurk around in the shadows, watching her drift from room to room, memorizing the way she moves, the way she sweeps her hair up into a bun when she's heading down to her examination room, the way she tucks her feet up underneath herself while she's watching TV in the evenings.

I've seen all of those things. But today she saw me, her big blue eyes meeting mine in my office as she told me that she had found my messages for her.

I drop back on the couch, still staring at her number on my phone, and her name beside it. I click the option to add a photo, and I scroll through the dozens I've taken over the last two years, almost all of them while she's sleeping. She tends to doze off while she's watching television, and more than once I've stolen in and snapped her soft, peaceful face before ducking back into the hallway, my breath fast and panting.

A few times, of course, I've watched her sleep while she's in her bed, when her sleep is much deeper and therefore safer. I'm not sure how I can tell the difference, but it's always obvious to me when she's under enough that I can sit beside her bed and watch the soft rise and fall of her breasts and the moonlit glint of her hair on the pillow.

It's one of those pictures that I go with. Abi on her side, her long eyelashes resting against her cheekbone, her expression peaceful. Then I stare at that for a while, her name in my phone, a picture beside the name.

I should see her tonight.

The excitement brims up in my chest. I haven't actually visited her house in a few weeks, mostly because I was planning for my most recent kill. It took more care than usual since I had to do it in the hotel. There's a pattern I'm leaving for her, a trail of breadcrumbs in the shape of a signature. I know she's found the letters I've left her, carved neatly into the skin of my victims. But I wonder if she's seen how carefully I've arranged them for her. I wonder if she realizes yet that they're words.

Words introducing my true self to her. The first volley in a conversation that I want to continue forever.

I sit up, excitement thrumming through my body. Yes, I'm definitely going to visit her tonight. Maybe I'll even leave another clue for her, something subtle—I've never gone down into the actual room where she does her autopsies before, so that might be a good place. Just something to let her know she's on the right track. That she should keep digging and not give up.

Because that's the *last* thing I want. And she did seem disappointed this afternoon that she didn't find any leads. I know it means that I did a good job of covering my tracks, exactly the way Uncle Nash taught me. And obviously, I can't have her going to the police.

But I still want to let her know how good she's doing.

I CREEP THROUGH THE SMALL, tidy cemetery that surrounds the funeral parlor Abi calls home, dressed all in black and wearing my killing face, a dark mask I had custom-made shortly before Abi came back to Rosado. Even though there's no one out, I still stick to the shadows offered by the row of pecan trees that run along one side of the cemetery, their branches all twisted sideways from the constant, beating wind blowing in off the Gulf.

All the lights are off in Abi's house save for the front porch light, which she always turns on around ten o'clock, the same time that she double-checks all the locks. Usually, if I'm going to visit her inside, I've already gone in by then. But I'm not planning on going in through the doors tonight anyway.

Instead, I'm doing something different. Something risky.

Talking to Abi this afternoon, getting her number, has made me feel emboldened.

When I come to the edge of the cemetery, I double-check Hatch Street both ways to make sure no one's coming. It's a quiet road, especially this late at night, but you can never be too careful.

All that's out here is me and the wind.

I dart across the street, taking off in a sprint so that I can minimize how long I'm out in the open. I wind through the wild patch of flowers that Abi grows in the front yard. In the mornings, she puts the flowers on the graves in the cemetery, something I'll watch her do on days when I don't want to take the risk of breaking into her house. Right now, they're mostly sunflowers, their yellow faces already facing east to greet the sun.

Normally, I'd go in through the side door, which has the flimsiest lock. But tonight, I keep going around the side of the house until I get to the long, narrow driveway that runs up to the part of the house where Abi receives bodies for her coroner work. There's a big metal garage here as well as a regular entrance, both guarded by an electronic lock. I've never bothered coming in this way before because I want to spend time with Abi when she's off work and relaxing in her living room. Tonight, though, I have other plans.

The lock on the entrance is easy enough to bypass. I pry the cover off easily—I've always been strong—and then it's just a matter of crossing the wires in a specific way. Uncle Nash taught me how to do this ages ago, before I ever even killed for him. I was his thief before I was his murderer.

The lock beeps and springs free, and I ease open the door, letting in a wash of overly cool air. It smells like a hospital, bright and sterile, although there's a faint, comforting layer of rot underneath it. I do like the smell of death. It's one of the things I like about Abi, the way that sweetness follows her around like a perfume. I doubt anyone notices it but me, which just makes it all the more special.

I slip inside, dragging the door shut behind me. All the lights are off, but I have good night vision. My shoes whisper against the tile floors. Normally, that'd give me pause, but I know Abi is tucked away upstairs. I doubt she can hear me down here.

I follow the scent of death to the autopsy room, which is also locked, although not electronically. I pick the lock easily and step inside.

My movements make the lights flicker to life.

For a moment, I freeze, breathing hard behind my killing face. I don't want to take it off, even though I'm not here to kill tonight. It reflects my true self more than my human face, so I always wear it when I visit Abi. After all, what's love if you can't be your true self around the object of your desire?

I creep forward through the overly bright light, peering out at Abi's workplace. She keeps it clean and tidy—all her instruments put away, all the surfaces gleaming. I stop in front of the weapons she has laid out, ready to be used. Well, not weapons, I suppose. Tools. She only uses them on people who are already dead.

I run my gloved hands over them, picking them up one by one to feel their weight. A thin, delicate scalpel, which is a type of blade I've never used before. A bone saw, which is one I have.

That was for Uncle Nash, though. My own kills, I prefer to be more creative. I never use knives anymore.

I turn away from the autopsy tools and take in the rest of the space. I don't see any bodies, but I do see a wall of gleaming metal drawers. I walk over, my footsteps soft and clicking.

They're labeled. Names, a date (death or delivery, I don't know) a string of identification numbers. Marcus Nielson is on the far left, and I pull him out and look down at him, his face much more peaceful than the last time I saw him.

"You served your purpose well," I say, my voice echoing strangely in this cold, sterile room.

I consider, briefly, leaving my message *on* him. But no. Neither the police nor the sheriff's department currently suspects foul play, even if my clever Abi does, and I want to keep it like that. I've no doubt she'll take this to them, and I fear marring Mr. Nielson's corpse might be a bit too obvious. I don't want the cops swarming my hotel in earnest.

So I slide him back in with a distressingly loud clang. Then I turn away from the cabinet, looking out at the room. For a moment, my eyes settle again on her tools. That could be a possibility, but something about it doesn't chime right. I keep scanning, looking over the sterile countertops, the pristine walls, until I land on a door.

It leads, I think, into an office; there's a window beside it, although whatever's inside is too dark to see. I stride over, my heart fluttering. An office would be intimate, wouldn't it? And subtle, if I play it right. I need something meaningful to her, but not to the cops.

I try the door, and find it unlocked. Unlike the autopsy room, the lights don't come on automatically, and I feel around until I find the light switch.

What that soft overhead light reveals makes my heart flop over in my chest.

A map of Rosado County. It's impossible to miss; the office is tiny, and Abi has pinned the map to the wall exactly opposite the door. But it's not *just* a map.

It's a model of all my work over the last two years.

I drift forward, my breath caught in my lungs. I have a similar map at home, neatly folded in a locked box I keep in the back of my closet. Every letter of my message is planned out there, every location of all seven kills marked with a blue felt-tip pen the same color as Abi's lovely eyes.

She doesn't have all of them, of course, because I haven't

finished my work. But she has pressed a red pin in the location of every single kill to date, each letter of my message printed on a little flag.

But what really makes my heart skip—and, if I'm being honest, what sends blood shooting into my cock—is the fact that there are a smattering of white pins, too, and a handful of them, enough to be impressive, are also my kills. Murders from before she came back to town.

Not all of them. She's being overly optimistic, I imagine. But she's clearly seen enough of my work to understand it.

I stumble up to the map, breathing heavily behind my killing face, and read what the flagged pins spell out.

YOUR DAR

My mind fills in the rest: *Your Dark Whisperer.* My signature, just for her. My way of introducing myself. I chose it because my true self doesn't really have a name, and this felt appropriate, given all the times I've knelt beside her bed and whispered truths into her ear while she was sleeping, hoping that she would hear them in her dreams.

Truths like, *You're the most beautiful woman in the world.*

Or, *You're the reason I finally freed myself.*

Or, sometimes, *I love you.*

I feel dizzy—with happiness. With excitement. Of course I knew she had found the most recent **R** and enough of the letters to see a pattern, but I didn't know, not until this moment, that she had all of them.

Plus some of the others. Before Abi came back to Rosado, I used to choose my victims purely by instinct, an instinct even I barely understand. I'd watch them at the hotel or on the beach. I'd wait until they were far away from anywhere tied to me. And then I'd find a way to trap them in their deaths.

And yet Abi still sifted through that chaos until she found me.

I suck in my breath and palm my cock over my pants, shuddering at the touch. I never masturbate in her home, mostly because I don't want to risk leaving evidence, but also because it feels uncouth somehow. I usually do it out in the cemetery, holding onto the memory of her lovely face while I spill my seed on some hundred-year-old grave.

But this is special. In fact, this might be how I send my message.

I choke back a groan as the idea takes form in my head. I imagine it: Abi coming into her office, a tidy bowl of my cum waiting for her on her desk. It's *definitely* uncouth, but I bet she doesn't go to the police with it. And it'll let her know she's onto something.

There has to be a bowl somewhere down here. Or a jar.

I don't go looking for one just yet, though, just unzip my pants and grab hold of my cock, giving it a few slow strokes. My grunts are dangerously loud in the quiet of her office. But they sound right, too.

God, what I wouldn't give to fuck her down here for real. I might whisper in her ear during our nights together, but I've never touched her, not even when she's sleeping. I don't want her like that. I want her awake and willing. I want her to lean back on her neat little desk and slide her skirt up her thighs and show me she's naked underneath. I want her to gaze up at my killing face with lust in her eyes and beg the real me to make her come.

Heat surges up into my cock, and I drop it, my heart racing. I need a receptacle. I'm not a fucking asshole who's going to shoot his load all over Abi's work documents.

But when I go over to the doorway, I hear something, faint but definite.

Footsteps. Soft, clicking footsteps.

And they're coming this way.

5

ABI

I jerk awake, dragged out of some pleasant dream and into my dark, disorienting bedroom. My alarm chimes softly beside my bed.

No, it can't be my alarm. It's still dark outside.

I roll over, fumbling for my phone. Is someone calling me? Any coroner business goes to the funeral parlor line, not my cell. Something with Penelope or Chloe, maybe? I can't imagine they'd have the kind of emergency that would warrant calling me in the middle of the night.

I finally grab hold of my phone and roll onto my back, squinting at it in the dark. The screen blurs without my glasses.

And then, with a drop in my heart, I realize what it is.

An alarm, but not my morning alarm. This is the alarm tied to the electronic lock on the back door.

I sit up, my heart pounding, and slide my glasses on. But then I see the flashing POWER FAILURE notice, and I breathe out, slumping against my headboard. This is not the first time this shit has happened, and it won't be the last. Any time the power flickers—and it does surprisingly often, given how old

41

the house is and how much the Gulf wind sweeps across the property—the back door lock has to be reset.

I want to leave it for tomorrow morning. But it's only midnight, and I can hear Uncle Vic's voice chiding me: *Those bodies are responsibility, Abi. You can't just leave them vulnerable like that.*

I sigh, defeated by my own memories. Then I whip off my blanket and roll out of bed and fumble around on my desk until I find my glasses. The house is quiet, save for the constant, murmuring hum of the AC. Guess the power outage didn't last long.

"Let's get this over with," I mutter, shuffling out into the hallway. I make my way downstairs, where everything feels even more still and quiet, following the narrow hallway until I come to the entrance to the funeral work space in the back of the house. I push the door open.

And freeze.

Something's wrong. It takes me a second to register what it is, because the work hallway is as still and undisturbed as the rest of the house.

Except that the light is on in the examination room.

The door is closed, so it's not immediately obvious. But I can see the thin line of brightness reflecting off the hallway tiles. Fear prickles over my skin.

Something probably fell over, I think. *And activated the light.*

I force myself to ignore the examination room and instead walk over to reset the entrance lock, telling myself I'm being paranoid. We've never had a break-in at the Hatch Street Funeral Parlor, and I have no idea why we'd start now.

You were literally investigating a murder this afterno—

Something thumps from the examination room. I whip around, my heart pounding, and stare at the light trickling across the floor.

Silence.

Part of me thinks I should go upstairs and call the police. Part of me also thinks that's a stupid fucking idea, because Kaplan's influence in the sheriff's department extends to the police department, too. Neither of them takes me seriously unless they absolutely have to, and a single thump isn't enough to convince them to come out here, even if my outer lock needs to be reset.

I creep down the hall, my eye on the door to the examination room. If *anything* looks wrong, I'll call the cops. But I need to give them something more than a sound.

I push the door open and peer inside. The light floods over everything, but nothing looks out of place. All the refrigeration drawers are shut. My supplies are laid out where I left them earlier, waiting for work to start tomorrow. My office door—

My office door is open.

I always close it. Always. I don't want anyone seeing my crazy-person red-string map. I always close the examination room door, too, but I can be careless about it. Not so with my office door.

I jerk away and move to run back upstairs. Fuck Kaplan. There's got to be one cop in this town who'll do their fucking job.

But I don't get far. I make it maybe two strides before a gloved hand wraps around my mouth.

I shriek into the soft, supple leather as fear ripples through my body. My attacker drags me backward, into the examination room, and I flail against him, the familiar space suddenly overwhelming and terrifying. For a moment, I'm sure he's going to toss me onto the examination table, but he pulls me past it.

Then he throws me into my office.

I slam against my desk and whirl around as he kicks the door shut, enclosing us together.

For a moment, I just suck in deep breaths of air, staring at him. He looks like he's wrapped in shadow: Dressed in head-to-

toe black, including the black leather gloves. His head is wrapped in a hideous, black rubber mask that hides his face and his hair. The only thing I can see of him, really, is the cruel glint of his eyes.

"I called the police," I spit out. "They'll be here any second."

"No, you didn't." His voice is low and graveled, soft behind the latex of the mask. I don't know what it's supposed to be, all that black rubber twisted into a sneer. If it's a horror movie character, it's not one I recognize.

I squeeze my hands around the rim of the desk, chest tight. I don't think this is a burglar.

"Wh-who are you?" I stammer out, even though I'm pretty sure I know.

It's him. The killer I've been looking for.

He tilts his head, studying me from behind that twisted, leering mask. He doesn't have a weapon that I can see. No gun. No knife.

But none of his victims were killed with guns or knives, were they?

"What are you doing here?" My voice shakes, and I squeeze the desk tighter, flicking my eyes around, as if I might find some escape out of this coffin of an office.

"What have you been doing here?" he counters, his eyes sliding off me to the map of Rosado County on my wall. "It seems you're hunting something, little detective."

I bite back a whimper of terror. "It's for my work," I say shakily. "It's—"

He moves on me, faster than I would have thought possible. His gloved hands wrap around my wrists, and his thigh slides up between my legs to pin me against the desk. My nightgown bunches around my hips. I cry out, too terrified to move, as his dark eyes drink me in from behind the mask.

"It's not for your work," he murmurs, his thumb stroking along my wrist, making me shudder a little.

With fear, I tell myself. *He's making me shudder with fear.*

Even if there's a soft coil of heat forming in the place where his leg meets my pussy.

"It's nothing," I whisper, staring at his masked face.

He tightens his grip on my wrists. *Liar*, the gesture says, and I cry out again.

"Tell me what it is," he growls, leaning closer. The movement makes his thigh shift against me, the rough fabric of his jeans evident through the flimsy cotton of my panties.

"A m-map," I whisper, his leering mask centimeters from my mouth. "A m-map of Rosado."

"And what do you have pinned on that map of Rosado?"

I flutter my eyes shut, as if he'll disappear if I can't see him. But he's still there. Still squeezing my wrists. Still pressing his leg, ever so gently, between my legs.

"M-murders," I whisper.

He sucks in a sharp breath. "I knew you would see me," he murmurs. "I knew you would get my message."

My eyes fly open, and he's still there, dark eyes boring into me.

"You're him," I say before I can stop myself.

He nods slowly. One hand slides down my arm.

"I watch the places where I kill," he says in that soft, almost seductive way. "You went to the hotel. You talked to that pathetic owner."

I think of Rowan, floppy-haired and sweet, and feel a sudden surge of panic for him.

"Who are you?" I ask, trying to get the conversation away from Rowan. "How did you see me? Do you work there?"

He chuckles. His hand glazes over my shoulder and then wraps softly around my neck.

Terror slams through me, and I scream and try to thrash away from him. But he presses his imposing body up against mine, his strength undeniable. The rim of the desk digs sharply into my lower back, and there's more force in that than there is in his fingers around my throat.

"I told you," he says, "I watch the places where I kill. I wait for you to come and investigate, little detective."

Horror flutters around in my chest. He knows who I am. He knows what I've been doing. He's been *watching* me—

But the thought evaporates when he presses the twisted mouth of his mask to my lips.

I freeze, too frightened—and too confused, really—to move. *He's kissing me*, I think distantly, even if he's doing it with his mask.

He grunts and pulls away. I swear I see disappointment flash in his eyes.

"What—" I whisper, and my fear takes on a new angle. "What was that?"

He keeps his hand around my throat as he lets go of my wrist, reaches up, and peels the mask just enough to reveal his mouth.

My mind whirs. *Memorize it*, I think, staring at his full, soft lips. The surrounding skin is slightly tan, with glints of reddish-black stubble. *White male*, I think in a blur. *At least a foot taller than me. Husky build.* There's nothing else for me to latch onto.

And then he presses his real lips to mine, and I forget everything I was thinking.

It's not the sloppy, angry kiss I would have expected. He's soft. Hesitant. He doesn't pry my mouth open, only presses his lips to mine, and makes a soft sound in the back of his throat. It only lasts a few seconds before he pulls away and slides the mask back down, covering that mouth. He even draws his knee away from between my thighs, and a darkness inside me whimpers at the loss of pressure.

I gape at him. It's been a long time since I was kissed. A long time since I bothered even trying to find someone to kiss.

But if I did go looking, I'd want someone who would kiss me like that.

"I just wanted to taste you," he says. "You've done so good, finding me."

I stare at him. Baffled. Terrified.

Turned on.

No. I shove that part of me away, lock it in the darkest part of my brain. No, I am not turned on by this. Not by his rough, soft voice. Not by his gentle kiss. Not even by his validation that I was right this whole fucking time, that those accidental deaths weren't accidents at all.

"Can I make you come?" he asks softly.

"What?" I wrench away from him, but he wraps his arms around my waist and pulls me up so my back presses against his chest. His mask brushes against my ear.

"I want to make you come," he murmurs. "A reward for finding me."

"I didn't find you," I say, staring at the far wall, feeling hopeless. And not because I'm trapped, either, although that's what I want to tell myself.

But because there's a heat between my legs, traitorous and evil, and I almost want to take him up on his offer. Because he asked. He didn't just take.

"But you did," he growls in my ear. "You found my messages. You tracked them on your map there. You went looking for me."

"You found *me*," I tell him, shifting like I might get away. I don't, of course, but I do feel an unfamiliar stiffness press against my ass.

Heat throbs into my clit.

"Yes," he says, sliding his hand over my belly. "Because I wanted to tell you what a good job you're doing."

He stops just before his fingers meet the seam of my legs. I don't know why he doesn't just take what he wants. That's what evil men do. I know that firsthand, don't I?

"May I touch you?" he asks roughly, his fingers tightening against my belly.

A new heat surges through me. A terrible desire to say yes. When was the last time a man asked to touch me?

"You're already touching me," I say. "You kissed me."

He goes quiet, his hand a searing heat on my belly. "That was a taste," he says, almost defensively. "I want to *touch* you."

"Why?" I twist against him, like I might look at him. What little of him I can see.

"Because you're beautiful," he answers.

I rip away from him, my heart pounding. He lets me go, even when I whirl around on him, my hands balled into fists. I can feel him staring at me from behind his mask, his eyes as hot as fire.

"Who are you?" I hiss.

"I am exactly what you think I am," he responds.

And then he ducks out of the doorway, leaving me alone with my map of his crimes.

6

ROWAN

I tear across Hatch Street Burial Grounds, adrenaline surging me forward. I can't believe I did any of that. I can't believe I touched her. Or *kissed* her.

Everything was heightened in the office. Abi herself was a riot of sound and scent: heartbeat and breath and fast-pumping blood. She smelled brighter and sweeter, like I was choking on hyacinth and funeral orchids. If she had run, I could have tracked her across the county on the trail of her scent alone.

That sort of thing happens to me when I'm going after a kill. But I wasn't going to kill Abi. I will *never* kill Abi.

I leap over the fence and land on my feet, never once slowing down as I leave the cemetery behind me. I fucked up, I know. I pushed her too far. I shouldn't have asked to touch her—

You should have just done it.

The thought comes to me in Uncle Nash's voice, because it's something Uncle Nash would say. But I'm not him. I won't hurt her. I shouldn't have even kissed her like that, but she was so close, her eyes huge behind her glasses as she drank in my killing face, and I wanted her to bless it with her lips.

And then it wasn't enough, that blessing. Nor was it enough when I pulled the mask away so there wouldn't be any numbing barrier between us. That's why I asked to touch her, and why I ran when she didn't give me permission.

Because I was afraid of what I would have done to her if I stayed. I know I'm a monster. I know my killing face represents my true soul.

I careen through the scrubby open field that juts against the cemetery, the barrier between the dead and the beach. This isn't a great place for me to be, and I force myself to slow down so I can stick close to the spindly mesquite trees that offer almost nothing in the way of camouflage. Beachside Boulevard is several yards to my left, and even though it's probably after midnight, I still hear the occasional sigh of a car as it drives past.

I don't want to think that Abi will call the cops on me. But I'm sure she has.

I keep myself low to the ground, moving quickly. I don't tire easily, which has always been a boon given what I like to do in my spare time, and the adrenaline of speaking to Abi twice in one day—once as Rowan, and once as myself, something I never thought was even possible—gives me an extra boost of speed. It's not long before the smell of the ocean overpowers Abi's lingering scent, not long before I hear the waves rolling into the shore.

I take my killing face off before I step out onto the cracked, weatherworn sidewalk that runs parallel to the beach. This isn't the main strand, but there are houses here, shabby little bunga-lows like the one I call home. Although my house is about a mile from here, right at the place where the string of hotels and restaurants begins.

No one's out, fortunately. The houses are all dark. Still, I walk as if I live there, sliding off my gloves and tucking them into my killing face, which I press under my arm so it's not obvious what it is. Dunes crest up ahead, the vines silvery in the moonlight, and I walk parallel to them until I come to one of the boardwalks, gritty with wet sand from the tar showers.

When I finally see the beach proper, with its pale, packed sand and dark mounds of seaweed, I can finally relax. I always feel safer on the beach. I suppose it's because I imagine I can dive into the waves and swim away from danger.

Or maybe it's because I always come this way when I visit Abi, and I know there's a bathroom up ahead, a standalone brick building locked up for the night. Two years ago, when Abi came back to Rosado, I loosened some of the bricks in the side of the bathroom so I would have an easy place to hide things. Like my gloves. My killing face. My shoes, too, which are black boots that look absurd on the beach. If the police somehow find me out here, I won't look like the monster who just finished terrorizing the woman he loves. I'll look like the insomniac I also am, wiling the night away by the shore.

I cram everything into my hiding hole and slide the bricks back in place. I'll be back tomorrow morning to fetch everything, but I tell myself it'll be safe for now. My gloves and shoes and socks I'm not worried about, but I don't want to lose my killing face. Especially since Abi—

Abi *kissed* it.

The thought floods me with a hot, dangerous lust. I jog down to the water, kicking the sand around to try and hide my footprints. I stop at the place where the waves crash frigid water over my bare feet. The night feels endless; the moon is tiny tonight, little more than a fingernail, and the sky and the water bleed together.

I reach down and rub my cock, listlessly.

There's so much to process. But all I can think about is Abi. The sound of her footsteps and then the sight of her in the cold, sterile hallway, practically naked in her nightgown. The shocking warmth of her body against mine. The quiet, fearful noises she made against my glove.

Her lips against my lips.

Her pussy against my thigh.

The throb of lust that I'm *certain* I felt from her.

I slip my hand into the waistband of my pants and pull my cock out, thrusting furiously into my hand. I know it's stupid, doing this out here. I know the cops have probably descended on her house already, that they're fanning out through the cemetery and surrounding streets.

But all I can think about is her scent, and her heat, and her mouth.

I kissed her. Finally, after all these years.

Cum erupts from between my fingers, disappearing into the pale surge of sea foam. I drop my hand to my side, breathing heavily, wondering what might have happened if I stayed. Where that cum might have ended up.

The sea wind gusts around me, bringing the scent of the oceanfront. People scents. Sunscreen, sweat, food, blood. None of it is as sweet as Abi, and all of it dulled down. Faded. The cops haven't come looking on the beach.

I tuck my cock away, feeling deflated after that paltry excuse for an orgasm. I conjure up Abi's face again, although this time, I imagine her in my office at the hotel, smiling and shy. I know she wasn't smiling at the real me, but I can sort of pretend.

There's nothing else for me to do but go home. I'm not going to sleep tonight, that much is certain, but I can plan my next kill. It's an auspicious one, because the victim will get a K somewhere on their skin. I like that. K for Kill. I already know the location: Neptune's Adventure, the mini golf course that looks out over the beach. A good place for a death. Lots of moving mechanical parts that can trap clothes or hair and murder someone in a way that doesn't look like murder.

Which has always been my speciality, even when I was killing for Uncle Nash.

I amble along the beach, walking where the water meets the sand. The night creatures are out. Ghost crabs, mostly, little pale streaks that slide into their sandy tunnels as soon as they feel the thunder of my feet. Prey hiding from a predator, although I'm not a predator they have to worry about.

The wind shifts, shoving my hair into my face. When it does, the scents change, too. The dull underscore of humanity is still there, the way it always is. But I smell something different.

Darker. Muskier. *Dangerous.*

I stop, the waves splashing around my ankles. I rarely experience fear, but a trickle of it rises in my throat now.

The cops? Did they track me here?

I turn around, my footsteps already disappearing into the wet sand. But I don't think this is the cops. Whatever this is, it doesn't seem...

Human.

The thought startles me. It's not an animal. Animals have their own presence, a wildness in their scent like gamey venison. This is closer to a human than that.

But it doesn't feel like the presence of the humans on the beachfront. It doesn't feel like Abi, either.

"Hello?" My voice is immediately swallowed by the wind, and the only answer I get is the rhythmic crashing of the waves. I tilt my head, listening.

I think I hear a heartbeat. Or maybe I'm just hearing my own, since my heart is currently pounding against my ribcage like it's trying to warn me of danger.

But there's nothing out here.

It's just me. The only monster in Rosado.

7

ABI

I pace around my darkened living room, feeling jangly and agitated. I know I should call 911.

But I don't.

I stop in front of the window and jerk the curtain back, peering out at my front yard, with its flower patch and neatly manicured grass, and then to the cemetery itself, everything illuminated in patches by the street lamps. No movement.

He's not going to come back.

I drop the curtain and stumble backward, my arms wrapped around my chest. I hate that the thought almost makes me feel disappointed.

I stifle it before it can get any further. That was a *killer* who pinned me to the desk and ran his leather-gloved hands up my bare arm like I was something precious. A killer who pressed his lips to mine and then asked if he could touch me.

Why did you want to say yes what the HELL is wrong with you—

I fling myself out of the living room and back into my bedroom for what has to be the third or fourth time tonight. After it happened, after the masked man—the masked *killer*—left me trembling and terrified in my office, I could barely move. Eventually, I managed to drag myself over to the back entrance, which he had left hanging open. I shut it. Activated the lock. Every second, I expected him to leap out of the shadows and wrap his hand around my mouth again.

It never happened.

I scoured the house, both the funeral parlor downstairs and my living space upstairs. Nothing. I picked up my phone a dozen times, but I could never bring myself to call the police.

I still can't.

Every time I look at my phone, I think about the last time I dialed 911, when I was 16 and Blake Fletcher was lying crooked and broken at the bottom of the stairs of his house. I had shoved him.

He had touched me, too. But he hadn't been gentle about it, like the killer. He had grabbed me and thrown me against the wall and ripped my shorts over my hips, hissing that an ugly nerd like me should be thrilled to give it up to a guy like him.

I squeeze my eyes shut, trying to block out the memory. When I think about it, I also think about everything that came after. The interrogation. The grand jury. All the newspaper stories and the harassment and the death threats.

It always felt like everything started because I called the police instead of running away.

I throw myself onto my crumpled bed, roll onto my back, and stare up at my ceiling fan. My sheets feel sticky and uncomfortable, and I squirm around to get them off of me. Somehow, I hike my nightgown up in the process. It bunches around my hips the way it did when the killer pressed his knee between my thighs and whispered in his soft, whiskey-rough voice.

I want to touch you.

Why?

Because you're beautiful.

I suck down deep lungfuls of air. I wish I knew what's wrong with me. It was *him*. He told me who he was. He confirmed my suspicion that all those deaths weren't accidents.

But I don't have real proof. Only my word. And I know how much stock Rosado law enforcement puts in that, coroner appointment or not.

I dig the heels of my palms into my eyes, but it's not enough to block out the memory of what happened. The killer's soft, chaste kiss. His hand splayed across my belly, asking permission to touch me.

That's the thought that sends heat down between my legs. He asked permission.

"No," I whisper, my voice thunderously loud in the silence of my room. *This* is the reason I keep stalking back and forth between my bed and the rest of the house. Because every time I lie down, I feel his silky touch on my skin, and I wish—

I wish I hadn't shoved him away.

A sick, heavy guilt squeezes my chest. He's murdered at least seven people. He broke into my home, presumably to murder me.

Although he didn't.

He kissed me instead.

The house creaks, settling into its foundations. I jerk up on my elbows, but there's no one in my bedroom with me. He's not here.

What if he was?

I slump back, hating myself for following the threads of my fantasy. What *if* he came back? What if he crawled in through my window, looking like a wisp of shadow? What if he slid into bed and ran his leather gloves up my legs until he pried them apart, and then ran his thumb along my slit until—

I hardly realize I'm touching myself. But I am, circling my clit over my thin cotton panties.

And I'm still imagining *him*, the killer I've been tracking since Uncle Vic left me alone in this stifling town. Imagining him sliding up the bottom of his mask like he did before, then kissing me in earnest. On the mouth. On the neck. On the cunt.

I moan softly, shuddering with fear and shame and lust, and slide my panties aside so I can stroke my quickly-dampening pussy.

May I touch you? The growl of his words echoes in my head.

"Yes," I whisper raggedly to the empty room. "Yes. Touch me."

I hate myself for imagining what would have happened if he had. Hate myself for imagining him bending me over the table and sliding my panties over my thighs and pressing his fingers into my slit. I don't know what a leather glove would feel like against my pussy, but god, I fucking want to.

I arch my back, hooking my fingers into myself as I remember what the killer's cock felt like when he pulled me up to him. I imagine him taking it out, sliding it into my waiting cunt.

I jolt beneath my own touch, shame shivering through me. No. I will not give in to this darkness I've worked so hard to carve away from myself. So I force my thoughts to go elsewhere, to something safer, and I settle, somewhat suddenly, on Rowan Hanover, grinning bashfully down at me in his sunny hotel office.

It's easy, at first, to sink into the fantasy. Me bent over Rowan's desk while he thrusts into me, his hands squeezing tight around my hips. But as my pleasure crests, the image changes. And suddenly, Rowan's wearing black leather gloves and a black rubber mask with a twisted, leering face.

May I touch you? he rasps, his cock already buried all the way in my pussy.

"Yes!" I cry out in my bed, my cunt too tightly wound for me to change course in my fantasies. "Fuck me!" I press my fingers deeper inside my pussy and flop over onto my belly so I can hump my bed as I fuck myself. And because it's easier to imagine a masked man thrusting his big cock into me from behind.

You did so good finding me, he rasps in my imagination. *Are you ready for your reward, little detective?*

"Reward me," I whisper into my pillow, my breath tight and choking. "Reward me for catching you. Please, sir." My hand is almost numb from how frantically I'm touching myself, sloppily rubbing inside and out as my orgasm crests from somewhere deep inside my core. It's the same deep place where I hide all my shameful fantasies—dark, blood-soaked fantasies. Fantasies full of bones and death and, tonight, black rubber masks. That evil has haunted me as long as I can remember. Usually, I lock it away. But a killer has unleashed it, and I don't know how to put it back in.

"Reward me!" I shriek, bucking against my bed. "Please! Please! Ple—"

When my orgasm rips through me, I can't speak. My words dissolve into a long, throaty moan, and I fingerfuck myself through each agonizing, exquisite pulse of pleasure.

And the whole time, I'm thinking of *him*.

My nameless killer.

My CELL PHONE RINGS, jarring me awake.

For a minute, I'm too disoriented to register anything. I'm in my bed, half naked. Sunlight pours in through the window. My sheets are on the floor.

My phone beeps over to voicemail.

"What time is it?" I mutter, pushing myself up. The light in the windows feels wrong. Too bright. Coming in at the wrong angle.

My phone chirps, letting me know I have a text. I must have finally fallen asleep last night, after I—

I shove my nightgown down over my thighs, heat flooding into my face.

My phone chirps again, pinging and insistent. For a minute, my thoughts whir around: did I have an appointment today? Something I missed by oversleeping? But no. There was nothing on my calendar.

Then a new fear works its way into my chest. That Kaplan and the rest of the sheriff's department *know* somehow. Know that a killer came into my home and I just—let him go.

I snatch my phone up, my heart pounding. Slide on my glasses so I can see. But the call isn't from the police. Instead, a name flashes on the screen that I haven't thought about in years: Heather Staunton.

My lawyer from when I killed Blake Fletcher.

An old, paralyzing dread grips me from the inside. My hands shake as I swipe open her text message, which just makes things worse:

> Call me as soon as you can.

I don't bother listening to the voicemail. Just punch my thumb against the CALL button and hold the phone up to my ear, my breath shaky and trembling.

I was acquitted on all charges two years after Blake's death. Why is Ms. Staunton calling me?

She picks up on the first ring. "Abilene," she says, her voice breathless. "Oh, thank god."

"What's wrong?" I stumble out of bed, my thoughts buzzing. The sunlight is too bright. It feels sharp, like a knife.

"I was worried you—" She cuts herself off. "I'm sorry to call out of the blue like this. But you need to know."

I freeze in the middle of my room, the wooden floorboards cold against my bare feet.

"Know what?"

I don't like this. It feels like I'm sixteen years old again, about to be led out of my parents' house in handcuffs.

She takes a deep breath. "Do you remember Olivia Pearce?"

I squeeze the phone, the name clanging around in my head. It's familiar, although I can't place it.

"She was the reporter—"

That's all Ms. Staunton has to say, the word *reporter.* It all comes back to me. Olivia Pearce was a reporter for the newspaper in my hometown. She had covered my case from the beginning, and she was the only one who believed my story about Blake assaulting me. She was young—well, probably the age I am now. Mid-20s. Pretty. When she interviewed me, she told me she had been a cheerleader at my high school. *When they're good at sports,* she had said darkly, the two of us sitting in the dusty little coffee shop in downtown Magnolia, *this town will let them get away with anything.*

"Abilene? Abi?"

Ms. Staunton's voice cuts through my memory. I stumble back until I'm sitting on my bed. "I'm here," I say. "What's wrong? Did something happen?"

Ms. Staunton goes quiet on the other end of the line, and I know something did. A killer broke into my house last night, and now my past is calling me this morning.

"I don't know any way to say this nicely," Ms. Staunton's voice is tight and rigid. "So I'm just going to tell you. Olivia's body was found this morning."

Blood pounds in my ears. "And I assume it's not..." My voice trails off. *Natural causes,* that's what I want to say, but I can't get my mouth to form the words.

"It looks like murder, yes."

My whole body goes numb. I stare at my closet, the door hanging open a little.

Just like the door to the examination room last night.

Bile rises in my stomach, and I lean over and retch before I can stop myself. There's nothing to throw up, just pale, foamy stomach acid.

"Abilene?" I can barely make out Ms. Staunton's voice on the phone.

"What happened?" I say, switching the phone over to speaker. "Where was she? How do they know it's murder?"

"They don't *know* it's murder," Ms. Staunton says. "As I'm sure you're perfectly aware. But it doesn't—"

"It doesn't look like an accident?" I stumble into the bathroom and fill my toothpaste cup with water to clean out my mouth.

All his *kills look like accidents*.

"No," Ms. Staunton says. "Her body was, um, mutilated. I don't want to frighten you, but—"

"I want to do the autopsy." I stare at my reflection in the mirror. I look like hell. Dark circles under my eyes, my skin wan and pale. "I'm a coroner now. Did you know that?"

"Yes," Ms. Staunton says gently. "Yes, I've seen your name around. That's actually why—"

"Who do I need to call in Magnolia?" I say. "To make sure I can do it? I know they're bigger than Rosado, but—"

"Abi, listen." Mrs. Staunton takes on that sharp, teacherly voice she used on me when I was panicking, back when I was a teenager. But I'm not a teenager now. I'm a grown woman.

And I need to know if there's a letter carved on Olivia Pearce's body.

It didn't look like an accident. He makes his victims like they were in an accident.

"—in downtown Rosado."

I freeze, looking over at my phone. "I'm sorry, say that again?"

Ms. Staunton sighs, clearly frustrated. "This is what I'm trying to tell you, Abilene. Olivia still lives in Magnolia, but her body was found in downtown Rosado. She was—displayed, for lack of a better word, on the gazebo in the town square."

"What?" I snatch my phone up and run back into my bedroom. "This morning?"

"Yes, a groundskeeper found her very early this morning. From what I've been able to get from the police, and it's not a lot, she was likely killed there overnight."

Could he have even done it? After he left here?

"I know you handle all the coroner cases in Rosado County, but I did not want you to have Olivia Pearce come in without warning."

"How did you find out?" I throw my closet door open and dig through my clothes, looking for my most professional outfit.

"Olivia's husband let me know," Ms. Staunton says gently. "Olivia and I have done a lot of work with victims' rights, and he was worried I might be in danger. But her being found in Rosado—"

I stop, a pale linen dress dangling from one hand. "You think I might be in danger, too."

"I don't know what I think," Ms. Staunton says. "But I felt obligated to let you know."

I throw the dress on my bed. "Thank you, Ms. Staunton."

"You can call me Heather."

It feels disrespectful, calling her Heather. Like we're colleagues. Like she isn't the reason I was able to convince a jury in Magnolia that Blake Fletcher's death was an accident.

Well, her *and* Olivia, if I'm being honest. Anxiety twists around in my belly.

"I'll let you know what I find out, okay?"

I hang up before she can argue with me. Then I strip out of my nightgown and get dressed.

I need to see that crime scene.

8

ABI

They have the whole block roped off, yellow tape criss-crossing over the road. I can still see the Rosado gazebo, though, a white-and-pink structure rising out of the center of a lush green patch in the middle of downtown. It's a historical marker, one of those things that Rosado's known for aside from the beach. The town has farmers' markets here once a month and a Halloween festival in the fall.

And now it's a crime scene.

My throat is dry as I walk up to the uniformed police officer guarding the area. I don't recognize her, although that doesn't mean she won't know my name.

"I'm Abilene Snow," I say, already pulling out my coroner's badge. "I need to look at the body."

She frowns at my badge. "I didn't realize Kaplan had contacted you yet. He's still talking with Detective Contreras about how they want to proceed."

I stiffen. I didn't expect Kaplan to actually be here, not with the crime scene being in the city limits.

"The police department contacted me," I lie, tucking my badge back into my pocket. "May I?"

The officer nods and pulls the tape away. I duck through and cut across the dew-damp grass, my heart thudding furiously in my chest. Officers from both the police department and the county sheriff's office are here, all of them swarming around the space like ants. I don't see Kaplan, but I'm sure he's around here somewhere.

But I'm not really worried about him. My vision's focused on that gazebo, though, gleaming in the morning sun.

I can already see the blood.

It spills down the steps like some bright, garish river. My stomach turns over, and I bite back the nausea rising in my throat. I deal with dead bodies every day. I am absolutely not going to throw up over this one.

Even if it's Olivia Pearce. Even if she protected me, more or less, when I was a terrified teenager.

As I get closer, I can see more of the damage: the entire floor of the gazebo is soaked in blood, and the deceased—

Oliva

—is positioned in the center. They've covered her up with a sheet, the white already marred with a few spots of blood.

"Ms. Snow? What are you doing here?"

I recognize Kaplan's voice immediately.

I sigh and compose myself before I turn around, hoping my expression looks bland and professional. Kaplan and Rick Contreras, a detective from the police department, both stand a few feet away. Rick gives me a friendly smile. Kaplan doesn't.

"I wanted to see the scene," I say stiffly, digging my nails into my palms. "I heard it was—"

"Heard from who?" Kaplan asks. "I didn't tell the department to contact you yet."

We stare at each other, Kaplan glowering at me from beneath his shock of grey hair. Rick clears his throat.

"Someone at the police department probably did," Rick says smoothly. I'm sure he believes what he says, but I still appreciate the cover. "It'll be good to have the coroner check things out. We don't exactly get a lot of murders around here—"

Kaplan fixes his gaze on me, like he's daring me to contradict it. I don't say anything.

"And this scene is—just brace yourself," Rick continues. "I'll let the CSI know you want to take a look."

"Do you know who the victim is?" Kaplan says coldly. "Not sure you're necessarily the right person for the job."

Rick looks at me apologetically before he slinks away. Coward.

"Yes, I'm aware of the victim's identity," I say stiffly, squaring my shoulders. "And I don't know who else would perform the autopsy. The body was found in Rosado. I'm the Rosado County coroner." I give Kaplan my iciest smile. "Now, I'd like to do my job, please."

I glide past him, my chin lifted as I make my way to the gazebo. I can feel him watching me, but he doesn't say anything more. Doesn't try to stop me, either.

Rick is up ahead, talking to one of the CSIs beside the gazebo. I circle around on the grass so I don't step in the dark, sticky blood on the sidewalk.

This her?" the CSI asks as I approach. "The coroner?"

"Yes. I'm Abilene Snow," I tell him. "Do I need to cover my shoes?"

"Nah, I've already got everything from the steps here." It's a second entrance into the gazebo, and it's far less bloody than the one I saw when I arrived. The CSI tilts his head. "Come on up."

I suck in a deep breath as I enter the gazebo. The stench of blood is everywhere, sweet and sickly like rotting flowers. I'm not used to smelling blood out in the open. In the frigid, preserved air of my examination room, scents fade into the background. Besides, we don't get a lot of mangled corpses here in Rosado.

Even with... him.

I shove his masked face out of my head. I'm still doubtful he did this. All this terrible theater isn't exactly how he operates.

"You ready?" the CSI asks, tugging on the white sheet covering the body.

I nod, afraid that my voice will crack if I speak. He peels the fabric back.

"Jesus Christ," I murmur, reflexively stepping backward.

It doesn't look like the Olivia I remember, the pretty blonde woman who bought me a coffee and listened without judging. The face barely looks human at all. It's nearly split in half, in fact, cut at her mouth so the top part of her skull falls backward, revealing the glossy, bloody mess of tongue and mouth.

Worse, the body is naked and black with bruises—around the throat, across the chest. Around the wrists, too, which are positioned behind the back, with the body arranged into a kneeling position. One of the breasts has been cut off, a black, oozing hole where it should be. The entire front of the body is drenched in blood. The same blood that ran down the steps and onto the sidewalk.

What patches of clear skin I can see, it's clear that lividity has already set in. She's been dead for at least a few hours. Probably longer, given the scent of rot on the air.

For a moment, everything seems to constrict around me. The cicadas are already screaming, and the sound draws tighter and tighter in until I think I might black out.

"Who found her?" I spit out the first question I think to ask, even though I already know the answer.

"A groundskeeper," Rick says. "We spoke to him already. I sincerely doubt he had anything to do with this."

I walk around her slowly, my steps shaky. "How did she get here? Do you know?"

Rick gestures at the CSI, who throws the fabric back over the body. I breathe out, relieved even though I don't want to admit it. Rick wouldn't hold it against me, but I can feel Kaplan watching me from the grass, and he would.

"That's what we're trying to figure out," Rick says. "Her husband's out of town. We confirmed that, by the way. Been in New Orleans for the past three days. Got tons of witnesses to back it up, too."

I nod, my throat dry.

"She was killed here," I say numbly. "There wouldn't be so much blood otherwise."

"Yeah," Rick says. "Unfortunately, the security cameras were vandalized a few days ago. Hadn't been replaced yet."

Of course.

"We're asking around some of the shops on the square to see if they might have any footage. Hopefully, we'll find something."

I keep walking around the gazebo. Nothing else looks out of place. But then, I don't normally look at crime scenes, do I? I look at the body.

"When did the last shop close?" I study a wisp of spider web in the corner. My killer—

You did not just think of him that way.

He broke in a little after midnight.

"The diner across the street closed at 10 P.M." Rick nods toward it. "I've got someone following up with the cook who closed last night, but the waitress here this morning said they're usually gone by eleven. So we figure the death had to happen sometime between eleven and five A.M."

I shudder. My encounter happened a little after midnight. I suppose it's possible that he broke into my examination room, kissed me, and then killed Olivia Pearce.

But it doesn't feel right. It doesn't feel like *him*. This wasn't made to look like an accident, for one.

But I'll only know for sure if there's no letter marked on her skin.

"Send the body to the funeral home when you're ready," I say, wheeling around and out of the gazebo. It feels better out in the thick, stagnant air, even though the stink of death hangs heavy around us. "I'll get the autopsy done today."

SEEING Olivia laid out on my examination slab is somehow worse than seeing her at the crime scene. At least out there, she was a victim of a terrible crime. In here, on the metal table and beneath the bright lights, she's meat.

Horrible, mangled, horribly mutilated meat.

The first thing I do after Hector delivers her to my examination room is search her body for another letter. I rinse the blood off in patches, scouring her bruised, mottled skin for one of those telltale marks.

It's not there. Not on her ankles or calves, not on her hip, not in the crook of her elbow. Not in any of the places the letters have been before.

But more than that, rigor mortis has already set in through the body, the limbs stiff and immobile. I take the internal body temperature and calculate backward.

The time of death, as best I can tell, is between eleven and one A.M.

When my killer was here. With me.

I look over at my office, the door closed shut and the lights switched off. By this point, it's been more than twelve hours, and I still haven't taken the break-in to the authorities. I guess I have to accept that I'm simply not going to.

If a letter had been on Olivia Pearce, I would have. It would have been definite proof—*look, I told you those others were murders*. But there isn't.

So, yes. *He* didn't kill her.

But someone did.

Which strikes more worry in my chest. Because Olivia wasn't just killed. She was tortured. She was arranged in one of the most prominent places in Rosado in a position of submission—kneeling, her hands tied behind her back, her skull split open.

I grip the side of the examination table, taking slow, deep breaths. I tell myself this is a coincidence, that this has nothing to do with the articles Olivia wrote in my defense ten years ago.

But it sounds absurd. It sounds like a lie. And I can't shake the deep-rooted, shuddery feeling that Olivia is dead because of me.

I force myself to focus on my work. An autopsy is the first step in finding out who did this and getting justice for Olivia. So I began the slow, methodical process, starting with a visual examination.

"Probable cause of death," I say numbly into my recorder. "Severe laceration to the head."

Then I move closer, studying the patterns in the cuts: jagged, angry, a bit amateurish. The bruising is intense, too, and suggests she was tied up for several hours, a thought that makes me queasy enough that I have to stop, stepping over to my supply cabinet to take deep, long breaths.

I've always told myself I went to mortuary school because of Uncle Vic. Because he was here for me, in Rosado, when it felt like the entire world loathed me, even my parents. Because I found peace in the calm, gentle way he guided people through their grief, the way he would spend hours applying makeup to the deceased so that they would look their best.

But it became clear to me early on that I'm not cut out to be a funeral director. That's why I went on to study forensic science. I didn't want to let go of working with the dead. And deep down, I've always wondered if that's because my life was touched by death so early on. A death *I* caused, even if I didn't mean to—

You did mean to you knew he would fall down the stairs you did it on purpose

I squeeze my eyes shut, but it's not enough to stop it, the sudden, terrible onslaught of memories. How Jessica and Ashley, who I thought were my friends, told Blake I had a crush on him. How he laughed like it was the funniest thing in the world, then called me a few weeks later and said he'd been thinking about me and did I want to come over? His parents weren't home.

And I did.

I did, and he kissed me, jamming his tongue into my mouth. It was my first kiss. I thought it was how things were supposed to go, even though I didn't really like it.

Then he started pulling my top off, and I told him to stop, and he hit me, hard, in the face. Hard enough that I had a black eye for a week. Ms. Staunton told me, two years later, that black eye helped save me.

Because it was photographable proof of what he did. Everything else he did, you couldn't see. The way he slammed me against the wall and yanked my shorts down and shoved himself inside me while I was screaming at him to stop. The pain was blinding. I can almost feel it now, a lance of fire slicing between my legs.

I press my forehead against the cool wall, trying to remember what my therapist taught me when I was a teenager.

Breathe in for four. Breathe out for four.

But it's like my lungs can't get enough air. And I keep seeing it: how I wrenched away from him and shoved him. Not once, like I told everyone, even Ms. Staunton. But twice.

Once to get him off of me.

And then a second time, when I realized he was lined up with the top of the stairs.

My stomach lurches, and I vomit up the remains of the

lunch I nibbled at earlier. The splat of it against the floor slams me back into the present.

I'm not sixteen years old. I have not just been raped. I have not just killed the boy who raped me.

I'm twenty-six. I'm a grown woman. I graduated from high school early and went on to study mortuary science and then forensics. I'm a professional.

You let a killer put his hands on you, and you didn't fucking stop him.

I rise on shaking legs. Olivia Pearce is still lying out on my examination table. I haven't even cut her open yet.

I should have asked to have her sent to Magnolia. I don't think I'm strong enough to handle this.

My phone chimes, the sound startling me but also grounding me enough that the overwhelming, sickening panic recedes. I throw down some paper towels on my vomit, peel my gloves off, wash my hands, and check to see who it is.

I assume it's Ms. Staunton again, as anything related to the investigation would have gone to the office line. Maybe Penelope or Chloe, although I haven't told them what happened yet.

But when I pick up my phone, the name I see on the screen is the last I expect.

It's Rowan Hanover.

ROWAN

I know something's wrong the second I step into the Palm Breeze lobby, and it has nothing to do with my precious encounter last night with Abilene Snow.

I've always been able to sense things. Uncle Nash called it my sixth sense and told me I was lucky to have it. My mother said I was possessed by a demon, which, coincidentally, is also why she sent me away when I was eight years old.

Whatever the reason for it, it's just another way I'm different from everyone else. I hear people, all the stuff moving around inside them, and I go from there.

And I hear it when I come into work. Fear. Everyone's afraid.

It's not like when Mr. Nielson died. I did my job well, so all that generated was a cloud of dark curiosity. Only my Abi knew it was a murder, and that's because I shared the truth of it with her.

This fear is different, though.

I wade through the thickness of it until I get to the front desk, where Judith has already taken over from Alberto, the night shift worker. When she sees me, her eyes get huge. "Oh my god, did you hear?"

"Hear what?" I adjust the display of seashells and dried starfish we have arranged around our check-in times.

"There was a murder," she breathes.

I freeze. For a moment, I'm struck with a terribly paralyzing panic that I've been caught.

Except I haven't *done* anything.

"A murder?" I say carefully, looking over at her.

She nods. "At the gazebo. I don't know the details, but Marielle's sister works in the coffee shop that's over on the square, and she saw *everything.*"

"Everything," I repeat numbly.

Julia leans over the counter, dropping her voice to a rough whisper. "The cops are all over the gazebo square," she says, her fear tightening the words closer together. "She said there was *a lot* of blood, that they were turning people away because they didn't want them to see."

Years of practice have made it easy for me to keep my expression neutral, even if a million neurons are firing off in my brain. Another killer is in town.

I don't like that. At all.

I think of last night on the beach, that odd, not-quite-human presence I sensed. My skin prickles; the hairs on my arm stand on end. Maybe the presence felt not-quite-human because they're broken like me.

"Do you know who the victim was?" I ask.

But Julia shakes her head. "Marielle's sister didn't know, and I don't think they've released the name yet." Her fear spikes suddenly through the air, sharp and unmistakable. "Do you think this has anything to do with that lady who came by yesterday? The coroner?"

The question cuts straight through me, and for a second, I forget myself.

"What?" I ask stupidly.

"That lady with the glasses," Julia says. "Didn't she think there was something off about the guy who died here a few days ago? I mean, I know that was an accident, but—it's a weird coincidence, isn't it?"

I'm suddenly aware of the weight of my phone. Abi. I should make sure Abi's okay. If that presence followed my tracks back to her house...

A hot, surprising rage twists up in my chest.

"It's just a coincidence," I say. "Mr. Nielson's death was an accident, not a murder. Now, do me a favor and don't talk about *any* of this in front of guests. Make sure everyone knows, okay?"

"You got it, boss. But if I hear anything more, you want me to let you know?"

"Sure." The rage is still there, a wall of fire behind my chest. If anything happened to Abi, there'll be blood on a lot more than just the fucking gazebo.

I leave Julia at the front desk and duck into my office, clicking the door shut behind me. It's easier to breathe in here, cut off from the rest of the hotel staff. I lean against the door and take long, deep breaths until I'm calm enough to pull out my phone and open up Abi's number.

Her picture is still there, her softly sleeping face. The idea of actually calling her is genuinely terrifying, but I think I can manage a text. Just something that will get her to reply, so I don't spend the whole fucking day agonizing that I got her killed somehow.

> Hey. I just wanted to check in to see if you need anything else from the staff.

I read over my text. It's stupid. She was here yesterday investigating a murder—one of *my* murders—but now there's *another* murder, and it's dumb not to mention that. Isn't it? Because Rowan Hanover, the owner of the Palm Breeze Hotel, wouldn't actually know that they're unrelated. He'd assume the worst, like Julia.

Abilene Snow wouldn't, though. She knows I was with her last night.

I delete everything. The last thing I need is for her to link my identities.

So I try again.

> This is Rowan Hanover. I heard there was another death. I hope they aren't related, but I wanted to check if there was anything else you needed from me.

I read over it. Better. I tell myself I just need a response. This is to make sure she's safe.

I send it off. DELIVERED, the message says.

My throat constricts.

I carry my phone over to my desk, open up my computer, and immediately search for the death. Julia's right; they haven't released the name of the victim. And what details are out there don't exactly make me feel better. They found the body early this morning. They have no current leads. Several local authorities are cooperating on the investigation.

I'm just about to tell Julia I'm taking the day off when my phone buzzes against my desk. I snatch it up, and relief slams through me.

Abi responded.

ABI SNOW

> Hi. Thanks for checking in. No, I don't think they are related.

I slump back in my chair and let out a long, low breath. Still, I feel jittery. I don't like the idea that there's another killer in my territory. Abi lives alone, and I know from personal experience that her house isn't exactly secure. What if this person comes after her next?

I pull up a map of Rosado on my computer, zooming in until I have a view of the intersection where Neptune's Adventure is. That presence I felt—it had the air of a predator. Of someone like me.

I wonder if I could lure him to the mini golf course. Two birds with one stone, as they say. I continue my message to Abi while clearing out this interloper in the process.

My phone chimes again, and when I glance over at it, my heart skips.

Another text from Abi.

> This is going to sound crazy, and you can say no if you want, but do you want to grab a coffee this afternoon? Maybe at Seaside Brews?

All my vision tunnels down to her text. Did she ask me out?

I think of her warm body, her soft panty breath, the heat between her legs.

She didn't know that was you, dumb ass.

I pick up the phone, still staring down at her message. Seaside Brews. That's just across the street from the hotel. I've never been, although my staff are always bringing in coffees from there, the cups emblazoned with neon-colored palm trees.

I keep expecting Abi's message to vanish, like it's a mirage. A hallucination. But it stays put, the cursor in the reply box blinking steadily. I wonder if she can see that I've read her message, a thought that fills me with a sudden torrent of panic. I don't want her to think I'm blowing her off.

> Yes, of course.

I can't believe I just did that. Can't believe this is happening.

> Oh, that's great! Meet in 30 minutes?

My heart thunders as I reply back with another yes. I'd meet her there in five minutes if she asked me. I'd do anything she asked me.

I stare at the map on my computer screen, the familiar roads of Rosado crisscrossing over my monitor. An auspicious kill in so many ways, it seems. Not just that it's **K**, or that it's completing the next word. But that it's the first kill after she came to me as Rowan, and after I went to her as myself. The first kill after she's spoken to both sides of me, the disguise and the truth.

I don't ask why it's all happening now. Maybe I should. I know Uncle Nash would tell me to be suspicious, but that's because he beat into me since I was a boy that the only person I could trust was him.

And that's just because he wanted to use my violence for his own purposes.

I clear out the map, erase my browser history, take a deep breath. Remind myself that, despite what happened last night, she's meeting Rowan Hanover. I have to keep my disguise in place, even if it tears at something in my chest, knowing she would never have asked the real me out to coffee at Seaside Brews.

It doesn't matter. The real me will still be there, lurking inside this shell.

10

ROWAN

The coffee shop has the same nervous energy as the hotel. Everyone seems normal on the surface, but I can feel their fear drifting around, taut as a wire. That murder really has everyone worked up, and I wonder, for the first time, what my rival did that was so terror-inducing.

I specifically craft my kills so they don't look like kills, and I take pride in that—in protecting myself, in being clever. But I suppose, wading through the fear in the coffee shop to a small table near the back, that I can see why someone might want to generate all this terrified energy. Why they might want to bask in it.

It certainly helps distract from my own anxiety over being on a date with Abi.

I get there early because I don't want to make Abi wait. I order a plain iced coffee and sip on it, watching the door while I count down until our meeting time. I also listen, because half the people in the coffee shop are talking about the murder.

"Can't believe something like that would happen here," says one woman to her friend, both of them older and clearly wealthy, the kind of people who live elsewhere but own a house on the beach for whenever they want to get away. "Can you *imagine?*"

"I heard it was a gang initiation," her friend says. "With Rosado being so close to the border and all."

I roll my eyes. I had more than my share of encounters with the gangs that run drugs through south Texas. Their kills are strategic, just like the assignments Uncle Nash gave me.

"Do they know who it was?" This question isn't from the two wealthy ladies, but from a surfer-type hanging around the bar, bothering the barista in his board shorts and flip flops. "ID'd the vic?"

"Not that I know," she says, sliding glasses down the bar. "I heard it was a tourist. An out-of-towner."

"Oh, yeah? Who told you that?"

She says a name, but I don't hear it, because everything in that coffee shop becomes overpowered by the sweet scent of lantana and orchids.

The bell over the door chimes, but I already know it's Abi. She's as pretty as she was last night, although she's pulled her hair back, and she's not wearing her thick-framed glasses. That just makes it easier to see her big blue eyes as she sweeps them around the space. When they land on me, my heart nearly erupts out of my chest.

I still manage to lift my hand in greeting.

And Abi *smiles*, right at me, and it's like the sun coming out from behind a cloud.

"Hey," she says when she comes over to my table. "You're here."

She says it like she thought I might not be.

"Well, yeah, of course." I hope my voice isn't too shaky. "Do you want me to get you something?"

Abi hesitates, just for a second. I think my question surprised her.

"Sure," she says. "If you don't mind."

I'm already pushing away from the table, my wallet in hand. "I'll get it for you. What do you want?"

Abi blinks at me. "Um, how about an iced lavender latte?"

"Coming right up."

It's interesting how easy it is to fall into the role of Rowan Hanover when twelve hours earlier she was pressed against me, and I wasn't Rowan Hanover at all.

I order her drink and wait for the barista to prepare it. When I come back to the table, Abi gives me a somewhat embarrassed smile. She's scared, too. I can sense her fear as much as I can sense everyone else's.

"Thanks for meeting me," she says, stirring her drink around with the straw. "I know—I know it came out of nowhere, but I just..." She looks up at me, gnawing a little on her bottom lip. "I just wanted to talk to someone, and you seemed nice when we met the other day."

An odd, wriggling feeling rolls through my chest. I think it might be guilt. After all, I'm not exactly who she thinks I am.

"I'm happy to talk," I say, a million other questions bubbling around in my head. I know she doesn't really have friends here in Rosado. I never see her going out with anyone. She certainly doesn't go on dates. She spends her holidays alone, which has always worked out for me, since it means I don't have to spend them alone, either.

But I want to know *why*. That's always been the missing piece.

"When you texted about the murder this morning," she says, looking down at her latte. "I don't know, I just needed to get out of my examination room. I—"

She stops, and I feel something drifting off her, a hesitation and a whiff of lust, a ghost of what I felt last night. For a second, I think she might tell me about it.

Instead, she says, "I agreed to autopsy the victim."

"Isn't that what you do?" I ask carefully.

Abi looks up at me, her long side-swept bangs falling across the tops of her eyes. "Yeah," she says. "But I knew her."

I freeze, my fingers tightening around my coffee glass. "Who was she?" I say softly, before I can stop myself. But I need to know. This killer, I need to know everything I can about him, if only to keep my Abi safe.

Abi bites her lips, more hesitancy coming off her. "I probably shouldn't say," she murmurs. "But I'm going to. It's gonna be in the papers soon enough anyway."

I wait, watching her.

"She was a reporter." Her voice is steely. "She lived in Magnolia."

I don't react. I don't show Abi that I know what that means, that I know about her past.

"Her name was Olivia Pearce," Abi continues, and I recognize the name immediately. I have copies of all the articles that Olivia wrote about Abi from back when I was a teenager, when Abi first moved to Rosado. All I knew about her was that she had killed someone and that she was beautiful. I wanted to understand everything I could about that kill, so I went to the library and pulled issues of the newspaper Olivia wrote for and copied anything that mentioned Abi's name.

I still have those articles, too, tucked away in a file folder in my desk.

But of course I can't let Abi know any of this. Rowan Hanover is a stranger to her.

"How'd you know her?" I say.

It's the right response. Abi jerks her gaze to meet mine, and I feel a flutter of her excitement. A kind of—lightness. Or relief.

She thinks I don't know about her past.

But I do know. And I really don't fucking like that this interloper killed someone who helped clear Abi's name ten years ago. I don't like that this murder has any connection to Abi at all.

"She helped me out with something when I was younger," Abi says carefully. "It's not—it's not important. But it freaked me out that she could—" Abi looks off to the side, her expression distant. "I'm sorry, I don't want to dump all this on you. I just needed to be around another living person, and you—"

"Seemed nice?" I offer. Abi smiles. Laughs a little.

"Yeah," she says. "I mean, you had a *Blood Raiser 3* poster in your office. You seemed like someone—" She shrugs a little. "Someone I could be friends with."

My heart races a million miles a second. *Friends. She wants to be friends.*

It's a start. A step closer to having her the way I want to have her. Not like last night, where I had to take. Maybe she doesn't want the real me, but I think if Rowan Hanover asked to touch her—not right now, of course, but soon—she would say yes.

"I don't have any friends who like the Blood Raiser movies," I say.

Abi laughs, a kind of tension-breaking laugh. I've heard it before, from victims. It's more hysterical-sounding when they do it. And not nearly as sweet.

"I mean, I guess I technically do," she says. "But they don't live here. One of them's always moving around, and the other's on the East Coast."

I know about them, too. Chloe Monroe and Penelope Noble. I've scoured every photo they've posted across social media. Parties from college. A vacation to Florida that they all took together. I know Chloe is a data analyst, and Penelope's an environmental activist who moves around to chase different protests.

I've spent hours learning about Abi. Killing and Abilene Snow, those are my two biggest interests.

But of course I can't let her know any of that.

"That sucks," I finally say. "Not having friends close by." I sip on my drink, barely tasting it. "I don't have a lot of friends, either. I have to spend all my time at the hotel."

"Oh, I can imagine," Abi says. "God, that seems like so much work. Running a hotel."

"I fell into it. My uncle left me the hotel when he died."

I wonder if she remembers Uncle Nash's death. She was still living here when it happened.

"My uncle left me the funeral parlor," she says with a laugh. "Funny. That's another thing we have in common, isn't it?"

"We both inherited real estate from our uncles?"

"Yeah." She smiles. "Well, real estate and a business." She pushes her hair behind her ear. "I don't do funerals, though. I wasn't really good at that part. Not like Uncle Vic."

"So what part were you good at?" I can't believe how easy it is to talk to her like a normal person, to learn things I can't find out from watching her in the dark.

Abi rubs her finger around the rim of her cup. "I liked working with the bodies," she says softly. "Uncle Vic would let me help with the preparation. Putting on makeup, that sort of thing. I liked how— unjudgmental they were, I guess."

All I can do is sit and stare at her. I'm afraid that if I say anything, it'll scare her off.

"God, I'm probably freaking you out right now," she laughs, shaking her head.

"No!" I say it too quickly, and she jerks her gaze up to mine. "No, I think it's interesting. I feel like maybe running a hotel and running a funeral parlor are kind of similar?"

I have no idea where I pulled that out from, but Abi tilts her head, waiting to hear more

"You have to make people happy," I say. "Make them feel welcome."

"Honestly, you're right," Abi says. "It's all hospitality, right?

That's why I like doing autopsies instead of mortuary science. The dead don't care what you do to them."

That's the same reason why I like killing people more than running a hotel. Another similarity between us that I can't say out loud.

"I wish my guests didn't care what we did to them," I say. "But, alas, they care way too much."

Abi laughs at that, and I can feel her anxiety lifting, just a bit. So I start telling her about running the Palm Breeze Hotel to see if I can lighten her mood even more. To my surprise, it works.

I tell her about the Patton family, who show up every July with their seven incredibly destructive children. And about Mrs. Gomez, a widow who spends the whole summer at the hotel, lounging by the swimming pool like an aging movie star. The more I talk, the more stories come out, and soon we're having a real conversation, me and Abi, our words crossing back and forth across the table.

I've daydreamed about this a million times, probably even more than I've daydreamed about fucking her. And it's just as exhilarating as it was to kiss her last night, and to feel her arousal seeping through her panties.

And it's just as disappointing when she cuts it short, too.

"God, I'm sorry," Abi says, checking the time on her phone. "I didn't mean to stay this long. I've got to get that autopsy done."

"Do you need—support, or something?" I imagine stepping into the examination room as Rowan Hanover. But Abi shakes her head.

"I just need to get out of my head for a while, and this helped. A lot. Thank you." Her blue eyes meet mine. "Really. I appreciate it. I know how weird—"

"It's not weird," I say quickly. "I like talking to you."

A pink blush creeps into Abi's cheeks, and, just for a second,

I catch the same heightened orchid scent from last night. My cock stirs.

"I like talking to you, too," she says. "Maybe we can do it again?"

"Anytime."

When she stands up from the table, I do, too. I'm a gentleman, after all.

"Thanks for the latte," she says. "I'll text you, okay? Maybe this weekend?"

"Sure." As if I'm going to wait until the weekend to see her again. I've never needed much sleep, which means I'll be watching Abi's house tonight. And tomorrow night. And every night until I make sure that the interloper who killed Olivia Pearce breathes for the last time.

I don't believe in coincidences. Uncle Nash taught me that. And it's certainly not a coincidence that Olivia Pearce died in Rosado, not Magnolia. I'm a killer who sends messages, so I know what a killer's message looks like.

"Thanks again," Abi says sweetly, lingering by the table.

"Let me walk you out," I say.

Let me do anything to protect you.

11

ROWAN

I crouch on the lower branches of the big, sprawling oak tree that grows in Abi's yard, right next to the window that opens into her living room. The funeral parlor is downstairs, so Abi doesn't spend much time there. This tree has proven to be a perfect place for me to be with her when I don't want to risk breaking in. It helps that her only curtains are these pale, gauzy things that let the sunlight in during the day. At night, when she has the living room lights on, I can see everything.

I've spent so much time with her like this. Joined her in her annual *Blood Raiser 3* viewings. Sat with her during Thanksgiving last year while she ate a dinner she cooked for herself and watched *The Godfather*. Or just hanging out in the evenings, both of us sprawled out: Abi on the couch in an oversized T-shirt after a long day at work, and me in my killing face on this thick branch that slings down like a hammock.

She's not alone tonight, though, nor is she watching movies. She's with her two friends on Zoom. I can't see or hear them, but Abi keeps waltzing around the living room with her laptop in hand, speaking to the screen. She smoked a joint earlier and then opened a bottle of wine, and it's made her light and giggly, loud enough that her voice spills out through the thick, distorted glass of the window. My hearing's always been good— uncannily good, Uncle Nash would say with a knowing wink, just like I'm uncannily strong and uncannily talented at killing —and I know they've been talking about some development in Chloe's life. But since I only hear Abi's side of the conversation, I don't know the details. Something about Chloe getting a house on a lake.

It doesn't matter. I'm here to make sure Abi's safe, not to eavesdrop. Although when I hear my name, my whole body lights up, and I lean forward, making the tree branches rustle.

"—coffee together," Abi's saying. She's stopped next to the window, holding the laptop like a waiter balancing a tray on one hand. She has her wineglass in the other. "He's really nice. A lot nicer than most guys around here."

I get that weird twist of guilt again. She wouldn't say the real me is nice. That encounter, she hasn't even mentioned to her friends.

She pauses, staring down at the computer, then gives a shriek and a giggle and cries, "Oh my god! No! It was just coffee!"

Heat warms my cheeks.

"Stop!" she cries. "I never should have told you two about him."

Abi turns away from the window, drifting out of my line of sight. I can still sense her inside—the quiet hum of her voice, too far away for me to really hear, and something else, a kind of underlying rhythm that feels reassuring. I settle back agains the trunk of the tree, staring at the window of light through the canopy of leaves.

She thinks I'm nice.

No, she thinks Rowan Hanover is nice.

I am Rowan Hanover.

You're a fucking monster.

That last bit, it's in my mother's voice, screaming and hysterical. She was drunk, too, when she said that to me. I don't even know how she knew what I was capable of. I was only eight. I hadn't killed anyone yet.

More laughter from inside. Abi's settled down on her couch, but all I can really see of her is her long, pale legs, stretched out on the ottoman.

Still, I don't want to leave her. Even seeing that little bit of her is an assurance that she's safe. That she—

The damp wind gusts through the tree, making all the leaves shimmer, and I sense something.

I sit up, adrenaline prickling over my skin.

Someone else is here.

I check my killing face to make sure it's secure. Then I slide out of the tree, dropping lightly on the grass into a crouch. I go still for a minute. Listening. *Sensing.*

It's the same presence as last night. Not human. Not an animal.

I rise up, my muscles tense. I can still sense Abi, too. She feels calm.

I move forward, following the trail on the breezy, salt-kissed wind. It leads me around to the front of the house, and I stop beside Abi's flower garden, the sunflowers bobbing in the darkness.

The presence is in the cemetery.

I sweep my gaze around, but I don't see much. The street lamps illuminate the road and the black wrought iron fence that wraps around the burial grounds, but even in the darkness beyond, I can't see much. Just the pale teeth of headstones.

But that presence is there. I'm certain of it. I *feel* it, hot and coursing and vaguely sinister, like spilled blood. The interloper. Olivia Pearce's murderer. Who else could it be?

I don't want to leave Abi alone, but if this is my chance to dispatch the interloper before he can hurt her, I'm going to take it.

So I dart out of her yard and across the street, keeping away from the street lamps. Something about the presence changes, somehow. It feels brighter. Clearer.

Does he sense me the way I sense him?

I weave through the cemetery's pecan trees, leaving the funeral parlor behind me. The presence shifts; I thought it was directly in front of me. Now it feels like it's off to the left.

I jerk my gaze up, and just for a second, a split second, I see a flicker of movement, like a rabbit darting back into the woods.

Like a victim giving chase.

I take off in a run, my feet pounding against the dirt, my breath quick and steady. Adrenaline surges up in me again, along with that inky blackness that starts to take over before I make a kill.

A kill. I can't kill the interloper here. I'm not ready for my Neptune's Adventure kill yet, either. Fuck. I hate killing without any preparation. As Uncle Nash *constantly* reminded me, that's how you get yourself caught.

Another flicker of movement, this time off to my right. I stumble to a stop, nearly tripping over a mossy hedge of gravestones, and I whip around to see a figure disappear into the shadows between the pecan trees.

I follow it, hungry for the pursuit. I don't chase my victims often. Not like this. Usually, I watch them from the shadows, the way I watch Abi, waiting for them to fall into whatever trap I set for them.

But I don't have a trap here. I just have a target.

I dart across the cemetery, moving through the darkness. I don't see much of anything beyond the pale headstones, but I can sense the trail my prey has left behind. It's not a scent, not a sound. Just an intuition, telling me where to go.

The wind howls, damp and smelling of the sea, and the trail vanishes.

"Fuck!" I whisper, skidding to a stop. I'm at the far edge of the cemetery, where the black fence juts up against the overgrown field that eventually rolls down the shore. I sniff, sweeping my head around, trying to catch on to that presence again.

Gone. It's gone. I squeeze my eyes shut and strain against the night, listening for something, although I'm not sure what. It's worked for me in the past.

I can sense nearby animals, small and cautious. But nothing human or close-to-human. Not my prey.

The wind settles into stillness. I open my eyes.

Still nothing.

Then something sparks in the distance. But it's not my quarry. It can't be. Because they disappeared into the open field, and this is coming behind me. It's coming from—

From Abi's house.

I whirl around, a thick, black dread coiling in my stomach. And I realize this *can't* be the presence I was tracking. Because it's human, undeniably so.

But that humanity is wrapped up in cold, terrible malevolence. Anger. A propensity for violence. I'd recognize it anywhere because for ten years these were the kinds of humans I was always killing for Uncle Nash.

And I realize, with a thud of despair, that I've completely fucked up.

Whoever I was chasing isn't Olivia Pearce's killer.

This is.

And he's at Abi's house.

12

ABI

"Truth or dare," Chloe announces. "Penelope."

"I'm not fucking doing this." Penelope leans back, shaking her head. "We are grown women."

"Fine. Abi. Truth or dare."

I take a sip of my wine before answering. My two best friends aren't here *with* me, technically, but at last I can see both of their faces blinking up from their computer screens. Chloe's out on her apartment balcony, so all I can see is her face lit up by the sallow overhead light. Not that it's going to be her apartment for long, since she's apparently going to move into that Appalachian lake house her grandparents left her. It's dark where she is, too, in North Carolina. All I can see of Penelope's background is a plain white wall. She's staying with her sister right now, she said when we first hopped on the call. In Chicago.

"Come onnnnn," Chloe whines. "Truth or dare. I want to play."

"Why?" Penelope asks. "We fucking know all of each other's secrets."

Chloe groans, and I laugh.

92

"She's right," I say. "She's got you."

"You two *suck*," she says. "Okay, how about a drinking game? I've got a bottle of gin here, and I want to drink it." She leans forward, tapping on her keyboard. "I bet I can find something online."

"So drink your gin," Penelope says. "No one's stopping you."

"You are so boring, Penny." The light from Chloe's laptop changes, illuminating her face as she squints at her screen. "It'd be like when we played D and D in the dorms, remember? Take a drink anytime someone rolls a crit."

"We're not playing D and D," I point out. "Although I guess we could."

"Do not give her any ideas." Penelope sucks on her vape pen, pale mist filling up her screen. "What do you want to do, Abs?"

"I don't need to play a drinking game, that's for damn sure." I've already had nearly half a bottle of this sweet red grocery store wine, plus the joint I smoked earlier. The world feels heady and bright and a much better place than it was before Chloe and Penelope and I got on this call together.

I know why Penelope's asking me, though. This call is for me. A distraction from everything.

"What if we watch a movie?" Chloe's still tapping on her laptop. "I can start a watch party or something."

"Let me guess," Penelope says. "We watch *Friday the 13th* and drink every time there's a kill on screen?"

"No." Chloe grins. "We watch my giallo marathon and drink every time there's a boob on screen."

Given the overly potent combo of weed and wine, this is legitimately the funniest thing I've heard in a while, and I dissolve into hysterical laughter, which sets Chloe off, too. Penelope's too cool for it, and she just sucks on her vape pen and stares at her screen with an amused sparkle in her eye.

I wish they were here, for real, the three of us sprawled out in my living room like we used to do our final year at college, when we shared a duplex a few blocks from campus. *I should move*, I think blearily, although I don't know where. To middle-of-nowhere North Carolina, with Chloe? It's not like Penelope stays put, really. She's always moving around, chasing causes. Living in hostels or couch-surfing.

North Carolina would be nice enough. I'm sure I could find a job. But leaving Rosado means selling the Hatch Street Funeral Parlor. And I promised Uncle Vic I wouldn't do that.

"Okay, but seriously," Chloe says. "There's the new A24 movie—"

"Abi doesn't want to watch that pretentious garbage," Penelope laughs.

"Oh, shut up. It's free on HBO right now. I can share my password and—"

Something thumps downstairs.

Immediately, the woozy, feel-good feeling from the weed calcifies into a sharp, paranoid anxiety. I take a deep breath, trying to calm down my suddenly racing heart as Chloe and Penelope argue good-naturedly on the computer screen.

Another thump, louder than the first, and I jump against my couch.

He's back.

"Abs? You okay?" Penelope's voice sounds far away. I blink at the computer. They're both staring at their screens. Looking at me.

"I'm fine," I say. "I just—I thought I heard something." I shake my head, force out a grin. "It's just this house. Makes a lot of noise at night. What movie were you thinking of—"

My cell phone lights up, buzzing against the coffee table. I grab it.

UNKNOWN NUMBER

"You need to take that?" Chloe says, and I can tell from the worry in her voice what she's thinking—more bad news, another death.

"No, it's a spam call." I silence my phone and throw it on the sofa beside me. "What are we thinking? Movie?"

My phone lights up, this time with a text.

"Can you even still do watch parties anymore?" Penelope says. "I figured they nixed all that shit after—"

I check my phone as surreptitiously as possible, hoping Chloe and Penelope can't see me on screen. The same unknown number—

And the text is a photograph of my front door.

Real fear lances through my chest, and I suck in deep breaths of air as Chloe and Penelope's bickering voices spill out of my computer speaker, tinny and far away. I should call the police.

What if it's him? My killer?

What if it is? He's a fucking murderer, even if he's apparently not the only one in Rosado. I shake my head, trying to clear out my thoughts. Trying to convince myself not to be stupid.

"Abi? Are you even paying attention?" Chloe says, sounding put out.

Something explodes downstairs. A loud, echoing *bang*, then the crash of splintering wood. I shriek and jump to my feet, dropping my laptop on the sofa.

My phone lights up with another text. Chloe and Penelope are shouting at me, asking if I'm okay, wanting to know what's going on. I don't know how to answer them. I told them about Rowan and our coffee date, but the whole time I was thinking about the masked killer who broke in the night before, who brushed his mouth against mine and asked if he could touch me.

I grab my computer and hold it up to my face. "I'll be right back," I tell them, hoping I can keep the panic down in my voice. "Someone's at the door, okay?"

"Ignore it," Penelope says flatly. "It's almost midnight."

More thumps from downstairs. My heart is going to erupt out of my chest. I have no idea why I'm not being truthful with them—

Because you think it's him, *you absolute fucking idiot.*

"I'll call you guys back, okay?" I exit out of the Zoom room and snap my laptop shut and grab my phone. A single text waits for me.

> Where are you hiding?

Terror squeezes my throat shut, and I know, regardless of whether it's my nameless killer or someone much, much worse, I need to figure out a way to get out of this house.

I stand still, holding my breath. I can hear someone moving downstairs, slow and purposeful. Fuck.

I immediately shut off the living room lamp, plunging me into darkness. Then I skitter across the floor, moving as lightly as I can, and stick my head out into the hallway.

No one's here.

I know damn well I should call the cops, and I know damn well why I'm not, even if I can barely admit it to myself. I want it to be him. The killer I've tracked for two years. I don't want the cops showing up and shooting him dead. I want—

Footsteps thump on the stairs. I stumble backward, staring at the stairwell at the end of the hall. I fumble with the phone, typing 911 into the dial pad but not pressing the call button.

And then I wait, my breath shaky and ragged.

A light dances across the stair landing. I slip backward toward my room, clutching my phone, fear and excitement wrapping tight around my thoughts. *Please be him. Please be him.*

A dark figure steps onto the top of the stairs. And for a

second, I feel a burst of relief. Because it looks like him—dressed all in black, his face disguised.

But he turns toward me and stops, and I realize how wrong I am.

He's shorter and thinner than the man who visited me last night. And he's not wearing a mask, like I thought. He has a stocking pulled over his face that distorts his features.

"There you are, you ugly cunt," he snarls.

I scream and, in a moment of panicked stupidity, I hurl my phone at him instead of pressing the call button. He ducks, and the phone sails past him and hits the wall with a crack.

Then he laughs. "Was that supposed to do something?" he chuckles, stepping toward me. He has something in his hand. Rope, I think.

"Get out of my house." My voice comes out thin and tremulous. I take a cautious step backward. One step closer to my bedroom. I have a lock on the door. I can barricade myself in. Find a way to call the police.

Because this definitely isn't my killer.

"No," the intruder says. "I've got big plans for you. Come on. You might even like it, little slut that you are."

"Who the fuck are you?" Another step backward. My bedroom feels like it's a million miles away.

"You haven't guessed yet?" he laughs, holding up the rope. "Come on, bitch. I thought you were supposed to be smart."

Tears brim in my eyes. I can see my phone sitting dark on the floor, but a murderer is standing in front of it. And not a murderer who's going to ask to touch me, either.

"You killed Olivia, didn't you?"

The intruder laughs. "Yeah," he says. "I made her suck my cock right before I split her face in half."

Revulsion and terror spike through me. For a moment, the room seems to spin. I press my hand up against the wall, trying to steady myself. The second-floor landing is wide, wide enough that I might be able to run past him and grab my phone and get out of the house.

"I fucked her real good before she died," the intruder says. "And I'm going to do the same thing to you. Now *kneel*."

He lunges at me. I scream and dart sideways, managing to shove him in the process so he slams up against the far wall. He lands with a thump, and I forget my phone. All I can focus on is tearing down the stairs in a stumbling panic.

"Get back here, you stupid fucking whore!" he bellows, his footsteps shaking the landing. I leap off the steps and whip around the hallway. Glass glitters on the floor, and the front door hangs crooked on its hinges, letting in curls of warm summer air.

That's all I focus on, getting to that door, even as I can hear the intruder thundering down the stairs behind me. If I can get outside, I can get away from him.

I fling the door open and leap out onto the porch—

And slam into a broad, masculine chest.

13

ABI

"**N**o!" I scream, despair coursing through me as I stumble backward, so sick with fear I'm about to throw up. How could I be so stupid? Of course I won't be safe just because I leave the house. Of course he's not working alone.

But then the man in the doorway speaks.

"Where is he?"

I recognize the voice immediately. Low, raspy. The same voice that asked, *May I touch you?*

I jerk my gaze up, my breath tight and panicky. It's him. He's wearing the same twisted mask, and I can smell him, a dark amber scent like the woods at night.

I drop my mouth open, but my throat doesn't work. I can't answer.

It doesn't matter. My nameless killer drags me by the shoulders and heaves me violently onto the porch, then steps in front of me just as the earlier attacker bursts through the doorway.

"Who the fuck are you?" the attacker asks.

My killer launches himself at him, a dark comet that slams into the intruder's chest and shoves him back into the house. I

99

can just see them through the door: two dark masses that bleed into one another as they thump against the floor.

One of them screams, sharp and short. Then it's caught off.

I brace myself against the banister, my entire body sheened with sweat as the hot, muggy air presses around me. The silence is overpowering.

I know I should run. There's a twenty-four-hour gas station about a half mile down Hatch Street. Once I get there, once I'm bathed in the buzzing fluorescent lights, I can call for help.

But I don't move. I'm petrified against the banister, my pounding against my rib cage like it's training to escape.

Footsteps.

I stiffen, whimpering with fear, my muscles tense. A dark shadow falls into the doorway.

It's him. It's my killer.

He stares at me through his mask, his eye gleaming in the porch light. For a moment, we just stare at each other.

Then he says, "Come inside. Now."

"W-why?" I whisper.

"He's dead," my killer says. "You don't have to worry about that. But you need to come inside. A car might drive by."

I look over Hatch Street, illuminated in patches by the street lamps.

"Who are you?" I whisper. "Why did you—"

"Inside."

I peel away from the banister, moving on slow, shaky legs. I could still run. My killer makes no move to attack me. He doesn't even have a weapon. Not that a lack of a weapon would stop him, clearly.

I can feel him watching me as I shuffle across the porch, my arms wrapped tight around my chest. When I'm close enough to the door, he steps aside, giving me room to come in.

My attacker lies sprawled in the foyer, his head bent at an impossible angle.

"What did you—" I can't say it. I can't stop shaking. "How did you—"

A bang as he lodges the broken door back into its frame. I jump like I just heard a gunshot.

"I've been watching you, my little detective," he says softly, right in my ear. I shriek and whip away from him.

His eyes move behind the mask, watching me.

"Who was that?" I gasp out.

"I don't know." He tilts his head toward the body. "Why don't you take that stocking off and find out?"

My breath lodges in my throat, and I shake my head furiously. "I can't do that. I can't mess with a—a crime scene—"

My killer grabs me around the waist, jerking me up against his chest. I don't know how he moved so fast. One minute he was there, the next he wasn't.

"You're not thinking of calling the police, are you?" He bows his head to speak into my ear, the cool latex of the mask smooth against my skin.

"What else am I supposed to do?" I whimper. "I can't—it happened in my house, and I—"

My killer snakes his arm tighter around my waist, pulling me closer into him. His body is soft and strong at the same time, and I have to fight against the urge to lean back into him, to wriggle my ass until I feel his cock.

You did not just fucking think that.

"You can't call the police," my killer murmurs. "Because then we wouldn't be able to continue our conversation."

"What conversation?" I gasp, even though I know:

Letters carved into skin, spelling out words only I can see.

He tuts. "Don't hurt my feelings, little detective. I don't want the authorities investigating me. I want you to do it."

"He killed Olivia." The words turn into a sob, and I doubt my killer even knows who Olivia Pearce is. Or cares. "He told me he did."

"And now he's dead." My killer loosens his grip, sliding his hand over the curve of my hip but not dropping it any lower. "Justice has been served, yes?"

I take deep, shaky breaths, staring over at the body. It looks like a pile of laundry in the middle of the floor. It looks like nothing.

"What am I supposed to do with that?" I hardly believe that I'm even *considering* doing what my killer asks. I want to tell myself I'm just playing along, that as soon as he leaves, I'll be on the phone with the police department and the sheriff's office, given his track record covers both their jurisdictions.

But I know I won't be.

"You don't have to do anything with it." He steps around me, moving with slow, steady strides. "I'll take care of everything, little detective. All you have to do—"

He glances over at me, the twisted expression on his mask leering and cold.

"—Is keep looking for me."

"I found you," I gasp. "You're here. Right here."

He shakes his head. "Not what I mean, and you know it."

He crouches down beside the body and gestures for me to come over.

"You're going to keep killing," I whisper. "I'm supposed to let you just keep killing—"

He looks at me again, his eyes an impossible weight. For a moment, I want to see his face. Not so I can know what he looks like, but so I can know what he's thinking.

"Of course," he says. "We're having a conversation. Each death serves a purpose." His eyes glitter. "It helps me reveal a little more of myself to you."

I suck in my breath, unsure how to respond to that. Or unsure why it sets my heart fluttering.

My killer reaches down and yanks the stocking off the attacker, then carefully tilts the face toward me.

He's older. That's the first thing I think. He's got to be fifteen years older than me, with shaggy brown hair going grey at the temples and tanned, leathery skin. His eyes are wide with shock, his mouth slack.

I don't recognize him.

"Who is he?" my killer asks, eyes fixed firmly on my face.

I shake my head. "I don't—I've never seen him before."

Still, I work through the possibilities in my head. He murdered Olivia Pearce and then came for me. It has to be someone connected to Blake Fletcher, doesn't it? But I've never seen this man before. And he's too old to have been one of Blake's friends at school. A relative, maybe?

"Hmm," my killer says. Then he balls up the stocking and shoves it in the man's mouth.

"What are you going to do to him?" I whisper.

My killer stands up. "Not what he did to poor Olivia Pearce," he says.

My heart thumps. So he does know about her death. Suddenly, I'm wondering about another killer's identity. He obviously lives here. The police didn't release many details about the case, but the Rosado gossips have been hard at work, no doubt.

"But I won't tell you anything else." He tilts his head, and his voice changes. I think he's smiling. "But you'll find out soon enough. Think of it as a test, Abilene—"

It's the first time I've heard him say my name, and it sends lightning bolts through my core.

"If you keep our secret safe, I'll know I can trust you." He moves closer, stepping over the body without looking at it. I hold my breath as he leans into me, his eyes dark behind his mask as he reaches up and cups my face with his gloved hand.

I shiver a little at the touch.

"I'll know you really are my little detective," he purrs.

"Good night, Abi. And go upstairs. Tell your friends you're all right."

How the fuck did he know about that? Another spike of terror in my belly. But something else, too. A sense of dark flattery.

"Don't come down until morning." He rubs his thumb against my jawline. I hate that I like the way it feels, that I don't want him to stop. "You'll see. In the daylight, everything will be all right."

14

ABI

My phone is waiting for me at the top of the stairs, and when I swipe it open, *911* is still eblazoned on the call screen. I stare at it, my breath tight, as sounds drift up from downstairs. Thumps. Rustles. Heavy footsteps.

My killer, making the nightmare go away.

I erase the numbers and open up the string of messages from my group chat with Chloe and Penelope.

PENELOPE

U there?

CHLOE

Call us. Everything okay?

Should we call the police?

PENELOPE

Don't be fucking stupid. I'm not sending the cops to her house. Abi, call us back as soon as you get this.

There are a couple of missed calls from both of them. I open up the group chat, trying to ignore my killer thumping around downstairs.

> Hey, I'm really sorry about that. It was someone from the sheriff's department checking in on me. They had a report of a lurker nearby, so they wanted to check in. Everything's fine.

I stare at the message. I hate lying to them. But I know I can't tell them the truth.

I hit SEND and go into my bedroom and lock the door. I doubt the flimsy lock could actually keep my killer out, but it gives me the facade of safety.

I can still hear him downstairs, though.

My phone dings several times in quick succession—Chloe and Penelope sending their flurry of responses.

CHLOE

> Girl you had us so fucking worried

PENELOPE

> Couldn't have spared a text for your old friends? A meager, simple text?

A meme of a sad-eyed cat.

I text back more apologies, my throat getting tighter with each one. Especially since my killer's presence is still wafting up from the first floor. And the fact that he's down there with a dead body makes me feel—strange. Afraid, yes. But relieved, too. Because he saved my life.

And there's something else, a darker undercurrent that pulses with my blood. I fall back on my bed and press my legs together, and it doesn't go away. Chloe sends another meme. I heart it without looking at it, then tell them both I'm going to bed.

I'm wide awake, though. Wide awake and throbbing with something dangerously close to desire.

A loud, decisive thump echoes from downstairs. My body quakes, and I honestly don't know if it's fear or anxiety or something else. Something I don't want to think about.

I squeeze my eyes shut, listening. The house is silent.

Don't come down until morning.

His words echo around in my head, and the truth is, I don't want to go down there. I feel safe up here, behind my door's lock. Insulated.

Even if I'm vibrating with adrenaline.

I push off my bed, my body shaking, and stumble into my attached bathroom. I lock that door, too, then peer out the small oval window. Not that I can see anything outside.

I move by rote to turn on the water and strip out of my clothes as it warms up. I stare at the spray, feeling numb and detached. I don't know if he's still down there. I don't know what he's doing, or did, to get rid of the body. I don't know why I'm trusting him not to frame me for his actions. Or do something worse.

But I need to wash the death off my skin. I need the numbing effect of hot water and scented steam. That death down there, it's not like what I deal with in my examination room. It wasn't sterile or scientific. It was terrifying. It was—

A warmth creeps between my legs.

I climb under the spray, hot enough to scald my skin as it streams over my shoulders and down the furrow of my spine. I hope it's hot enough to burn this terrible clenching away.

It's not. And yet here I am, in a fucking shower. Who gets into a shower with a killer downstairs? I've watched hundreds of classic horror movies with Penelope and Chloe. I know what happens when you mix killers and showers.

But nothing happens. There's no creak as the bathroom

door slides open—and it always creaks. There's no heavy thud of my killer's boot steps on the tile flooring.

Just the water.

Just the heat.

Just my memories. Of the death. And of my killer snaking his hand around my waist, telling me he would take care of everything.

I shudder and run my own hand over the place where he touched me, marking it like a map. I tell myself I don't want him coming upstairs, but that's not entirely true. Because I imagine it.

Imagine him creaking the door open.

Imagine his heavy footsteps on the tile.

Imagine his gloved hand sliding the shower curtain aside so he can see me, naked and soaked.

I think of his chaste, soft kiss last night. *May I touch you?*

I think of him crouching beside my attacker's body, tilting the dead face toward me like a gift. He did that for me. He killed for me.

He's been killing for me.

The idea sparks like lightning. I suck in a deep, shuddery draft of air and drop my hand lower until I'm teasing my clit, shame coursing hotly out from between my legs. I can't believe I'm giving into my darkness again.

But I am, and my body is wound tight with need. Not just from my killer's soft, careful touches or his low, raspy voice, but from what he did.

I brace my free hand against the shower wall and hike my leg up on the ledge, opening up my pussy so I can slide two fingers inside myself. I'm drenched, my cunt hot and slippery. It's *been* hot and slippery. Ever since I heard my attacker's scream cut off and knew, with a shiver, that I was saved.

I rub against my G-spot with a quickening desperation, one image after another sliding through my head—memories braided together with dark, devious fantasies. My thoughts settle on a terrible image of my killer bending me over the body of my attacker to fuck me from behind, the two of us desecrating the corpse of a monster.

I cry out, then bite it back, afraid he's still downstairs, that he'll hear me. But that fear just sends another pulse of lust through my body, because the thought floods me with a new fantasy, of him dragging me out of the shower and bracing me against the wall in the hallway, me dripping water everywhere as he wraps his hand around my throat and fingerfucks me the way I'm currently fingerfucking myself.

My body quakes and jolts. My legs shake. I'm close, and I swirl my thumb about my clit to coax my orgasm along. But all I can do is skirt along the edge.

I moan in frustration, bucking my hips into my hand, and freeze my killer's form in my mind's eye. Tall, broad, imposing. Dressed all in black. His leering mask.

I imagine him rasping, "Suck my cock," and then I imagine kneeling in front of him, taking him out, and swallowing him whole. He's big, in my imagination. Porn star big. Impossibly big.

"I did this for you," he says, thrusting his hips against my face, his impossibly huge cock sliding down the back of my throat. "I do all of this for you. I kill for you, Abilene. And you like it, don't you?"

And it's with that shameful, terrible truth that my pleasure finally erupts. I shriek and slap my hand over my mouth, jamming my fingers in and out of my pussy as my orgasm pulses like a heartbeat, making my entire lower body contract. I keep touching myself until it hurts, and I still don't stop, because I don't think he would. I think my killer would keep going.

I flip around, pressing my back against the damp shower wall. Steam clouds around me, the water's still scalding hot in punishment. But I don't stop. I slide my fingers out of my pussy and zero in on my clit, which flutters against my touch. This time, I give in completely, and I think about my attacker's death.

His short, aborted scream. The thump of his body. I didn't see it, the moment of death. But I wish I had.

I squeeze my eyes shut, tears streaming down my cheeks and mixing with water from the shower. The shame is almost as intense as the lust. Almost.

I can picture how he did it, my killer. How he broke my attacker's neck—simply, neatly, efficiently. From the angle of the head, he came at him from behind. Grabbed him. Twisted hard to the left.

My clit throbs, jolting me with pleasure. I play it over and over in my head. My killer calm and collected. The snap of my attacker's cervical spine. His body collapsing like a marionette with its strings cut.

"Again," I whisper. "Kill for me again."

And my second orgasm tears through me until I'm sobbing.

15

ROWAN

It's nearly four in the morning by the time I'm able to drive my latest victim down to Pier Fourteen, about six miles outside of town. Still firmly in Rosado County, though, which means when he's discovered, my Abi will get the call.

I park my car at the pier and cut the engine. This part of the beach is isolated. It's too rocky and dangerous for swimming, so it hasn't been built up like the ocean front in Rosado proper. No beach houses, no hotels, no cheesy pirate-themed seafood shacks. No one's ever here.

More importantly, there are no surveillance cameras. No floodlights. Just a rotting pier that ought to have been condemned ten years ago.

Which makes it perfect.

I climb out of my car, bringing the case of Lone Star beer I bought at the Walmart on the edge of town. Liquor would have been better, but this'll do fine. I carry it onto the pier, moving as quickly and methodically as I can. I don't let myself get distracted by my memories from earlier. Not the feeling of Abi's warm body against mine. Not the sound of the water running through the house's pipes as I tidied up downstairs, my cock throbbing at the thought of her wet and naked in the shower.

And definitely not the sweet, honeyed scent of her arousal that I *know* I smelled when she saw what I had done.

That's the hardest one to ignore, though. The sense memory of that scent is the reason my cock is still half-hard even though I'm focused on setting my scene.

I carry the beer halfway down the pier, tear open the box, and one by one, pour the contents of the beer cans into the ocean. Then I crunch them up, toss them at my feet.

Looking good so far.

The next part is harder. I go back to my car and pop the trunk, and Abi's would-be killer stares up at me with a frozen, terrified expression. I've already stripped him of his shirt, gloves, boots, and the stocking he used to conceal his face. Those are in a pile in the back of the trunk. I'll burn them when I'm done.

Stupid motherfucker, thinking he could come after my Abi.

I drag him out, grunting with the effort. I'm strong —*stronger than you have any right to be*, Uncle Nash used to say, his cruel, judgmental gaze dropping to my belly—but dead weight is always a chore. Especially dead weight that's already starting to stiffen.

Still, I manage to wrangle him up on the pier and over to the pile of empty beer cans. I step up to the pier's edge to study the rocks that run alongside and beneath it. The moon's out, and they look silver with sea foam.

I tip the body forward, angling it so his head crunches against a rock before it flips over itself, flopping like a rag doll, and splashes into the shallows. The waves splash around him, making him ripple and dance.

He'll be found easily. The tide's going out, leaving him exposed to the elements. With any luck, he'll get nibbled on by birds or crabs before someone happens to spot him.

I want him found, though. Mostly for the reason I told Abi: to see if she'll protect me as willingly as I protected her. It should be easy for her to fake a toxicology report, to confirm he was as drunk as the cans suggest. She'll know what I did when she hears about the scene, I'm sure of it. She's smart.

But I also want him found because I want to know his name. It'll be in the papers once they identify him, and I want to know what stupid piece of shit tried to hurt my girl.

I turn away from the body and stare down the long path of the pier to the empty, rocky beach. I'm still in my killing face—not that it really matters. There's no one nearby. The night is empty.

I leave it on, though, as I walk down the pier. It gives me a hot, coursing strength, especially when I'm around Abi. As Rowan, I would never wind my arms around her, never press her body to mine. Never kiss her.

But as myself, I can do those things. And I can sense the difference in how she reacts to me, too. She's not afraid of Rowan, although I guess she likes him, because her heart does beat a little faster when he's around.

But with me, the real me, she becomes a firestorm of heat. I wasn't sure when I sensed it on our first night together, mostly because I was overwhelmed being near her. But it was undeniable tonight, the way her body flared when she looked at me over the corpse of her attacker, seconds after I had killed him.

My half-hard cock swells. I'll have to take care of myself when I get home.

I unlock my car but look out at the pier one last time. The beer cans glint like stars, and from this angle, the body looks like a mound of seaweed

Everything is in place. The rest is up to Abi.

But just as I'm about to slide into my seat, something freezes me in place.

That feral, dark presence. The presence that nearly got Abi killed. It's back.

I straighten and turn around, scanning the shadows. I don't see anything, not like I did earlier. But I can feel the presence, his eyes crawling over my skin.

Did Abi's attacker have a partner? The thought makes my muscles cord up, like I'm preparing for a fight. I don't sense the same malevolence, though. Just a weird, inhuman energy that hums along the wind.

"Who are you?" I bellow, my voice catching on the wind and then disappearing into the roar of the waves.

No answer.

I step away from my car, moving in slow, loping circles across the packed sand. "I know you're there!" I shout. "You almost got someone killed tonight!"

The air shifts, and I tense up. I shouldn't have done that. I just staged the best crime scene I could, given my circumstances, and I don't need to fuck it up by announcing myself to the entire beach.

Even though I don't feel any humans here. Just—the presence.

"Were you working with him?" I call out, my voice sounding hollow. I let the rest of my threat hang in the air: *Because if you were, you're fucking next.*

There's still no response. Just the constant, beating wind and the crashing waves and the sense of eyes watching me in the darkness.

16

ABI

Olivia Pearce is still waiting for me the next morning.

I drag her out of the refrigeration unit and pull back the plastic I covered her with, trying to hide the mess of her body. Then I wait for the panic and nausea to hit.

It doesn't come.

I transfer her to the autopsy table and go about the ritual of setting up my supplies, moving by rote. I'm exhausted. After my shower last night, I sat on my bed, listening for some proof that my killer was downstairs, that he was still in the house at all. But it was unnervingly quiet, and I eventually went downstairs even though he told me not to.

The body was gone.

The foyer was clean.

The only evidence that anything had happened at all was the front door, with its shattered window and broken hinge. And even that, he had fixed into place rather than leaving everything open to the warm night.

After that, I took an overdose of melatonin that sent me to a dark, dreamless oblivion for exactly four hours. I shuddered awake this morning, my whole body vibrating, and found more texts from Chloe and Penelope on our group chat, most of them dumb memes. My two best friends both believed the lie I told them, a thought that makes guilt knot in my chest.

Now, I'm here. At work. Olivia Pearce is still dead, but so is the man who mutilated her body. Who raped her and killed her.

I feel nothing for him. No guilt for my involvement in his death. Only a sick, coiling uneasiness that said death will be traced back to me, and I'll be punished for it.

And yet, when I start the recording on my laptop and begin my visual report, I don't get overwhelmed. I describe the wounds, as awful as they are, with a calm, clinical detachment. My voice doesn't shake when I give the probable cause of death, and when I pick up my scalpel to begin the internal evaluation, I'm able to make the cuts as easily as if this were the body of a stranger.

I tell myself I don't know what changed, but of course that's a lie. I can do this because I saw the face of her killer, and I know he got what he deserved. Honestly, he got better than he deserved.

It takes me two hours to complete Olivia's autopsy, to take her body apart like a doll and examine the inside of her. I feel numb to the whole process, the way I do when I'm examining someone I don't know. And while I do a thorough job, I don't have the weight of expectation on me to find that key piece of evidence that will lead to the killer's identity.

Because he already confessed to me.

And now he's dead.

I don't find anything anyway. No semen, no loose hairs, no clothing fibers. And as I sew her back together, I realize I'm grateful for what happened last night.

Grateful that my killer was here to save my life, and avenge hers.

When I'm finished, I clean up and head into my office to

prepare my report. The light on my office phone is blinking, though. A message.

For the first time since I woke up, anxiety tightens through me.

I play the message over the speaker phone, my eyes fixed on the map behind my desk. Seven red pins marked with letters.

"Hey Abi, this is Lorraine from the Sheriff's Department. We're sending a body your way. John Doe. Looks like someone slipped and fell while they were drinking over on Pier Fourteen."

Relief flushes through me. A run-of-the-mill death, then. We usually get a couple of these a year.

Lorraine gives me the rest of the details, telling me the body should arrive around 11 A.M. When I check my clock, I see that's in fifteen minutes.

I start typing up my findings about Olivia Pearce, my emotions numb the whole time. I'm only about halfway through when the bell chimes, letting me know someone's at the back entrance.

I move to close up the report but get stalled, staring at it until the words blur together on the screen. I wish there were some way I could tell Olivia's husband that her killer paid for what he did. I'd like to tell Ms. Staunton, too. Because I know, for the rest of their lives, Olivia's unsolved death will be a wound that never gets to heal.

That's my biggest regret about last night, I realize.

The bell chimes again, jarring me out of my thoughts. I push away from my desk and make my way to the back entrance, where I slam my palm against the button to make the door roll up. It creaks on its chains, letting in the sweltering, humid sunlight and revealing Hector piece by piece. He's leaning up against the refrigerated truck, squinting at me.

"Wasn't sure you were here," he says.

"Sorry," I say. "I was just finishing up that—" My voice

wavers, and I swallow it down. "That murder from yesterday morning."

"Jesus." Hector shakes his head. "Bad fucking business. You find anything?"

I smile thinly at him. "You know I can't answer that."

He laughs, lifts his hands. "You're right, you're right. Just not used to that kind of shit around here." He unlocks the back of the truck, pulls out the stretcher. "Good news, though. This one's not bad. Probably an accident, but the cops wanted to be sure. You know. After—" He tilts his head sideways. Toward downtown Rosado, I guess.

"They were found on Pier Fourteen?" I'm changing the subject because I don't want to hear anything more about Olivia Pearce.

"Yep. Usual story." Hector drags out the stretcher and drops it on the cement driveway with a clank. The body bag jostles a little on the frame. "Poor guy drank too much, fell, broke his neck on the rocks. Seems open and closed to me."

As soon as Hector says *broke his neck*, my whole body goes rigid. Despite the sweltering heat and glaring sun, goosebumps rise on my arms.

"Broke his neck?" I ask lightly. "Didn't drown?"

Hector grins at me. "Well, I mean, that's really for you to figure out, isn't it? But yeah, guy's neck is broken for sure. You ready for him?"

I nod and step aside so Hector can roll the body into the hallway. I trail behind him, my heart pounding.

Think of it as a test, Abilene.

And suddenly, I realize what my killer meant when he said that. In my haze, I had just assumed he was going to get rid of the body completely. Dismember it, weigh it down, throw it in the ocean. Because surely someone like him, someone who has killed so many times, knows that it's better for a body to disappear than to be found.

But no. I see it now. He's roping me in. Making me participate in our shared cover-up.

I swallow down a surge of bile as I follow Hector into the autopsy room. He looks over at me expectantly.

"On the examining table there." I manage to keep my voice calm as he does the transfer. Manage to keep my hands steady when I sign off that the delivery's complete on his tablet.

"Good luck," he says. "See you around, Abi."

I nod, force myself to smile. My heart feels like it's going to explode, it's beating so fast.

I suddenly wish I had some way of contacting him, my killer. It's not fair that he knows who I am, but I don't know who he is.

As if fairness has anything to do with this.

I stand in the doorway of the autopsy room and wait until I hear the entrance door slide and lock back into place, until I know Hector is gone for good. Then I close the examination door behind me and stare at the body bag on my counter.

It won't be him, I think, walking over to it with slow, trembling steps. *It will be someone else.*

I draw the zipper down, my breath tight in my throat. Just enough to see the face.

I gasp and jerk my hand away, my adrenaline spiking. Because of course it's him. Olivia's killer.

I suck down a deep breath of air and force myself to pull the zipper down further. There's no sign of the stocking that my killer shoved into his mouth, and his shirt and gloves are gone, too. Still wearing his black black trousers, which are wet and heavy from the saltwater. No shoes.

I play back what Hector told me, that the victim had been drinking. How did he know that? There must have been evidence at the scene. Liquor bottles or some such. I'm sure there's a report waiting in my email, and if not, I can ask for it.

But I don't move. I just stare down at the body of Olivia's murderer, nothing but cold meat in a half-open body bag.

This feels like a challenge, like my killer is drawing me deeper and deeper into his world. A challenge, or an invitation.

I snap on my gloves and work the body bag away from the corpse, my thoughts tumbling over each other. It's standard, in cases like this, to order a tox report. But I already know that it won't show the level of intoxication they're expecting.

He wants me to fake it, I think with a sudden, violent jolt. That's the test.

I drag the body bag away and let it float down to the floor. Then my eyes settle on the ID tag dangling from the corpse's toe. I pick it up, flip it over. JOHN DOE. Of course, Lorraine mentioned that in her message, didn't she? I usually run the John Does through the database to see if I can find a match.

And suddenly, my killer's test feels more like a gift. A chance to find out who the hell murdered Olivia Pearce.

I stumble backward, feeling dizzy. The corpse of my attacker lies unmoving on the table, his head still twisted sideways, his body bloated and pale from being in the water overnight.

A gift, I think numbly. *What if this is supposed to be a gift?*

What exactly does that say about me?

I curl my hands up, my skin already sweating beneath my medical gloves. I should not be as okay with this as I am. I should be horrified, actually. I should turn myself in, tell the police everything. It's not like *I* killed him, and even if I did, it would have been self-defense.

It was self-defense with Blake Fletcher, too, and plenty of people didn't give a shit about that. Include Sheriff Kaplan.

The body lies there, waiting for me. Fingerprints. That would be the first step to finding out who he is. See if he's in the system. Dental work comes next. He doesn't have any tattoos that I can see. No other obvious distinguishing marks.

And somehow, I get to work.

ROWAN

I t's been nearly a week, and it seems my Abi has passed her test.

I keep an eye on the news all week, checking it compulsively when I'm at home or alone in my office at the hotel. There was a single story about a body found off Pier Fourteen on the local news, and then nothing more. "The police do not suspect foul play," the pretty newscaster says in a segment uploaded to YouTube. "But the city would like to use the incident to remind anyone visiting the beach to mind all safety and warning signs before entering the water."

They don't share the man's name, which irritates me. As pleased as I am that Abi understood what I needed her to do, that she covered up the death as beautifully as she tends to the cemetery before the heat of the day settles in, I want his identity.

I lean back on my couch as the video ends. There are a handful of comments underneath it, all variations on what a terrible tragedy it was. More irritation rankles in my belly. It wasn't a tragedy at all. He deserved his death. Certainly more than most of the people I've killed since Uncle Nash.

I toss my phone aside. The sun's just starting to set, which means it'll be time for my nightly visit to Abi's house. I've been watching her every night since it happened, of course. As soon as full dark hits, I'm patrolling the cemetery and her property both, checking in on her through the windows when I can. I haven't gone inside, though, not even when she's asleep. I know that if I do that, I won't be able to stop myself from touching her.

So I stay out in the hot, humid night, my killing face keeping me hidden. No one's come for her. I haven't even felt that odd, inhuman presence again. Not at her house, not on the beach. Nowhere.

It's vanished.

That makes me a bit nervous, I'll admit. I tell myself I scared him off.

When night falls, I make the trek to Abi's. On foot, like always—the last thing I need is Rowan Hanover's car to be spotted by the Hatch Street Burial Grounds. But the walk isn't far. It's why I bought the beach bungalow where I did. To be closer to her.

Her house looks as it has all week. Dark. Shut up tight. I keep a wide berth around the front porch—there's a camera installed there now, right above the doorbell. It appeared at the same time the door was repaired. I don't blame her for it, not really, but it means I can't check the integrity of the lock.

I make the rest of my rounds as usual. I sniff the air to see if anyone's close by. I double-check that the darkened windows downstairs are locked. I try the back entrance. When I'm satisfied, I make my way to the oak tree and shimmy up the trunk.

She's watching TV tonight, the way she does most nights. I don't recognize what's on the screen, but it looks like science fiction. A ship in deep space, dark industrial corridors, computers blinking like Christmas lights.

I wish I could be in there with her. She's anxious, as she has been all week, although it seems worse tonight. I don't like that. I don't like not knowing why.

Whatever she's watching ends, the credits blinking by on the screen. Abi sits forward and rakes her fingers through her hair, then stands and, to my dismay, walks out of the living room.

Damn it. I had just settled in, and there's no other tree that lines up with any of the other second-floor windows.

I slide out of the branches, keeping my eyes on the house. The lights in the window tell me where she's going. I assumed it was to bed, even though it's still early, but no—the light in the stairwell window snaps on, bright and unexpected. I watch her shadow move past it, then follow the trail of illuminated glass until she gets to her kitchen.

The kitchen is the only part of the living quarters that's downstairs, since everything else down there makes up the funeral parlor. Unfortunately, it only has one small window that doesn't show much of anything. I stick to the shadows, watching Abi move back and forth in front of it.

Then the kitchen light goes out.

I creep around the side of the house, waiting to see where the light trail takes me. But everything stays dark. I close my eyes and try to see her that way—through sound and presence. I can feel her, a heart beating inside the house's wooden and brick walls, but I can't tell where she's going. There's only the sense of movement, and sadness, and fear.

It cracks my heart in two.

And then suddenly, all of Abi's stormy emotions are blaring like an alarm. And then I smell her, a sweet and honeyed ribbon on the wind.

She's outside.

For a moment, I'm paralyzed with uncertainty. Did she hear me? Are there more cameras that I can't sense? Is she *leaving?*

No. I don't think it's the last one. And her fear is dull and quiet. A background fear, not the spike of adrenaline I would expect if she had seen an intruder.

I melt into the shadows along the edge of her yard, following the trail of her scent until I find her standing on her front porch, elbows resting on the railing, the salty wind blowing her hair away from her face.

She's holding a small, clear glass, and even from here I can smell the alcohol in it, something floral and antiseptic all at once. She picks the glass up distractedly, the ice clinking as she brings it to her lips.

I wish I were that glass.

For a moment, all I can do is watch her. The porch light is unnaturally bright and washes out her pale skin, making her look like a ghost. She's in thin, flimsy shorts and a long, flowy tank top that clings to her breasts, but when she moves to take a drink, I can see the dark outline of her areolas through the fabric, which makes my breath quicken.

I move closer, my steps slow and careful as I skirt around the flower garden. The sunflowers bob their heads in the wind. But Abi's looking straight ahead, at the cemetery, and her emotions are so strong that I almost feel them for myself. The fear and anxiety, yes. But something else, too. Confusion, maybe. Guilt. Whatever it is, it cuts like a knife.

Abi straightens her spine, takes another drink. There's nothing to separate us. No walls or thick, distorted windows.

I step forward again, and this time I let my step fall heavy.

Immediately, Abi's fear spikes. She jerks her gaze toward me, although she blinks blindly behind her glasses.

"Hello?" she calls out, her fingers tightening around the railing. "Who's there?"

My heart is thundering. I don't think I could turn back even if I wanted to.

"It's me, little detective." I take two large steps, moving into the edge of light cast by the porch.

Abi gasps, jerking herself back so her drink sloshes around in the glass. "You," she breathes, and beneath my killing face, the skin on the back of my neck prickles. "What are you doing here?"

I step up to the porch. Her emotions have shifted again. The fear's abated, which makes my chest warm. The confusion is still there. Heightened, if anything. But there's also a curl of heat beneath it. A sparking of excitement.

"Making sure you're safe." I step onto the porch steps and into the light. I can feel the buzzing heat of it, even through my killing face.

"What do you care about that?" Abi asks.

The question cuts through me. How can she not understand what she is to me?

Because she's terrified of you, dumb ass.

The voice sounds like Uncle Nash, and I hate it, especially since I know, deep down, he's right. I can sense the fear coming off her, even if it's nowhere as intense as the fear from the night she was attacked.

Abi stares up at me, lips parted, eyes big and glossy behind her glasses.

"Someone attacked you," I say slowly. "I want to make sure it won't happen again."

"Why?" Abi's voice wavers. "So you can attack me instead?"

Another slice of despair. "No," I snap. "No, I wouldn't do that."

We stare at each other in the sallow porch light. The air smells like her. Like funeral flowers and sweet fresh lemonade.

I take a step closer. She doesn't pull away.

"Can I ask you a question?" she asks softly, curling her glass up against her chest.

I stop; it brings me up short. But then I nod silently, my curiosity burning hotly.

"When you—" She stops and looks out toward the cemetery.

"No one's here," I say. "Just us. You can say whatever you need."

"How can you know that?" She looks over at me again, her eyes narrow.

I don't answer because I don't have one. I just know when people are around. I always have.

"Well, when you—*helped* me." She stresses the word. "When you, ah, *cleaned up* afterward, I thought you were going to—" The glass shakes, making the ice clink. "Take it to the dump? Get rid of the trash completely? But instead you—"

"I told you, there's no one here but us." I clear the space between us so that I'm close enough that I could touch her, if I wanted. Abi gazes up at me, her breath shuddery and soft. She's afraid, yes. But she's not *only* afraid.

I wrap my hand around hers and move to set her drink down on the railing. She doesn't fight me, and I'm glad, because it was mostly an excuse to touch her, and I keep my hand draped over hers as I speak.

"You're asking why I let the body be found," I say softly.

Abi sucks in a breath. Then she nods.

I draw my hand up her arm—slowly, cautiously. If she told me to stop, I would. But she doesn't, not even when she glances down at my gloved hand and bites her lip.

I tuck my fingers beneath her chin and make her look at my killing face again.

"There was an investigation, wasn't there? Were you asked to autopsy the body?"

"Yes." Abi breathes out the word like a sigh. She glances out at the darkness again, then says, "And I—I had to fake my report so they wouldn't—"

"Good girl." I slide my hand around to the side of her neck. Even though the leather of my gloves I can feel her pulse fluttering. My cock throbs, stiffening even further. "That's what I wanted you to do. A test, like I said."

"I didn't have a choice," she says tightly. "If his tox report came back clean, they would have known something was wrong."

"But it didn't come back clean." I stroke along her neck, wishing desperately that I could kiss her again. I refrain, though. "Did they find a name?"

"I found a name," Abi says stiffly. "His fingerprints were in the system."

I sense a shift in her emotions then, a flash of anger like a sun flare.

"And?"

"Julian Bernet."

The name feels anticlimactic. I thought I wanted to know who tried to hurt her, and I do. But the name doesn't actually tell me that, I realize. I've never heard it before.

"Who is he?" I ask.

"I don't know." Abi picks up her alcohol, but I stop her before she can take a drink. I want her clear-headed.

"Why do you keep doing that?" she asks me darkly.

I pull the drink away from her. "So when I ask if I can touch you, I'll know your answer is honest."

It comes out before I can stop it, something I would never say as Rowan Hanover. But it has an immediate effect on Abi; her body flushes, her lemony orchid scent deepens.

"Why do you want to touch me?" she whispers.

"I told you before," I say. "You're beautiful."

Then I tilt the drink on its side so the alcohol pours into the morning glory twining around the porch lattice.

"But first," I say. "Tell me about this Julian Bernet."

Abi gapes up at me, stunned like a deer. Then she blinks and sputters out, "I don't—he was arrested for breaking and entering a few years back. That's why he was in the system.

Didn't serve time. I—" Her voice tightens again. "I spent hours trying to find out more about him," she whispers. "He's not from here. He was born in Montana and lived along the West Coast for a while. I don't understand what he has to *do* with any of this."

I cup her cheek in my hand and tilt her face up toward me again.

"Some people are just killers," I tell her. "Maybe it was random."

"He was coming after me," Abi says darkly. "Olivia Pearce, then me? That's not random." She hesitates, staring up at my killing face. I can feel something opening up inside her. "Olivia Pearce helped me with something when I was younger," she says softly. "She helped keep me from going to jail."

"You think I don't know that about you?"

Abi's eyes widen. Her fear spikes. God, it smells fucking good.

"And you still think it's random?" she manages to sputter out. "And not a message?"

A weighted silence passes between us.

"Like one of my messages?" I finally ask. "No, little detective. It's not the same."

Before she can protest, I rub my thumb over her cheek. She doesn't pull away. Doesn't tell me to stop.Not even when I trace my thumb over her bottom lip.

But god, do I feel her tremble.

I think that's why I ask what I do next. Because I have a name, even if I don't have much else. I can look into it later. But not right now. Right now, I want to feel Abi tremble again.

"Now," I murmur. "Can I ask you a question?"

Abi stares at me, drinking in my killing face. The scent of orchids is overwhelming.

"May I touch you?"

18

ABI

The question throbs on the thick, sultry air. The last time he asked it, in my office, I shoved him away.

I don't shove him away tonight.

"You're already touching me," I finally say.

"You know what I mean." My killer presses himself up to me, his other hand coming to rest on my hip. "I want to make you feel good, so you'll forget about all this, just for a little bit."

Why? I scream internally. It makes no sense. I know what he's capable of. I've seen it firsthand. And yet—

And yet his hand on my hip is impossibly warm. Impossibly heavy.

"Out here?" I whisper.

He doesn't answer right away. Then he pulls his hand away from my hip and slides up his mask. Not enough for me to see his face, but enough that I can see his full, sensual lips.

"May I?" he asks, tilting in toward me.

A too-small part of me is screaming to stop, to run, to call the police. Too small, and it's getting smaller by the second.

I nod, my throat too dry to speak.

130

He gives me another one of those soft, chaste kisses. Electricity ripples through my body, and I tilt my head and return it with the barest hint of pressure.

My killer deepens the kiss, parting my lips with his tongue. I let him. Not only that, but I open up to him. His tongue slips over mine, and he presses closer against me, his hand tangling up in my hair.

For a long time, that's all we do. This slow, meditative kiss. It's not a lot, but the tenderness of it sends heat pooling between my legs.

My killer's the first to break it. He pulls away, his gloved fingers still twining around my hair, and I stare at his mouth, at the scatter of five o'clock shadow across his chin. The same dark brown with red highlights that I noticed earlier.

And then he jerks his mask down, recovering his mouth.

"Inside," he says, the voice coming from the mask's twisted, leering lips.

"W-why?" I stammer out, bracing against the banister.

"I want to touch you properly," he says. "And I can't do it out here."

My heart thunders. I can't possibly be considering this.

But that kiss—no one's ever kissed me like that. Slow and sweet. Almost worshipful. I press my thighs together, trying to relieve the pressure there. Or hide it.

"Why me?" I ask.

My killer stares at me, his eyes dark behind his mask.

"Because you're perfect," he answers.

I'm too stunned to say anything to that. Even when he takes my hand in his, braiding our fingers together. Even when he tugs me gently toward the door. My feet slip over each other to follow him.

"That's it," he says softly. "I told you. I'm not going to hurt you."

He eases the door open, and I blink at the rush of AC spilling out into the hot, humid night. Then we're standing together in the foyer, only this time there's no dead body lying on the floor. There's only us.

My killer pushes the door closed and turns to me. I suck down a deep breath, my hands trembling. That tension pulls taut inside me: the knowledge that I should tell him no. The fact that I don't want to do.

He moves up to me and spreads his hands over my hips and looks me straight in the eye. I catch just enough of them to see that they're brown.

"May I?" he murmurs.

I can't speak. My tongue is a weight in my mouth.

But I'm still able to nod.

His eyes change when I do. Lighten, somehow, like he's smiling.

Then he slides his hand down, easing it between my legs. I suck in my breath as he finds the heat there and makes a small, surprised noise in the back of his throat.

I widen my stance, giving him access. His eyes never leave mine, but his gloved hand slips up beneath my loose, flimsy shorts, shoving them aside. Then he's stroking me over my underwear, his breath soft and ragged.

Heat surges through me, and I fall into him, winding my arms around his big shoulder. He's solid and tall and reassuring, something I can cling to as he hikes my thigh up around his hip.

"Stay," he murmurs. "Just like that."

Then his fingers are on me again, only this time he's slipping them inside my underwear so the leather of his gloves slides along my damp, aching pussy.

I gasp, digging my fingers into his shoulder blades. I'm afraid that if I don't, I'll fall.

Fall more than I already have. This is a killer, and I'm letting him touch me.

"You're so warm," he breathes as he slides his gloves up between my folds. "And you open up to me so easily."

I squeeze my eyes shut and try to pretend someone else is touching me. Someone who isn't a murderer.

It doesn't work. Because I can smell *him*, my killer, the dark, sweet earthiness of his scent, and I bury my head into the crook of his neck.

One of his fingers slides into me. This time, I can't bite back my moan. Nor can I ignore the way his body shudders as he pushes his finger into the wetness there.

I should not be wet for him. But I am. Wet enough that his thick leather-covered finger goes in easily. He pushes it back and forth, making me keen softly and twine my arms tighter around his shoulders.

"Do you like this?" he says roughly.

I don't answer except to roll my hips against his hand. *More.* I want more of him. Pressure's already building in my core, hot and traitorous.

My killer slides a second finger inside me, pressing up against my walls. I cry out sharply, the intensity of it thick and unexpected. Then he presses the pad of his thumb against my clit, and my legs shake with need.

He knows what he's doing. He knows exactly how to touch me.

"That feels good for you," he says. It's not a question, and he moves his hand faster, fingers and thumb working in tandem. My whole body shudders, and the only reason I'm still standing is because I'm clinging to him in desperation.

"You're going to come soon," he adds, tilting his head toward me, pressing the mask's mouth against the top of my forehead.

"H-how can you tel-tell?" I choke out. He's right, of course. Pleasure swirls around in my belly.

"I can hear it." He shifts something in the way he touches

me, pressing his fingers in even deeper. I gasp and dig my nails into the fabric of his shirt, feeling his skin relent beneath them. "The way your blood beats faster."

I keen softly. His words introduce a new vein of fear into my pleasure, but that fear just makes everything better.

"How can you—" My words catch as his fingers fall into an exquisite, perfect rhythm against my G-spot. And then I can't get anything out at all beyond a low, panty keening.

My killer laughs softly.

"I told you." His mask presses against my hair. "I can smell it. Sense it."

My pleasure builds until it's almost unbearable. All I can do is roll my hips against his hand, too caught up in my ecstasy to care that this is *wrong*. But I don't want to be moral. All I want is to come all over his fingers.

And then he jerks his hand away.

I shriek in protest, the sudden lack of his touch devastating. "What are you—"

He sweeps me up and over his shoulder.

"Put me down!" I shout on instinct. My fear spikes, a cold vein of ice against the pulsing heat of my aborted orgasm. I was so fucking stupid, letting him touch me like that. Now I'm going to die.

"I will," my killer says, carting me unceremoniously down the hall. I struggle against him, still distracted and shuddery and impossibly turned on. "I'm just looking for a good—"

He steps into the viewing room and switches on the light, revealing the rows of neatly-placed chairs and the soft drapes falling around the big picture window that looks out at the flower garden. Uncle Vic would always set the deceased in front of the window so they could have a view of the flowers.

There hasn't been a deceased person in here since Uncle Vic's funeral, although the dais is still in place, draped in black.

I could never bear to touch this room, which is why I left everything the way Uncle Vic always kept it.

But now, my killer flips me over and lays me out on the dais, like I'm a dead body waiting for her funeral.

I blink up at him, fear making my breath tight and lust making my legs spread. He pushes his mask up again, giving me another tantalizing view of his lips.

"This is the first place I ever saw you," he rasps. "In this room. In front of this window."

A million thoughts surge through me: every funeral I ever worked, every body I ever watched over. Thousands of faces. Hundreds of tall, dark-haired men.

And then I'm not thinking of any of them, because my killer is yanking my shorts and panties down over my legs.

"I want to taste your orgasm," he says, throwing them aside and then crawling up on the dais with me. "I bet your pleasure's as sweet as ice cream."

For a moment, I'm too stunned to respond.

Then he hooks his arms around my knees and hoists me up, practically bending me in half, and latches his mouth to my cunt.

I moan in pleasure, dropping my head back against the dais and relenting to him completely. He slides his tongue along my slit and then presses it inside me to lap at my inner wall. He kisses me as deeply and slowly as he did earlier. Deeper, even.

"Fuck," I whisper, my thighs trembling wildly on either side of his head. I drop my gaze over to the window. Unlike the dead, I can't see the flower garden because the night has turned the window into a mirror. Instead, I see my legs wrapped around a masked killer's head as he feasts on my cunt.

Lust surges up through my core. I stare at the reflection, panting and hungry, watching as I roll my hips up against him, thrusting and jerking. He never stops licking me. His tongue probes through my folds and over my clit, and I give a desperate, shuddering moan. It occurs to me, distantly, that if someone were to drive by on Hatch Street, they would see everything.

And *that* thought sends even more lust surging toward my core.

"Don't stop," I pant. "Please. For the love of god. Don't stop this time."

My killer chuckles against my pussy, then drags his tongue hard over my clit. I shriek, arching my spine up to him. He presses down on my thighs, spreading my legs wider. I'm so close to spilling over. I'm just about to—

He pulls away.

"Fuck you!" I scream, jerking myself up to sitting. But my killer shoves me back down, pinning me by the arms. Every part of his face not covered by the mask is glossy with my arousal. And some of it's streak on his mask, too.

"I'm sorry, little detective," he purrs, leaning close. "But there's something I want from you."

He kisses my mouth then, and I moan into the salty taste of myself. Then he jerks back, his eyes blazing behind his mask.

"What do you want?" I whimper.

He rubs his thumb against my wrist, like he's feeling for the blood in my veins. "I want you to beg for it," he says softly. "Beg for my mouth. Beg for your release."

I shiver, curling my hands into fists. His own hands are wrapped around my wrists, and when he shifts his hips against me, I feel a thick, hard ridge.

The idea of his cock sends another pulse of pleasure through me.

"Why?" I manage to ask, not taking my eyes off him.

He smiles. There's something almost familiar about it, that smile, and I jolt.

I've seen him before.

I don't know where, though. And I can't think about it

further, because he slides one hand between my legs to roll my clit around in slow, teasing circles.

"Because," he says. "I want to know that you want it."

Then he's eating me out again, and I don't see his mouth or his smile, just the dark curve of the mask's leather between my legs.

I glance sideways at our reflection again. At my thick thighs, my breasts swelling beneath my shirt.

At my killer, devouring me whole.

"I don't hear you begging," he says from between my legs. "If you want to come, you'd better get started."

I watch our reflection as I answer. "I thought you wanted to taste my orgasm."

He laughs again, which just teases my oversensitive pussy even more. "I'm a killer, Abi. I know how to wait for what I want."

The word *killer* ricochets around in my head. It makes my pussy ache.

"Please," I whisper, watching my reflection's mouth form the words. "Please, um—" I swallow, and lift my eyes to the track lighting overhead, warm and tasteful and designed to soften the hard edges of death. My killer's running his tongue over my cunt in long, slow licks, like he's savoring my desire. "What should I call you?"

He stops, his breath warm on my pussy. "I don't have a name," he finally says, and he rubs my clit softly as he speaks.

"Everyone has a name," I say shakily.

My killer kisses along my thighs, still teasing my clit. "My name belongs to someone who isn't really me," he says. "The real me, the man who's going to make you come, is nameless."

"Nameless," I breathe out. I hadn't realized I wanted his name until now, and this, it seems, is the closest I'll get. "Please, Nameless. Make me come."

Overhead, the lights blur until they look like stars.

"Oh, Abi," he purrs. "You can do so much better than that."

He sinks his teeth into the soft flesh of my inner thigh—gently, like a warning. I yelp, startled more than anything, and he chuckles and slides his tongue inside my pussy.

At that, I groan and press my hand onto the top of his mask, pinning him in place between my legs as his tongue swipes and curls into my cunt.

"Please," I cry, thrusting against his mouth. "Please. I want to come. I'm so fucking clo—oh my god! Right there!" He's doing something to my clit that makes my whole lower body quake in pleasure. "Don't stop! Please don't fucking stop!"

I'm peaking against, pleasure surging up in me like a riptide. I think he knows it, too, because he pulls his tongue away with a slow, lazy swipe. I screech in frustration.

"I'm begging you!" I scream, thrusting my hips against his face. "Please! Nameless! Whoever the fuck you are! I'll die if you don't let me come!"

He groans when I say that, a deep throaty sound that sends another pulse of pleasure straight through my core. "Say that again," he growls into my pussy, right before he latches onto my clit.

"I'll die," I gasp, my words coming out panty and desperate. I can feel the window to my right, exposing our sin to the world. "If you don't make me come, I'll die. You'll—" I keen as he thrusts his tongue up inside me. "You'll fucking kill me if you don't—"

I'm tilting over, the knot of tension tightening deep in my core. "Please!" I scream, tears streaking out of my squeezed-shut eyes. I dig my fingers against the rubber of his mask until it shifts beneath my touch, and he kisses me harder. "Please, Nameless, I'm begging you to *let me co*—"

The tension breaks, and ecstasy floods through me. I lose all my words and can only shriek and flop against the dais as Nameless, my killer, licks me through one hot, fluttering contraction after another. The world falls away, and I'm just floating on a bed of pleasure. It seems to stretch on for hours, and Nameless never stops kissing me.

Then I snap back to reality. I'm in the fucking viewing room, spread-legged on the dais where a casket is supposed to go. A murderer is still kissing between my legs, although those kisses have softened, each one leaving a little pulse of heat in its wake.

The window is open.

I gasp and sit up, scooting backward to get away from him. He doesn't move to stop me. Instead, he just stares at me, his mask slightly askew, his lips swollen.

As I watch, he runs his tongue over them, cleaning his mouth like a cat. Then he pushes back to standing.

I pull my legs closed. Then I reach over and grab the curtain and yank it over the window. Well, half the window. I can't reach the other side.

But Nameless does it for me, drawing the curtain shut with a low, lazy movement. I'm suddenly afraid of what's going to happen next.

He turns to me and slides his mask back down.

"Thank you," he says softly. "For letting me touch you."

A strange warmth surges through my belly. No one's ever said anything like that to me before, and I don't know how to respond. So instead I just ask, "N-now what?" The question comes out shaky, and I hate that my eyes drop down to the visible bulge of his erection. I suddenly want nothing more than to have him in my mouth.

But if he notices, he doesn't say anything. "I'll keep watching you, little detective." He steps around the dais, coming up close to me. But all he does his tilt my face upward with his finger. His eyes blaze beneath the mask. "I won't let anyone hurt you."

"You killed the man who wanted to hurt me," I say carefully.

Nameless doesn't say anything, just keeps staring at me. His silence is unnerving,

"There could be someone else," he finally says.

And before I can register all the things that could mean, he slips away from me—out into the hallway, and out into the dark night.

19

ROWAN

I can barely think straight as I stumble across the yard, past the sunflowers, and out onto the empty street. The night is heavy and thick with humidity. The insect song is deafening.

But I swear I can still hear Abi's heartbeat inside the house, soft and steady and safe.

I climb the cemetery gate and slump down on the other side, sucking in deep breaths of air. My cock is so hard it's painful, and I adjust it listlessly over my pants, half-expecting to come from the friction. I nearly came earlier when I got my first taste of Abi's pleasure. Her orgasm coated my face with slick, salty-sweet arousal, and I can still taste it. Still smell it.

I groan softly, slumping against the fence, absentmindedly rubbing my cock over my pants. I've jerked off in this cemetery plenty of times in the last few years. But it's different tonight.

Tonight, Abi got to come, too.

I push myself up and lurch toward the trees, holding the memory of Abi's long, shuddery orgasm in my head. The way she begged me for release, screaming that she would die

141

without my tongue, calling me *Nameless* like it's a secret between us—

I groan and lean up against a big marble slab, the memory hot and throbbing. I need my own release. That way, I can get back to making my rounds around Abi's house. No one's out here that I can sense, but I don't like the idea of leaving her alone. Not one damn bit.

I fumble with my buttons and zipper. But before I can grab my cock and finish myself off, I feel her.

Abi.

I whip my gaze around and there she is, standing on the light-flooded porch again. Only this time, she has a flashlight with her, the light bobbing as she floats down the steps.

For a moment, all I can do is freeze in place, watching as she cuts across her lawn. Then I shove my cock back into my pants, but I don't run. I'm too enraptured by the sight of her coming this way.

"Hello?" she calls out, her voice thin and wavery. A little afraid. "Are you out here?"

I step forward, my heart thudding. I don't understand what she's doing. Why she's coming after me like this. I go to her. That's always how it's been, ever since I first laid eyes on her ten years ago. The only time she came to me, sort of, was when she met me for coffee a few days ago.

But that wasn't me. That was Rowan.

Abi curses softly, the word carried on the wind. She stops at the street and swings the flashlight around. It's too small to catch me from that distance, and I'm not sure what to do. Because I don't understand why she's here or why she's looking for me.

But god, I want to find out.

"Hello?" Abi calls out again. "Seriously, I—You just ran off, and..."

Her voice trails away. For a second, I think she's going to give up and go back into the house.

But she doesn't.

Instead, she crosses the street.

I wait for her, standing there with my aching, rock-hard cock and confusion tightening up in my chest. But I don't want to run from Abi, and so I just keep watching her light dance around as she approaches the cemetery gate. She unlocks it, the keys jangling, and shoves it open with a creak.

Then the light swipes around, blurring like a comet. Abi's steps are soft and rustling through the grass.

"What the hell am I doing?" she murmurs. Speaking to herself, I know, but even with the distance between us, I can hear her. "Fuck, I'm going to get myself killed."

That sends a twist of pain through my heart. I can't let it go.

"I told you I won't let that happen," I say, loud enough to announce myself.

Abi screams and drops the flashlight, plunging us into darkness. I can still see her, though, limned by the street lamps. And I can feel her: the spike of her heart rate, the soft tangle of her confusion.

"Fuck!" she says. "Where are you?" She fumbles around in the grass and then lifts the flashlight, sweeping it around again. When it lands on me, I swear I can feel it, all the warm molecules of its light.

"Hey," I say stupidly.

Abi blinks at me. We stare at each other from across the cemetery, the markers jutting up like teeth.

"Why'd you run away?" Abi calls out, her voice soft. Almost shy, maybe.

I step toward her, walking into the sphere of the flashlight. When I'm close enough to her, Abi tilts it away from my face, which I'm grateful for. I prefer the dark.

"Well?" She says it the way a victim will, when they're trying to be brave and talk back to me.

"I finished what I came to do," I say carefully. "And I wanted to come back out here to pick up my rounds again."

"Your *rounds?*" The word trembles. "What, like, you're looking for someone to ki—"

"No," I say sharply, right before I clear the rest of the space between us. Abi gasps softly and drops the flashlight to her side. She looks so pretty out here, drenched in moonlight.

"Turn it off," I tell her. "The flashlight."

"Why?"

"Because you're prettier in the dark."

She blinks, gives a shy, nervous titter. "Where you can't see me, you mean?"

"I can see you fine." I tilt her gaze up to meet mine, and for a moment, I swear I can feel her staring straight through my killing face to see me. The real me.

My cock is so hard it's painful.

"You should go back inside," I tell her. "It's safer in there."

"From who?" she counters.

I drop my hand. I don't want to tell her about that strange presence I felt, or my theory that her attacker may not have been working alone. I don't want her to worry needlessly, not when I can protect her. "I don't know," I finally say. "But if someone tries to hurt you again, I'll be here."

Abi sucks in her breath. Curls her hands up into fists.

"Why did you come find me?" I ask softly.

Abi hesitates. I can sense something like fear coming off her, although it's not the fear she felt when she was attacked, nor is it the same fear I felt when she discovered me in the shadows. She takes another breath. "I—" she starts, then glances away, off into the darkness. The cemetery rustles around us, moving in the sea wind. "I didn't understand why you ran away. Why you—did what you did and then didn't expect—"

Heat courses through me. My cock throbs.

"Didn't expect anything in return," she finishes in a rush.

"I got what I wanted," I say carefully, although that's not *entirely* true. Of course I would love to be inside her, to feel the tight clamping muscles of her cunt. But only if she wants it. Only if she gives it to me willingly.

Abi digs her toe into the graveyard dirt. She's wearing flimsy sandals, her toenails painted black. I hadn't noticed that earlier, the black toenails. I'd been too focused on other things.

"I just thought," she says softly. "It wasn't—wasn't fair, you know? For you to—not get to receive—you just gave—"

It takes me a second to realize what she's getting at. To realize what she's offering.

"You want to do that?" I ask. "With me?"

Abi jerks her gaze up to me. Even in the dark, I can feel the blood rushing close to her skin, perfuming the air around us.

"I just thought it would be fair," she whispers, the words strained.

Then, to my shock, she steps closer to me. Puts her hand on my chest.

"You saved my life," she whispers. "Then you made me come harder than—" She laughs, shakes her head. "Then *ever,* if I'm being honest."

Pride swells up in my chest. My cock strains against my pants.

"I just—I thought we could keep going." She looks up at me, her eyes bright in the darkness.

I don't want to fuck her. Not right now. I won't last long, and I want to do it right. I want to relish every line of her body and all the silky expanse of her skin.

But Abi Snow is staring at me with a hot, dark hunger in her eyes.

"Kneel," I breathe out.

And she does.

She doesn't protest. She doesn't fight. She just sinks into the damp grass, her eyes never leaving mine.

I drag down my zipper and ease out my cock, trying not to touch it too much because I'm afraid that if I do, I'll come. Abi watches me the whole time, her breath tight and shuddery until she sees my cock. Then she gives a soft, murmuring gasp. I don't know what to make of it.

And then it doesn't natter, because she wraps her fingers around my base and pulls my cockhead into her mouth.

I groan at the wet heat of her tongue, hardly believing that this is happening, just like I could hardly believe it when I was buried between her legs, feasting on the cunt I've dreamed of so much. But it *is* happening, and Abi makes a soft *mmm* noise in the back of her throat and pulls me deeper into her mouth. I braid my hand through her hair, although I let her take the lead as she bobs up and down my length. She's not quite able to swallow all of me, but it doesn't matter. I still sink into her, groaning, dropping my head back to look at the stars.

"Perfect," I growl. "You're fucking perfect."

That makes her moan again, and the reverberations send pleasurable jolts through my belly. My balls tighten, hot and hard against my body. I knew I wasn't going to last long.

I wind Abi's silky black hair around my gloved hands, tugging on it a little. She peers up at me over the rim of her glasses, my cock still buried in her perfect mouth, and I nearly topple over at how gorgeous she looks.

"I'm going to—" It's hard to get the words out. Hard to remember how to speak, with her kneeling at my feet like that. "Going to c-come."

I feel a flash of her surprise, and I guess I don't blame her, even if it is a little embarrassing to finish so quickly.

"You tasted so good," I add, tightening my grip on her hair. "Nearly came while I was eating you."

Abi moans at that, louder, and I grunt at the way her voice wraps around my dick. Then she bobs her head faster, urging me on. It takes every ounce of my willpower not to thrust into her mouth, not to fuck her face as roughly as I want to fuck her cunt. But I don't want to scare her away. Not when she came out here and willingly kneeled for me—for *me*, not even Rowan Hanover.

"Just like that," I gasp out as she braces her hands on my legs. All I can feel is the heat of her tongue and the heat of my own pleasure. I'm going to erupt soon. "Don't fucking stop, little detective."

And she doesn't. The rhythm of her soft sucking mouth is like falling back into oblivion. I squeeze her hair in my fist. Squeeze my eyes shut. Imagine how she looked laid out on that dais, her pussy wet and pink and swollen, her face flushed from coming.

Ecstasy tears through me. My cum shoots out, straight into her mouth, and I feel the convulsions of her throat as she swallows it down.

Then it's all too much sensation, and I pull away from her, my cock gleaming with her spit in the moonlight.

Abi falls back on her heels, looking stunned and beautiful with her glossy, swollen lips. For a moment, all we can do is stare at each other.

Then I can't stand it anymore. I kneel down, my softening cock wet against my thigh, until I'm eye-level with her. She looks into my killing face, and I can feel all these disparate emotions crashing around inside her. I would do anything to calm them, but I don't know how.

So I just cup her face. She jolts a little but doesn't look away from me.

"I didn't expect you to do that," I murmur.

Her hand snakes up and lies over mine. She's afraid. She's been afraid. But she's all turned on again. I can smell the sweetness of it, and part of me wants to devour her again, out here in the graveyard, until I'm hard again. Then we could just keep going back and forth until dawn.

But I don't want to overwhelm her. I don't want to frighten her away. So I peel my mask up and lean in and kiss her instead, sliding my tongue through her lips until I taste my cum on her tongue.

She kisses me back—shyly, with the faintest hint of hesitation. And I can already feel my cock rising again.

I jerk back. Abi watches me warily, and I wish, suddenly, that I wasn't the way I am. That Rowan Hanover was a real person, not a disguise. She would be with him for real, I think.

Darkness floods through me. I run my thumb over her lips, and her eyes search my face like she's trying to find my humanity.

I know she won't.

"Thank you," I say softly, and then I kiss her again, lingering this time. The truth is, I'm not Rowan Hanover. I'm not normal. I'm not sure how human I really am at all.

But I will protect her.

Abi breaks the kiss with a sigh. "Now what?" she asks.

I brush her hair away from her face, tucking it behind her ear. "Go back inside," I tell her. "Go to bed. I won't let anything happen to you."

Abi gazes up at me, eyes glimmering.

"I promise."

ABI

I don't want to think about why, but I sleep through the night for the first time since Olivia died. Since longer than that, even.

I wake up a little before my alarm, although the sun's already up, pouring hot and bright around the curtain. It's easy to move through my morning routine, and I don't feel that cold, sinking dread that's followed me around since Olivia's death. It's like giving in to my killer—giving into Nameless, which is how I've started thinking of him—has snapped something inside me. Something that was strangling me in place.

I feel good enough that I decide to tend to the cemetery, something I haven't done for a few weeks. Partially because of the heat, but also just because of everything else that's happened.

I fix up a cold brew coffee before I go out. Tidying up the cemetery and laying blossoms on the empty graves was Uncle Vic's favorite chore and one of the first things we did together when I came to live with him. He never skipped it, no matter what the weather was like.

Just a few minutes each day, he told me that first morning, the two of us winding through the cemetery with our arms full of flowers from the garden. *That's enough to keep them from being forgotten.*

Uncle Vic was surprisingly superstitious for a mortician, a fact I only discovered was odd when I went off to mortuary school for myself. Still, I've tried my best to keep up the routine since his death, even if I've been lax lately.

But when I step out onto the front porch, it's not Uncle Vic I'm thinking of. It looks different out here in the daylight, in the glare of the merciless sun. My cocktail glass is still in the grass where Nameless pushed it over, though, a reminder that it all really did happen.

I set the glass back on the railing, the memory of his touch playing over in my head. Everything we'd done had been so disrespectful to the dead. So why does it feel right? As right as plucking sunflowers and carrying them out to the cemetery?

I pick my way across my yard, sucking down the chilled, sweet coffee through a metal straw, my hair piled on top of my head to escape the heat. There's no sign of Nameless. Not when I cut a bouquet of sunflowers. Not when I cross the still street. Not when I step into the cemetery.

I stop beside the gate, staring out at the graves. Uncle Vic *certainly* wouldn't have approved of what I did out here last night, and I honestly can't believe I did it myself. Not just that I did it, but that I sought it out. That a murderer left me alone, and I followed him into the darkness so I could take his cock in my mouth and swallow his seed.

Heat flushes through my body at the memory. God, it had felt so good in the moment, though. So *right*.

I weave my way around the gravestone, dropping sunflowers one by one on the graves and reciting the names of each of the deceased like a prayer, the way Uncle Vic taught me. "Good morning, Edith," I say to the gravestone of Edith Barlow, who died in 1942. "And you, too, Albert." Albert's her husband, dead in 1938.

It's all so familiar. Comforting, even. But my thoughts aren't on any of that. They're on the way the grass felt as it crushed beneath my knees, and the way Nameless's tongue plunged up inside my pussy as I was displayed in the viewing room, and the way he denied me over and over until all I wanted was release at his hands.

I stop next to one of the cemetery's old statues, a shrouded figure worn away by the elements. It was around here where I knelt for him. And if I look back at the house, I'll see the window where he put my pleasure on display.

My body tightens at the memory, and I wonder, in the harsh morning light, what the hell is wrong with me.

But then I hear the soft rumbling purr of a car engine.

I turn around in time to see a blue SUV pull up in front of the house. I don't recognize it, and I sway a little in place, clutching my metal coffee cup as tightly as I can. But then the driver steps out, and I breathe with relief when I see the tall, blonde figure of Ms. Staunton.

That relief evaporates quickly enough, though. What's she doing here?

Dread twists up in my belly as I watch her walk toward the front door. I don't know exactly what I'm afraid of. Surely, if the police knew that I had faked the tox report for Julian Bernet, they would have been here well before her.

Unless she's come to warn me.

She rings the doorbell and steps back, waiting. I shove my nausea aside. I can't look suspicious. I can't let her know the truth about me.

"Ms. Staunton!" I shout, forcing myself to walk toward the cemetery gate. "I'm over here!"

She turns around, face hidden behind a pair of oversized

sunglasses. I know she sees me, though, because she smiles and lifts her hand in a wave.

That smile smooths my nerves a little. I know what she looks like when she's bringing bad news, and it isn't that.

"Abi!" she calls out, jogging down the steps. "Good, I'm glad I'm not too early."

I lay the rest of my flowers next to the gate and go to meet her in the yard. The sunflowers in the garden are all turned to face us, the petals brilliant in the morning light.

Ms. Staunton smiles at me again, brushes her hands through her hair. I squeeze my tumbler, my stomach churning too much for me to take a drink.

"Sorry, I was cleaning up the cemetery." I'm surprised how even my voice comes out. How normal I sound. "I hadn't done it in a while, and I don't have any bodies to look at today."

"Oh, that's fine. I was worried I might be interrupting your breakfast or something. I know I ought to call first, but I was heading to court and passed by Hatch Street and I thought— well, I thought I'd check on you."

The dread melts away, most of it. For a minute, my mind's a whir—what the hell do I say to her that won't let her know about the obstruction of justice I did the other day?

Or the murderer I almost-fucked instead of reporting to the cops.

"That's sweet," I finally say.

Ms. Staunton pushes her glasses up on the top of her head, her face a mask of motherly concern. "How are you doing?" she asks. "Are you handling everything okay?"

I breathe out and look over at the sunflowers. "As well as I can be," I say carefully before taking a drink of my watered-down coffee. "Do they, um, know anything?"

I risk glancing over at Ms. Staunton even though I'm terrified my face will give everything away. But she just shakes her head, looking sad and a little angry.

"No," she says sharply. "Nothing. The Rosado police are as incompetent as the ones in Magnolia."

I can't disagree, even though it certainly works out in my favor.

"No leads?" I say, hoping I don't sound too suspicious.

"Nothing," Ms. Staunton says darkly. "Absolutely nothing at the scene, from what I've been told. None of the cameras show anything. All the potential suspects they brought in have solid alibis." She shakes her head. "I don't like it, knowing that killer is out there."

He's not, I think, but I take a long drink of my coffee to stop myself from saying anything.

"Anyway!" Ms. Staunton takes a deep breath and smiles at me, bright and dazzling. "Like I said, I just wanted to check on you. Make sure you haven't—" Her voice wobbles a little, belying her smile. "Haven't had any odd experiences."

Despite the sun's baking heat, ice races down my spine. "What do you mean?"

Ms. Staunton's smile widens a bit more, enough that it starts to feel forced. "I just want to make sure you're safe," she says. "We don't know who did that to Olivia—"

"And you think he's going to come after me next," I say flatly.

Which is fair. Because he fucking did.

Ms. Staunton barely flinches, though. "I just want you to be safe," she repeats. "You live alone out here, not a lot of neighbors—" She gestures toward the cemetery.

"Well, not living ones," I say wryly.

Ms. Staunton doesn't laugh, though. "I saw you have a camera on your front porch. That's good."

Anxiety knots in my belly. Images flash through my head: Nameless standing over the body of Olivia's killer. Nameless watching me in the shadows of the cemetery. Nameless stepping into the light of the front porch.

"Did something happen?" I say carefully. "Something I should know about?"

Ms. Staunton gives me another one of those strained smiles. "No," she says, and I'm not completely sure I believe her. "But —I'm worried. Worried this ties back to what happened when you were sixteen."

My heart pounds furiously. "Why? You said they didn't know anything."

"They don't." Ms. Staunton's face softens a little. "Let's just call it an attorney's hunch, okay? I feel like—like something's missing here. Something that should be obvious."

Another blast of ice down my spine. I go to sip on my coffee, but it's all gone. For a single, dizzying moment, I consider telling her everything. She's a lawyer, after all. If anyone could keep me out of jail, it's her.

Keep *me* out of jail. But what about Nameless?

The idea should be absurd. But I think about his soft, gentle kisses and the way he edged me into oblivion. His gloved hands on my skin. His dark eyes watching me from behind the face of a monster.

So I don't say a word.

"I appreciate you stopping by," I tell her. "And if anything happens—you'll be the first to know."

ROWAN

I can't stop thinking about my night with Abi. It fills me with a hot, surging fire, and trying to get through my work at the hotel is practically impossible. I'll be in the middle of some mundane task—ordering more linens, meeting with Julia about making the weekly staff schedules—and the memory of that night will wash over me.

How sweet Abi tasted.

How warm her mouth was as she swallowed my cock.

How she sighed when I kissed her.

It's better than remembering my kills, and those have certainly bothered me to distraction before. But not like finally *having* her, my Abi, in any meaningful way.

I continue my vigil of her house at night, slipping around the perimeter with all my senses on alert. I don't go to her again, as much as I want to. As magical as it was to taste her like that, to feel her mouth on me, it was also unfamiliar. Strange. This thing that happened, this interloper attacking her, had interrupted a conversation between the two of us. And the truth is, I want to continue that conversation.

So while I keep watch on Abi's house at night, I use the free time I have during the day to plan my next kill.

This feels much more comfortable than everything else that's happened in the past week. It's something I've done before dozens of times, and I've always liked the methodical nature of it. There's something quiet and meditative about researching a kill's location and deciding on a method. Finding the right victim.

Every kill requires me to put on a new face. The last one was the easiest; I did it as Rowan Hanover, since it had to happen at the hotel. But for this kill, I just need to take up mini golf, and that's easy, too, since I can walk to Neptune's Adventure from both my beach cottage and my office at the motel.

I plan my first visit for a Tuesday afternoon, when it will be less likely to be busy. Things at the hotel are calm, and I leave Julia in charge. Then I walk down the beach, just out of reach of the water.

It's the peak of the tourist season, but Olivia Pearce's murder has had a noticeable effect. There are fewer people out —fewer kids building sandcastles, fewer adults drinking beers and roasting themselves as they watch the waves roll in. We're down at the hotel, too, although I'm not terribly worried about the finances. We have the wiggle room.

I can just see the big fiberglass pirate ship that marks the entrance of Neptune's Adventure when I hear someone shout my name.

And then I smell it. Lilacs and lemons and orchids.

Abi.

She's walking barefoot across the sand toward me, a pair of jogging shoes dangling from one hand. She smiles, the wind blowing her dark hair across her face, and I'm paralyzed in place, seeing her out in the sunlight.

"Hey," she says. "I didn't expect to see you out here."

Abi usually saves her beach walks for the off-season, and it's one of my favorite things, watching her from my office window during the cool winter months. Or maybe it's just too crowded this time of year for me to pick up on her.

"Yeah, I was just—" I glance over at the entrance to Neptune's Adventure and think about the afternoon we got coffee together. It was so normal, wasn't it? "Just going to play a round of mini golf."

Abi gives a delighted laugh. "Seriously?"

"Yeah." I force myself to look at her, reminding myself that she doesn't know the truth about Rowan Hanover. Something like jealousy twists in my belly, but it's a jealousy of myself. "It's, ah, a new hobby. What are you doing on the beach?"

Abi sighs and squints out at the water. "Going for a walk," she says. "Things have been... weird, lately. And I needed to clear my head."

A part of me wants to tear down all my carefully constructed walls and take her right here, the way I did at the funeral parlor the other night. I wonder if she would realize the truth as Rowan Hanover licks her orgasm.

The idea's enticing. But also stupid. Still, I don't want to walk away from her, now that she's here. I don't want to let her go.

"You want to play with me?"

The question is out of my mouth before I can stop it. I know I'm not asking her to play with *me*-me, but with Rowan Hanover. Still, her eyes light up, and she smiles. A big, dazzling smile that she's never given my killing face.

"You don't mind?" she says. "I wouldn't want to impose—"

"You're not imposing," I say quickly, although my head is whirring like a hurricane. This is not how I'm supposed to do things. I'm not playing eighteen rounds at Neptune's Adventure for fun but to research the next beat of my conversation with *this* woman.

But god, she looks so beautiful, standing there in the wind, her hair whipping around. And maybe I want to have a real conversation with her. Even as Rowan Hanover.

"Then I'd love to." She smiles at me again. "I've never even been to that place before. Isn't that funny? I've hardly done any of the tourist stuff around here, though."

"Yeah, me neither." We drift toward the golf course. My whole body is on high alert. My brain is screaming at me that I'm a fool. That she'll recognize me—my voice, my eyes. Something. And then all my carefully constructed plans will blow with the wind.

But I also don't want to miss another second with her. And besides, as long as she's with me, then I know she's safe.

We walk up to the ticket counter, and the teenager in the back looks at us, bored. Even with Abi at my side, my brain still clicks through the checklist of preparing for a kill. There's the scene to set, the accident to emulate. And, of course, the victim, the centerpiece of the whole operation.

I glance sideways at Abi, wondering if she can feel my thoughts the way I can feel hers. But she just meets my glance and smiles a little, her cheeks pink.

"How many?" the teenager drawls, like we've irritated him. If he were older, he might make a good victim. And if Abi hadn't seen his face.

Shit. Abi. My little detective might make the link between Rowan Hanover and me, won't she? This was a mistake. A big, big mistake.

But it's also too late, because Abi's saying, "Two, please," and pulling her credit card out of the little purse she has slung over her shoulder.

I panic, briefly. Partially because I may have laid the groundwork for her connecting my two identities, and partially because I feel like I'm the one who's supposed to pay.

"I've got it," Abi says suddenly, almost like she really can read my mind. "Since I forced myself on you and all."

"You didn't. Really."

She's already sliding her card across the counter. The teenager looks like he'd rather be anywhere but here.

"I know. It was just a joke." Her eyes gleam mischievously, which makes my heart flip around. "But you also paid for my coffee last time. Figured it was my turn."

The teenager gives her back her card along with a couple of bright orange mini golf clubs. "Can grab your score pads there." He tilts his head vaguely. "Or download our app."

Abi grins brightly at me as she hands over the club. "Want me to download the app?"

"We don't need to keep score." As soon as I say it, I wonder if it's the wrong thing. "I mean, unless you want to."

She shrugs. "That's fine with me. I'm not really competitive."

We go over to the first hole, which is guarded by an over-sized fiberglass tortoise. It's simple, with no moving parts. I'm gonna need moving parts for my kill. I'm thinking a mechanical accident.

Abi, though, lets out a little laugh of delight. "Look at that," she says. "A big-ass turtle."

"This entire course is big-ass animals," I say, which makes Abi laugh. My chest constricts. Rowan Hanover can make her laugh. But *I* can't.

I let Abi go first, like a gentleman, and then we settle into the game. It's nice out here. Hot, yes, but the wind is up, and it blows Abi's scent over me as we move from one hole to the next. Here's one with a giant ant. Here's one with a glittering fish. Here's one with an enormous, pearly pink conch shell where you have to shoot the golf ball into its spiraled center and out the other side.

This one causes Abi an endless stream of consternation. There's only a narrow slot where the ball can fit, and she keeps missing it by a few centimeters. "Oh my god!" she shouts on her fifth try. "It's the wind!"

"You want me to do it for you?" I peer around the corner of the shell, where I'm tapping my own ball toward the hole. Abi just huffs, blowing her hair out of her face.

"No," she says darkly. "It's a matter of honor."

I chuckle at that. She squares up her shoulders like she's a golfer on TV, switching her gaze back and forth between the ball and the shell. Then she pulls back, takes a deep breath, and swings.

The ball slams against the shell's wall and ricochets off the green.

"Motherfucker!" Abi shouts, then promptly slaps her hand over her mouth, her eyes wide. "Sorry," she stages-whispers to me. "Did you see where my ball went?"

"Yeah, it's in the palms there." I step off the green and over to a big spray of leaves bobbing gently in the wind. A couple of men are on the other side of the plant bed, laughing raucously. I can smell the tequila and lime on them. Tourists.

They glance over at me as I fumble around for the ball. One of them says something, although I'm not paying enough attention to hear. The other laughs, mutters something back. Look at me again.

No. Not at me. Past me. At Abi.

Rage flares in my chest, and I remember, with a sudden, vicious clarity, why I'm here. I've been having fun with Abi— trailing alongside her, cheering her on when she makes a hole, laughing with her when she misses one. But I'd forgotten that I'm actually here to plan my next kill.

I remember now.

The two tourists snicker and smirk and move onto the next hole. I stare after them, my blood pulsing. *Now* I can hear them, the twin rush of the breaths. It sounds like waves crashing on the sand.

"Rowan?"

Abi's voice drags me out of it. I whirl around, and she studies me, frowning a little.

"Did you find the ball?" she asks.

I force myself to focus on her. The pretty light in her eyes—she's not wearing her glasses today, so it's brighter than usual. The soft, wind-blown muss of her hair.

"Yeah," I say, swooping down into the palms. Fortunately, I find the ball easily. A white spot in the middle of the dirt. When I hand it over to Abi, she smiles at me, and I can feel myself calming.

A little.

We work through the rest of the course, and I feel like I'm being pulled in half. Rowan is doing his best to be charming, to say stupid shit that makes Abi laugh, because it's addictive, how sweet and musical her laugh is. And the real me never makes her laugh, so I want to relish the novelty of this as much as I possibly can.

But the real me is also very cognizant of why I'm here. I watch the two tourists like a predator, tracking them through the whimsical sculptures that guard each of the holes. They're two stations behind us, a constant, nattering presence. At one point, as I'm attempting to finagle a ball around a glittering waterfall, they shift downwind of me, and I catch their scent: Beer. Aftershave. A salty, peculiar fragrance that I've always thought of as the blood inside a body, even though I know that's ridiculous. But everyone's is unique, and now I have theirs.

Worse, they keep talking about Abi. That's something else I sense radiating off them: lust, hot and sour at the same time. But they keep laughing. Laughing at her? At us?

I tamp down on my rage. Focus on Abi. She's trying to knock her ball past an animatronic butterfly, its wings flapping in a slow, steady rhythm, and I like how she looks standing next to it, like she might ride it away from here.

Away from me.

I shove the thought aside. She doesn't know who Rowan Hanover really is. She doesn't fear him.

She didn't suck his dick in the graveyard outside her house.

Abi swats the ball, and it vanishes past the butterfly's wing just in time.

"Got it!" she cries, turning toward me with a big, bright grin on her face. "Well, got it through, anyway."

"I bet I can get it in a hole-in-one," I tell her, because I've noticed that when I tease her like that, she wrinkles up her forehead and sticks her tongue out at me, and it makes me feel normal, a little.

I try to turn my attention away from my potential victims, at least while we're here. I'll need to track them after we're done, but for now, I try to enjoy my time with Abi. As we play, she talks to me in a way she never does to my true self. She asks me about the Blood Raiser posters in my office, and we go off on a long, spiraling tangent about horror movies, which she knows a shocking amount about. She tells me about her two best friends, Penelope and Chloe, how they met in college and how she misses them. She does not talk about the murder of Olivia Pearce or the fact that they haven't caught her killer yet.

She thinks I'm normal, after all.

Eventually, we come to the eighteenth hole. It's a big, animatronic pirate ship, the cartoon version of which is slapped all over Neptune Adventure's many billboards around town.

"Good lord," Abi says. "Finally seeing it in person is something, huh?"

"It looks exactly like it does on that one billboard on the highway," I say. "The huge one? I see it every time I drive out to Walmart."

Abi laughs, and like the dozens of other times she's laughed this afternoon, it makes my blood spark like lightning. "Tell me about it," she says. "God, that billboard is ugly."

She moves closer to the pirate ship, scoping it out. I've already gotten a sense of how it works, though, because I've been eyeing it as we played the other rounds. It has the moving parts I was looking for: cannons that slide in and out of their cubbies, an animatronic crew that makes the ropes move through pulleys so the sails rise and fall. You have to shoot the golf ball off a big curving ocean wave that keeps sliding back and forth, so it flies into the ship's deck, where you then have to send it through a maze of moving crew members and other pirate-themed obstacles.

The movement, that's what caught my eye, though. All those little metal pieces that could pinch and trap and shred.

Male voices rise behind us. My victims. I glance back at them over my shoulder, just in time to see one nudge the other and point.

At Abi. She's climbing up onto the pirate ship, and the wind has blown her skirt up, revealing a flash of her pale underwear underneath.

The two tourists snicker. And then one of them—the taller and more muscular one, the one with his hair shorn close to his scalp—lets out a loud, piercing whistle.

Abi freezes halfway up the ladder. And I feel the way her emotions shift. She was happy to be here with Rowan—

to be here with me

—but she's not happy anymore. Something like fear surges through her, although it's more acrid. Embarrassment, I think. Humiliation. She scrambles the rest of the way up the ladder.

"Hey, don't stop!" shouts my victim. "I was enjoying the show!"

His friend dissolves into laughter. I glare at them, blood coursing through my body. I'm afraid to do anything else, though. Afraid to speak. Afraid to move toward them. Because if I do, I don't think I could stop myself from slaughtering them, even out here in the open.

When I look at them, rage boiling inside me, I see dead men. I see dismembered limbs. I see blood dripping from that stupid giant crab they're leaning against.

"What're you looking at?" my victim taunts. "You got something to say, fat ass?"

"Rowan, ignore them." Abi's voice is like a cool breeze in the heat. "They're just drunk."

I glance over to find her standing on the edge of the pirate ship, the wind blowing her hair back. She seems pale. Worried. It reminds me of how she looked after I killed the interloper in her house.

My two victims laugh again, jeering and cruel. I force myself toward Abi, who looks down at her hands. And I hate them in a way I never hate my victims. I hate that they ruined this for her.

But it's going to be so satisfying to watch them die.

2 2

ROWAN

I'm parked outside the La Arena condos, wrapped in shadow because I smashed all the lights in the parking lot. It's nearly midnight, and my fingers are itching for death.

It was torture, parting ways with Abi at Neptune's Adventure. I sensed the sadness radiating off her when she walked off, like she was disappointed that I didn't want to stay with her. I wish I could have told her I'd see her later, that she'd hear from me soon. But I knew she was sad about Rowan, not me.

No matter. I couldn't go with her as Rowan because I needed to follow my victims when they left the mini golf course. I waited on the little bench on the boardwalk, scrolling idly through my phone without really looking at anything, until I caught the whiff of their scents. The two of them spilled out, still laughing, still drunk, and made their way toward the beach.

I followed.

That was how I found out they were staying here, at La Arena, a shabby little property that's half locals and half short-term rentals. Not exactly a competitor to the Palm Breeze Hotel.

165

This was all the information I needed to put my plan into motion. I saw what unit they were staying in, and I saw them leave this evening, presumably to go drinking. They took a big pickup truck covered in sand and salt. That was when I got my own car from my house and drove over to Neptune's Adventure to set everything up.

Now, it's just a matter of waiting.

I don't have to wait too long. A little after midnight, the SUV pulls into the lot. I slouch down in my seat, watching over the rim of my steering wheel, as my two victims stumble around, arms wrapped around each other, clearly drunk. Idiots, to be out driving like that.

Their voices clatter out into the night. I stay put, waiting for them to disappear into their condo unit. This is always the hardest part, getting all the pieces into place. But I have plenty of experience.

Once the victims are inside, quiet falls over the parking lot again. Clouds cover up any moonlight, accentuating my work with the broken security lights.

Which is perfect, because it's dark enough that I can move unseen. Good thing I've always had great night vision.

I put on my killing face.

Then I slide out of the car and make my way up the stairs, moving quickly and quietly. This kill is going to be extremely complicated, and I know I could have made it easier on myself by choosing someone else. Someone who worked at the golf course, for example. But these two deserve to die, and so they will.

I'm prepared to pick the lock, but I try the knob first, and the door swings open. Lucky me.

I peer into a small, empty living room. I don't see either one of my victims, although I can smell them, and I can hear them. Not just their voices, although one of them is singing loudly from the back of the condo. But their heartbeats. Their breaths.

I ease the door shut behind me and step into the hallway, listening. One of them, the one that's singing, is in the bathroom. The other is in one of the bedrooms, and I go to him first, moving in the soft, careful way that Uncle Nash taught me when I was a child. I trained to do this on men who would know to expect someone like me, and these two tourists are—not that. So that's something in my favor.

I peer into the bedroom and find the guy who catcalled Abi. He's facing away from me, fumbling drunkenly around in the closet, and I hear his sharp whistle in the back of my head.

His friend is still in the bathroom. I intended to kill both of them, but fuck it. I can streamline this if I work fast. And this asshole's the one I *really* want, anyway.

So I act. I slam forward and hook my arm around my victim's neck and slap my free hand over his mouth. He makes a muffled *hmmph* sound and tries to kick out of my grasp, but his movements are sloppy and lazy from the alcohol he clearly drank earlier. And the other drugs, too. I'm not sure what, but I swear I can feel them pulsing through his system.

I brace my arm around his throat, squeezing with all my strength. He wants to fight, but I'm much, much stronger than him, fat ass or not. I swing him around and heave him onto the bed, pressing my body against his back so his face is pressed down in the mattress and he can't scream for help.

I squeeze his neck, tighter and tighter like a boa constrictor, until he finally passes out. The other one is still in the bathroom, still singing drunkenly.

I sling my victim over my shoulder and stalk out of the condo. I move like a shark—constant and unthinking. If I stop, I'll get wrapped up in my thoughts and risk getting caught by the other one, and I'll have to drag both of them into my car.

This way is easier.

I carry my victim out into the pitch black parking lot. I throw him in the trunk. Get in behind the wheel. Peel away. The whole thing takes less than ten minutes.

It's less than ten minutes to get to Neptune's Adventure, too. I pull up to the front gate and climb out of my car and breathe in the damp, salty wind. The place looks untouched, but I know the truth: Snapped wires on the cameras and broken streetlights that will hide me as I go about my business. The missing activation key for the pirate ship, which is currently in my pocket after I filched it when the bored teenager wasn't paying attention.

Thumps come from inside my trunk, soft and confused. My victim is stirring, waking up, but he's not all the way there yet. No matter. I can handle it either way.

I'm ready for him when I lift the cover. He sits up and opens his mouth to scream, but I slap my hand over his mouth and jerk him out so I can loop my arm around his throat again. He passes out even faster this time.

I dig out my crowbar and cart him up to the entrance gate with the same fireman's carry I used to get him to my car. He's not so heavy, even with all his sleek, cultivated muscles.

It's easy work breaking the lock on the gate and getting him inside. I go straight for the pirate ship, all the animatronics still for the night. They won't be for long, though.

I heave him up the stairs and drop him on the deck. This afternoon, when Abi was trying desperately not to let his jeering get to her, I studied the structure to keep myself focused. And I saw the latch that opens up the innards of the pirate ship.

I pry it open now, using the hooked end of the crowbar. When I see the tangle of gears and wires and metal rods inside, my cock jolts.

This is going to be the perfect gift for my Abi. Even if I

can't let her *know* it's a gift. Can't let her link me and Rowan Hanover.

The idea makes me sad. But I don't have time to be sad. Not tonight.

I turn back over to my victim. He's stirring again, moaning a little, dropping his head from side to side. I grab him by the ankle and pull him across the deck. He groans in protest.

"Ethan," he mutters, which I suppose is the name of his friend. "Ethan, what the fuck is this, man? Why do you keep..."

The words dissolve into nonsense. I loop one of the ship's ropes around his ankle to hold him in place while setting the scene that this was all just a drunken, stupid accident.

"The fuck?" he mutters, shifting around more earnestly. He kicks at the rope in confusion, then twists around, whipping his gaze back and forth. "What the fuck? Where the—"

His eyes finally settle on me.

For a moment, all he does is stare up at me, and I savor the quick flicker of emotions across his face. Confusion, fear, adrenaline. They're all softened by the drugs and alcohol in his system, and he squints at me, like he's trying to convince himself I'm real.

"Who the fuck are you?" he finally spits out, belligerent.

When I knot the rope off, I see him make the connection. He kicks again, more furious this time. "What the fuck?" he shrieks. "What are you doing? Why am I—"

He looks up at the ship mast, the pirate flag fluttering in the night wind.

"What are you doing?" he whimpers, his voice small and terrified. "Why is this happening?"

I consider telling him. But I never talk to my victims, just like I don't talk to any of the other pieces of my scenes. This man may have dimmed the bright, sparkling light in Abi's eyes, but he's not a man anymore. He's an object, same as that rope or the metal gears that are going to grind him into meal.

I step over to him, my boots heavy against the pirate ship. My victim tries to squirm away from me, but I lash out and jerk him over to the gaping entrance to the ship's innards.

"I'll pay you, man!" he shouts, trying to fight against me, his muscles tensing beneath my hands. "I've got money! How much do you want?"

I drop his arm and grab him by the back of the head and slam his forehead down on the ship deck, right next to the open hatch. It's not enough to knock him out, but it is enough to surge him with adrenaline, and he starts trying to fight me in earnest, even as blood pours over his forehead. He swings his arms, kicks against the rope. I manage to keep my grip, although it's a reminder that I need to finish this up.

"Let me go, you Halloween-ass motherfucker!" He swings a punch at me, but I catch his fist. He stares at me, eyes wide with fear.

Then I shove him back, hard enough that he cracks into one of the animatronics. I cringe inwardly; I wanted the ship untouched. But I suppose that adds a touch of verisimilitude, considering he's meant to look like he was stumbling drunkenly around up here.

It also stuns him, which gives me a chance to dart over to the button that activates the ship's mechanisms.

I jam the key into the ignition, turn it, press the button. With a groan and a clatter, the pirate ship creaks to life. For a second, I just stand there, listening to the symphony of mechanical groans from inside. All that metal grinding together.

I climb back up the ladder. My victim stirs against the animatronic pirate captain, who twists back and forth despite the crack in his peg leg. I grab my victim by his hair and heave him toward the open hatch.

For a moment, I think he might be knocked out, given how

heavy his body feels. But as I hold his head over the hatch, he wakes up, screaming.

"No!" he howls. "What the fuck! No! Don't do this, man! I told you, I can pay! I can—"

I shove him inside, face-first.

For a second, his screams drown out the grinding mechanism of the pirate ship. He kicks furiously, trying to drag himself out, but my rope holds him in place. And eventually, his screams fade into a kind of wet squelching, and blood splats out against the dark of the night. I step back, watching his body twist and flop as the ship's mechanism chews him up. And then there's a loud, sighing groan, and the ship jolts sharply and comes to a halt. I can smell something going wrong, the hot metallic scent of metal parts jammed together.

I kneel beside what's left of my victim. It was his shoulder that broke the ship, the way it jammed in at an angle. The other shoulder juts up, his arm flopped against the deck.

Very carefully, I push his shirt sleeve up, revealing a smooth patch of skin. Then I pull out my pocket knife and press the blade there, making a single tiny mark. Then another. Another. Three simple lashes to form the letter **K**.

"I'll talk to you soon," I whisper, holding Abi's bright smile in my mind.

23

ABI

"Got another one for you."

It's Deputy Muñez on the end of the line, sounding put out. Fear knots up tight in my belly, though. "Another one?" I echo, staring at my computer screen. *Like Olivia?* I think, even though I know it's impossible. That killer is dead.

"Yeah, another drunk tourist fucking around where he shouldn't."

Relief floods through me, but just for a second. It's immediately replaced with another squeeze of—not fear, exactly. Anxiety, maybe.

Anticipation.

"What do you mean?" I push away from my computer and stare out at the examination room. "What happened?"

"Some college kid broke into Neptune's Adventure—"

I freeze, hearing the name. I was just there yesterday. It had been nice, with the sea wind keeping me and Rowan cool as we worked through the menagerie of fiberglass animals. The only dark spot had been those two dickbags at the pirate ship, but that was a minor thing. Mostly, I remember Rowan: sweet, caring, shy.

Fuck, what if Nameless saw us together?

"—mangled pretty bad, so I did want to give you a heads up. I should have the body to you by this afternoon."

I blink, trying to catch up to the conversation. "That's fine," I say, working backwards through what he told me. An accident. The victim fell inside the pirate ship while it was running.

"Do they have an ID?" I ask, my heart hammering furiously. I'm terrified it's Rowan. Terrified that Nameless saw me with him and went after him, a thought that makes me nauseated.

"Oh, yeah. The wallet wasn't damaged. A college kid visiting from Dallas."

I breathe out. Not Rowan, then.

"His friend reported him missing around three in the morning," Deputy Muñez continues. "Said they'd been out drinking and that the victim was pretty sloshed. Probably went wandering and wound up at the mini golf course. It wasn't far from where they were staying."

My head buzzes. Maybe it's not Nameless. Maybe it really was just an accident—

But you could say the same about all his other kills, too.

The rest of the morning is a waste. I'm too anxious about the delivery to take care of the other bodies on my list, two elderly people who died in the local nursing home. I at least try to catch up on paperwork, but it's hard to concentrate.

Part of it is that I'm still worried about Rowan. The death being at Neptune's Adventure feels too pointed to be a coincidence. Now, I can't shake the thought that Nameless will do something to Rowan out of—I don't know, jealousy?

It seems a strange word to describe a killer. But it also fits.

To calm my jangling nerves, I send Rowan a quick message.

Hi, I had fun yesterday.

Which is true enough, but mostly I want him to respond, to know he's okay.

At least he responds quickly.

ROWAN

Me too! Glad I ran into you!

I stare down at the text, a thick darkness eating away at my chest. I like Rowan. I do. We have identical tastes in movies, and I appreciate a guy who apparently cuts out of work to play mini golf. I like his dark, curly hair and crooked smile and big, reassuring body. I like the way he always seems nervous about looking me in the eye.

He's the kind of awkward guy I would always get a crush on in college. And sure, I've gushed about him to Penelope and Chloe. But there's a dark, bitter truth:

He's not the one I want.

The one I want is a killer, and I think he may have killed again.

THE BODY from Neptune's Adventure arrives right when Deputy Muñez told me it would, and I hang back as Hector wheels it into the examination room.

"Table or fridge?" he asks, hands still clutching the gurney.

"Table," I say, hoping my voice doesn't come out shaky.

"Brace yourself." He transfers the body over. "It's fucked up. Good reminder not to go drinking and golfing."

I give him a thin smile.

Hector arranges the body on the table for me. When he's done, he steps back, and I see the damage for the first time.

The head is crushed. Mangled. It doesn't even look like a human's head at all, just a mess of meat and bone.

"Guess you got a strong stomach, huh?" Hector glances over at me. "Officer Whitehead puked when he saw it."

"I don't blame him." I circle the body, heart fluttering. I'm not interested in the mangled head, though. I'm looking for the one thing that will prove this is Nameless's work.

And that proves—what? He watches me during the day?

"You good?" Hector asks, dragging me out of my thoughts. "Ready to sign off?"

"Yeah, I'm good." I scribble a line on his touch pad, give him a wave goodbye, and wait until I hear the clank of the garage door to approach the body.

I snap on my gloves. Grab the fabric scissors. There's an order to performing an autopsy, and technically, I do follow it. I cut the clothes away, my eyes scanning the pale, mottled flesh. There's nothing to indicate a struggle, not really. Some rope burn around one ankle, but the report Muñez sent over said the victim had been found with one of the ropes from the sails tangled around his foot. I can see the story as they would: a frat boy stayed out late drinking, broke into Neptune's Adventure to cause some mischief, got himself tangled up, tripped, and fell in. We've seen other things like this in Rosado.

And how many of those were because of Nameless?

I run my hands over the body's leg, lifting it to look under the calf. Work my way up to the hips, the belly. Nothing. No suspicious marks.

The further up I go, the more my heart pounds. Maybe this really was an accident. Maybe Nameless only watches me at night, under the cover of shadows. Maybe Rowan is safe.

God, I hope he's safe. He doesn't deserve to die just because I like him. He hasn't even touched me.

I examine the hands. The wrists. The arms. Still nothing. I tell myself what I'm feeling is relief, not disappointment. Only a monster would be disappointed that an accident is an accident and not a murder.

But then I get to the shoulder.

Only one hasn't been damaged. The other was crushed by the same mechanisms that crushed the head, and it's nothing more than meat and bone. But the other is smooth and unblemished.

Except for a single, simple mark. So small, so faint, that it almost looked like nothing.

Except I know it's not nothing. It's a **K**.

I stare at it for a long time, my head buzzing. Then, moving slowly and methodically, I peel off my gloves and pick up my phone.

I snap a single picture.

"K," I whisper, drawing up to other letters in my head. **YOURDAR**.

YOUR DARK

The camera slips out of my fingers and clatters across the tile. "Your dark," I murmur, and I think of Nameless brushing his gloved hand against my face. *It's a conversation.*

I leave the phone and the body and step into my office. I haven't looked at the map closely in a while. Not since Olivia died.

Not since Nameless came into my life as a living, breathing person, and not a killer I'm trying to catch.

With a shaking hand, I write out a **K** on one of my little paper flags. Then I find Neptune's Adventure on the map and slide the pin into place with a red pin.

It feels empty, doing this.

"Your dark," I say again, feeling numb. "Your darkness."

But it's a conversation, he said. He's speaking to me.

And I wonder, with a sharp, shuddery thrill, how long he's seen the darkness hiding inside me.

24

ABI

It's torture, waiting for nightfall.

I haven't seen Nameless in a while. A week, maybe. But I also haven't gone looking for him like I did the night he made me come on the dais.

The night I knelt in front of him and worshipped his cock.

But tonight, I wait for him, sitting on my front porch as the sun sets, drinking a Coke instead of a gin and tonic. My hands shake as I bring the glass to my lips, making the ice clink. I'm not sure I'm more afraid he'll show up, or more afraid that he won't.

Darkness falls across the yard, cloaking the cemetery and then the sunflower patch. The street lamps switch on. I scroll idly through my phone, half-watching the videos that Penelope sends to the group chat. They're all animal-themed, the way they are with her. Otters holding hands and whatnot. But my mind isn't on cute animals right now.

Something cracks in the yard.

I set my phone down and stand up, blinking into the darkness. "Hello?" I call out. "If that's you, I want to talk."

For a moment, the only answer is the sea wind. I go up to the banister, squeezing my glass tight. "Are you there?"

I feel stupid, calling out to the darkness like that. But then one of the shadows moves. A figure steps forward, and my breath tightens.

It's him.

He steps right up to the edge of the porch light and looks at me through his mask. Seeing that twisted, leering face sends a shiver of heat between my legs.

I squeeze my glass tighter.

"You did it again," I say softly.

"I did." His gravelly, rough voice works under my skin. I take a sip of my Coke to calm myself. Then I grin sheepishly at him and say, "It's just soda."

"Good."

Heat blooms inside my clit. I try to ignore it. I can't do that again. Not with him. He's a *murderer*.

"Can we talk out here?" I ask.

Nameless tilts his head, and at first, I think he doesn't understand the question. But then he says, "Safer to talk inside. There are people around. Not like before."

I peer out at the dark and wonder again how he could possibly know that. The night feels empty to me.

I shouldn't let him in my house. I should go inside, lock the door, call the police.

I don't do any of that, of course. I just step backward over the porch and push the door open.

Nameless steps into the light, big and imposing in his dark clothes. My eyes drip, unbidden, to his gloved hands, and my clit pulses.

I go inside. He follows, his steps heavy against the wooden floor. When he swings the door shut, my breath catches. When he locks it, lust flares in me again.

I will myself not to look at the viewing room.

"What did you want to talk about?" he asks.

I stare up at him, feeling dizzy. I'm not sure what to do, really. Should I invite him upstairs to my living room? Should we stay down here in the funeral parlor, which feels more like a neutral territory?

Should I take him to see the body?

That thought startles me. I shove it aside.

"You were following me," I say, setting my drink and my phone down on the entrance table, next to the stack of pamphlets. They still have Uncle Vic's face on them, smiling pleasantly at the camera. I flip the whole stack over and look at Nameless.

"You know I watch over you," he says calmly.

"No." I shake my head. "During the day. You were following me. Neptune's Adventure? Really?"

His chest lifts, like he's taking a deep breath. When he doesn't say anything, I keep going

"You saw me go there, didn't you? With Rowan?" I tremble a little, saying his name. "Promise me you won't—*hurt* him."

I can't bring myself to say *kill*.

Nameless watches me, and I wish, suddenly, that I could rip that mask off and see his face. To have a sense, however vague, of what he's thinking.

"Rowan is the man you were with," he finally says.

"So you were following me," I say. "Why would you—*do that* at some place I was just at? Don't you know that Kaplan—" I stop myself, hearing the way the panic rises in my voice. "The Rosado sheriff already doesn't trust me," I say stiffly. "Because of what happened when I was sixteen. And if death follows me—"

"Death isn't following you," Nameless rasps. "It was a terrible, terrible accident."

"It was not! And we both know it!" My voice trembles.

"Who was it, anyway? I was so fucking afraid you had killed Rowan—"

"I'm not going to kill Rowan," Nameless says. "And the victim doesn't fucking matter. What matters is the message. Did you find the message?"

"Of course I did!" I spit out. "Why are you doing this? Why me?"

The question hangs in the foyer. Nameless steps toward me with his heavy boots. I don't run away from him. Not even when he touches me, sliding his gloved hand around my neck, spraying his fingers across my cheek.

"That thing you did when you were sixteen," he says softly, tilting his masked face toward me. I'm frozen in place, a deer about to be hit by a speeding car. "I thought that would make you someone who could understand."

It's suddenly hard for me to breathe. *Your dark.*

He does see it, the rot inside of me. But I've suppressed it for ten years, and I shake my head in protest. "It wasn't the same," I say tightly. "It was an accident. I panicked and—"

"All my kills are accidents, too," Nameless interrupts.

I jerk away from him, anger flushing in my face. "I'm not a killer!"

It feels hollow, though. It's always felt hollow when I say that, and I've said it a lot, especially back when the investigation was going on and I was a terrified teenage girl. But I know the truth sitting in my heart like a black diamond.

It wasn't an accident.

"You're not a killer like me," Nameless says, dragging me back to him. He runs his thumb over my lip, and I resist the urge to drag it into my mouth, to suck on it the way I sucked on his dick a week ago. "I know that. But you still—you understand something about killing, don't you?"

I stare at him, trembling. *Yes,* I answer in my head, but I don't say it out loud.

"It's all right," Nameless says, shifting his body closer to me. "You can tell me. You know I won't betray you."

"I—" My mouth is too dry to speak. The words can't catch hold there. And I remember being sixteen and seeing the stairs through the veil of my tears, my body screaming in pain, and I thought, *I can push him, and it will be over*. And then I did.

Nameless brushes his fingers down my cheek with a soft, gentle patience. "Say it, Abi," he murmurs. "You know what killing feels like."

"It was self-defense," I manage to choke out.

"I know." Nameless wraps his hand around the back of my neck, making me shiver. "What did I say? I know you're not like me." He presses his head to mine, the rubber of the mask cool against my skin. I can smell him, dark and musky, and my body floods with heat.

"But you still know what it's like, to feel that power." Nameless tightens his fingers against my neck. "And that's why I choose you, Abilene Snow."

Then, before I can react, Nameless picks me up and throws me over his shoulder. I cry out, startled by his sudden show of strength, but he grips my waist tightly and carts me off down the hall.

"What are you doing?" I cry out, trying to twist around to see where he's taking me.

"I want to admire my handiwork with you," he says calmly.

It takes a second to register what he's saying. His *handiwork*.

A strange, distracting heat flares in my core. I feel like I should protest and scream at him to stop. But I don't. Instead, I relax against him as he pushes open the doorway leading to the work area. And then he's carting me down the dark corridor toward the examination room.

He knows exactly where to go, I realize, chills rippling down my skin.. He knows his way around.

He's been inside my house before.

It's another realization that should disgust me, but instead just floods me with a hot, terrible sense of flattery. I press my hands against his back, my thoughts a confusing tangle wrapping around a single core truth:

I want him.

Why do I want him?

We arrive at the examination room, and he drops me to the floor but keeps his arm hooked around my waist to hold me close. I like it, the feeling of his firm chest against my back.

"Unlock the door," he rasps into my ear, his fingers splaying across my belly.

I do, even though my hand trembles as I press in the code. I can feel him watching me, but I don't try to hide it from him.

The lock pops open, and Nameless shoves in the door, making the examination lights flicker to life. Everything is clean and bright and sterile.

"Where is he?" Nameless asks.

I twist around in his embrace, trying to look at him. His mask tilts down. For a second, I see the gleam of his eyes, burning straight into me.

You can stop this, I think, but I don't fucking want to.

"Cabinet seven," I breathe out.

Nameless releases me and walks over to the refrigeration unit and pulls out the drawer. I laid transparent plastic over the body after my autopsy, a show of respect. Nameless yanks it off and lets it flutter to the ground.

The red of the victim's ruined skull is striking against the silver of the examination room.

Nameless looks down at the body and runs his gloves along the cold, mottled flesh. I stare at him, shivering, waiting for his next instructions.

He looks up at me. The mask leers.

"You were right," he finally says. "I followed you to Neptune's Adventure."

Blood pounds in my ears. "Why?"

He stares at me for a long time before he answers. "Because you're the focus of everything I do, Abi. I always want to be near you."

It's the last thing I expect him to say, and it knocks me breathless

"I want to protect you," he continues. "Not from someone like Rowan Han—"

He stops abruptly, like he can't even get Rowan's name out. My insides twist around. "Please don't hurt Rowan," I whisper. "He doesn't deserve it."

Nameless looks at me through his mask. Then he hooks his finger, beckoning me to come over.

And I do, like I'm on a fishing line, like he's reeling me in. As soon as I'm close enough, he yanks me up to him by the waist and positions me so both of us are facing the body.

It feels different, looking at it with him.

"Do you know who that is?" Nameless growls in my ear.

I shake my head.

"He was there," Nameless says, his voice ragged. Rough. "At the same time you were."

I stare at the torso and think back to my report. *Young Caucasian male. Early 20s.*

"He insulted you," Nameless says.

I jerk away from him and look up at his mask again. No, not his mask. His eyes. Trying to see him. Neptune's Adventure had been somewhat busy. It's summer, after all, peak tourist season. I play through the faces of everyone who had been there. Not trying to find the victim.

Trying to find my killer.

Nameless grabs my wrist and pulls me up to him, then grabs my chin, directing my gaze down at the body. "He *insulted* you," he says darkly. "Insulted your friend."

Rowan.

"And you killed him," I whisper.

"Yes." Nameless jerks me to face him, and the roughness is surprising but not unpleasant.

Neither is the presence of the body.

Or, the most terrible realization, the fact that the body only exists because of me.

"That's why you killed him," I whisper.

Nameless nods. Then he brushes his hand over my hair, smoothing it away from my face. I can see his eyes searching mine. They aren't as dark as I thought; they look hazel in the glaring light of the examination room.

"Why did you destroy his face?" I ask.

"I wanted to be here when you found out who he is," Nameless responds.

Then he reaches up, his eyes never leaving mine, and lifts his mask to show me his lips.

Did I see that mouth at Neptune's Adventure? I imagine him hanging off in the shadows, watching me. Faceless except for his red tongue slipping out to lick his lips as I moved to each station, laughing with Rowan. It's all I can see of him—his mouth, his eyes. The rest of him is hidden.

I can't grasp onto an image, even though the idea of it, him watching me in the sunlight, sends hot prickles over my skin.

"You wanted to be here?" I echo. "Why?"

But Nameless doesn't answer.

Instead, he kisses me.

ABI

I didn't realize how desperately I'd been waiting for Nameless's kiss until it happens, until he's pulled me up against his warm, strong body, his arms wrapping tight around my shoulders. His tongue probes into my mouth, deep and searching, and all I can do is slump into his embrace and kiss him back.

"I wanted to see your face," he whispers, breaking the kiss to speak into my skin. "When you saw what I did for you."

He moves his mouth down to my throat and sucks hard on the skin there, right against my pulse. I moan and slump backward. When my bare thighs bump up against the drawer, I startle at the cold against my skin.

"You shouldn't have done that," I protest, although it sounds feeble even to me, especially as Nameless slides his hand up to squeeze at my breasts, his mouth still exploring all the sensitive places along my neck.

"He deserved it," Nameless mutters, shoving up my flimsy T-shirt. I don't stop him. I should stop him. But before I know it, the shirt is gone, and my skin shivers in the cold air of the examination room. "No one has any right to talk to you like that."

He shoves me back, lifting me onto the drawer.

The drawer with the body.

"What are you—"

Nameless swallows the question with a kiss and unlatches my bra. I moan into his mouth, fear and disgust and desire twisting together. This is wrong. This is so fucking wrong.

And yet the space between my thighs is on fire.

Nameless slides his hands down to my shorts and fumbles with the button, still kissing me with a furious hunger. I can't feel the corpse, but I'm aware of it behind me. The guy who catcalled me, who humiliated me over nothing. Reduced to cold, ruined meat.

Nameless pulls down the zipper on my shorts, slow and teasing. At the bottom, he stops and pulls back and looks at me, his lips swollen from kissing.

"I'm going to fuck you," he says in a voice brimming with smoke and sin. "Right here."

Dark, dizzying lust shoots straight through me. No. No, I *have* to stop this. This is wrong. This is depraved. This is—

This is the hottest fucking thing that's ever happened to me.

Nameless drags my shorts down, bringing my panties with them. He kneels in front of me, guiding one leg out, then the other. I shiver—from the cold air. From my horror at myself. From the scorching desire brimming in my clit.

"Are you going to tell me to stop?" he murmurs against my calf, kissing it softly, working his way up.

The cold metal presses into my thighs, making me shake. I don't know how to answer, so I don't.

"Are you?" he asks, more sharply. Then he looks up at me, the mask distorted above his red, eager mouth.

"No," I whisper. It hangs on the frigid air, a terrible, terrible truth.

Nameless grins. "I told you," he says. "You understand me."

Then he kisses my cunt. The sudden heat of his mouth makes me cry out and jolt backward, and my hand brushes against the corpse's lifeless flesh.

Heat surges through my body.

I tell myself it's from Nameless and his talented, dexterous tongue, which is currently swirling around my clit like he's determined to make me come as quickly as possible. But I know that's a lie. And as Nameless licks me, I move my hand back, centimeter by centimeter, until I feel the flesh again.

Another shudder of desire wracks through me.

I squeeze my eyes shut, my breath coming out in short, frantic gasps. Nameless moans against my pussy, and the heat of his mouth is a startling, delicious contrast to the cold slab of flesh beneath my hand.

It's not that I have any desire to fuck the dead. It's *this* body in particular. This man who humiliated me. And I don't want to fuck his corpse, anyway. I want to—

I want to desecrate it.

"More," I whisper, rolling my hips against Nameless's face. He makes another soft moan and then, to my despair, pulls away.

The cold air washes over my drenched pussy.

"I'm going to fuck you on top of him," he says, rising to standing. "You tell me if you want to look at him or not."

My thoughts are like static. My cunt throbs with a need to be filled.

"I want to look at you," I say softly.

Nameless gives me the smile of a predator. "You're a fucking angel."

I am no such thing, and we both know it. But it's not a thought I can dwell on, because Nameless hoists me up by the waist and slides me onto the drawer. When the ice of the metal hits my ass, I cry out at the shock of it, at the contrast to the liquid heat between my legs.

And then he shoves me a few inches further until I bump against the body, the flesh cold and clammy against mine.

"Beautiful," he says, and there's a kind of wonder in his voice. He slides his mask down, hiding his mouth but giving me a view of his eyes again, and I shudder as they drink me in, naked and splayed out across a dead fucking body.

"Touch yourself," he orders.

I do, snaking my arm down to circle against my clit. I'm drenched. Honestly, I'm not sure I've ever been so wet. I can feel it pooling on the metal.

I'm going to have to sanitize this, I think, just for a second, before all I can focus on is my pleasure.

Well, my pleasure, and the sight of Nameless pulling out his cock.

I might have had it in my mouth a week ago, but I didn't really get a good look at it, not in the dark. Here, beneath the bright, gleaming lights of the examination room, I see it in all its glory: thick and slightly curved and already beading with precum.

He steps up to me and pulls my hand away from my clit so he can replace it with his cockhead. I moan and tilt backward, draping myself over the stiff, freezing flesh of the man he killed. Nameless rubs his dick along my slit, slowly easing himself in.

"Do you like this?" he murmurs, teasing me with his cockhead. "Pressed between me and my victim?"

"Yes," I gasp out. There's no hesitation. I can't deny it. Not anymore.

"So do I," he says.

Then he slides his full length into me.

For a moment, he doesn't move. Just buries himself in my

pussy, his masked face inches from mine. His breath shudders softly as his dark, glittering eyes search my face.

"Finally," he breathes, slowly starting to roll his hips against mine. "You've no idea how long I've waited for this."

I whimper as his thrusts quicken, his cock sliding against my drenched, slippery walls. Then he pushes himself on top of me, pinning me against the body of his victim. That cold flesh sears into my skin, although I can feel it warming beneath me. After all, my own body is on fire.

I hook my legs around Nameless's hips and thrust against him, dragging his cock deeper inside me. It's been years since I've had sex, mostly because it never, ever felt like *this*. It was always short and perfunctory and frankly boring. I was better off taking care of myself.

But for the first time, sex feels like something I can't do on my own. Nameless pushes his cock inside me with hard, pounding thrusts, each one grinding me down against the corpse, like a reminder that he did that for me. Killed someone.

Just for insulting me. Just for making me uncomfortable.

I scream out my abandon, thrusting up into him. The examination room floods with a wet, slapping sound, and Nameless groans and runs his hands up to my waist to squeeze my breasts. The leather of his gloves is soft and satiny, and it feels just as good here as it did between my legs.

"Are you going to come for me?" he rasps. "On top of this corpse that I made for you?"

I nod, gasping. And I think I am. I can feel the swell of my pleasure building,

"Say it," he orders, wrapping one hand around my neck, holding me down as he thrusts into me. "Say how happy you are I brought you this dead man."

"Yes!" I choke out, my legs already starting to quaver. "Yes! Thank you! I knew it was you when I heard abo—"

I cut myself on as Nameless angles himself against my clit, making my whole core quake with need.

"Is that it?" He presses the mask's twisting mouth against my ear. "Is that the spot you like, little detective?"

He does it again, striking my clit like a flint. I scream and flail my arms out to run my hands over the cool, rubbery skin of the dead body beneath me. This refrigerated meat is all that's left of that asshole at the golf course.

I whimper wordlessly. Nameless keeps his rhythm steady, and I'm so wet that I can feel it slicking down my thighs. His cock slides through my folds like a knife through hot-melted better.

"I want you to come," he pants. "I want to feel it around my cock. Can you do that for me, little detective?"

His hand tightens slightly around my throat, and I stare up at him. At the mask. At the eyes, boring into me.

"Faster," I whisper. "Fuck me faster."

He does. Faster, and harder, too. Hard enough that the drawer shakes on its tracks, and I bounce against the corpse, and my body seizes up.

"Just... like... that..." I choke out, grabbing at his arms. His eyes flash. He obliges, sliding his cock through my wetness so the base of it massages my clit. "Don't... fucking... stop..."

"I'll never stop," he growls, fingers tightening just a little bit harder.

I don't know what it is—if it's his words, or if it's the faint pressure of his grip threatening to cut off my air—but I come. My pleasure pours through me, hot and molten, and I arch against the corpse and howl with ecstasy. My lower body convulses, each contraction another ripple of pleasure, and Nameless doesn't stop fucking me. He drives into me over and over, and I can see a wildness in his eyes. A needy, desperate hunger.

Then he makes a strangled sound and shudders against me.

"Fuck," he breathes, pressing his forehead to mine. "Fuck, that was perfect."

I wind my arms around his shoulders, pressing him into me. He nuzzles my neck, then grabs my waist and heaves me up, lifting me off the shelf entirely. I cry out in surprise and cling to him as he slowly lowers me down to the floor, pulling his cock out of me in the process.

I can't believe the hot, slippery mess between my legs. Can't believe I came like that—

On top of a corpse.

I look over my shoulder at the body. Our desperate fucking slid it sideways along the shelf, and the arm hangs off the side, along with the ruin of the head.

"You looked so beautiful," Nameless says suddenly.

I jerk my gaze back over to him. He's watching me intently, his cock still out, wet from my arousal.

"On the body," he says. "I always wanted—"

He steps up to me and trails his fingers along the side of my neck, and I can't move. Or tear my own gaze away from him.

"I always wanted to see you like that," he says softly. "Screaming with pleasure on top of my work."

I shiver, unsure what to say to that. I know it's so fucking wrong, what we did. The worst kind of disrespect.

But he deserved it, whispers a cold voice in my head. *Just like Blake Fletcher*

And then there's the worst thought:

I don't care that he deserved it.

I would have loved it anyway.

2 6

ROWAN

I shove the body back into the refrigeration unit and scoop Abi up in my arms and carry her upstairs. Best of all, she lets me, her head pressed against my chest, her breath soft and steady. I lay her down in her bed and arrange the sheets around her naked body, and she blinks up at me, her expression dazed.

"Stay," she whispers. "Please."

"I always stay until morning," I answer, sitting down beside her. She rolls onto her side, the silky sheets slipping down to reveal a flash of her breasts. She doesn't cover it up. "That's how I make sure you're safe."

She frowns, and I sense fear rippling off her, just for a second. "I'm glad," she finally says, settling her head down on the pillow. "If you hadn't been here that night I was attacked—"

I brush my hand over her mouth, and she looks up at me, eyes wide above my glove. "Don't talk about that," I say, even though I feel a tight knot in my chest. Yes, I killed the man who killed Olivia Pearce, who tried to kill Abi. But I still can't shake the feeling that the danger hasn't totally passed.

It's that presence. Not human. Not animal.

I don't say any of this to her, though, just lift my hand away and run it over her hair. "Sleep," I say. "I'll be here. I won't let anything happen to you."

Her eyes glimmer a little as she looks up at me. Studying me. Studying my killing face.

"You aren't going to sleep?"

"I don't need sleep."

"Everyone needs sleep."

I smile, even though I know she can't see it. "I'm not like everyone, little detective."

Abi's still studying me. Frowning a little. "Are you going—going to take your mask off?"

My whole body goes still, and for a moment, I'm very aware of the blood pumping through my veins.

"No," I finally say.

Something darkens in Abi's expression. A flicker of disappointment.

"Oh," she says, and the disappointment is even clearer in her voice.

"You want to see my face," I say carefully, trying to keep my voice measured. "But this is my face." I gesture at the mask. "This is who I am."

She lifts her hand to run it over the mask's twisted mouth. "You don't look like that," she murmurs. "You don't look like a monster."

That word lodges in my thoughts as I run my hand down her hair until I reach her shoulder, pale and soft as moonlight. Monster. That's what my mother called me when I was eight years old, when she sent me to live with Uncle Nash. *I gave birth to a monster.*

I didn't think I was a monster, not then. But she wasn't wrong. After all, when I look in the mirror as Rowan Hanover, I don't see a monster there either. But that's why I wear my killing face. To show my victims—to show Abi—what I really am.

"I am a monster, though," I say. "Although not one who will ever hurt you."

Abi's breath hitches into a soft little sigh. There's a small, stupid part of me that does want to take my killing face off, but only because I can't kiss her properly with it on. Rowan could, though. Rowan could press his nose into her hair and breathe in her scent and feel her hands trace the skin of his face. But Rowan isn't real.

I am.

Still, I do reach up and push the mask up so I can lean over and brush my lips against her forehead. She tilts her face and catches them in a real kiss, her mouth on mine. It surprises me. I think it surprises her, too, given how quickly her heart starts beating.

I can't stop myself from deepening the kiss, though. Tasting her mouth with my tongue. And she gives in to that, too, moaning softly.

"Good night, little detective," I whisper, pulling away. "Go to sleep."

Abi's eyes flutter. And I watch her in bed, the way I've watched her dozens of times before. Except tonight, I'm not hiding in the closet like a secret.

I'm staying with her out in the open.

I LEAVE RIGHT AT DAWN, when the sun is just a thin pink line along the top of the Gulf. Abi's sound asleep. All night, I watched her, just like I promised.

Nothing happened. No one came sniffing around.

It hurts to leave her, but I know I can't stay with her as myself during the day. I'm afraid the sunlight will reveal too much, even in my killing face.

I go out through her window rather than one of the doors downstairs. I don't want to leave them unlocked, and I like the idea of her waking up to the warm sea breeze filtering through her curtains.

I jump down, landing hard on the dirt. *Bones of steel,* Uncle Nash used to say whenever I'd make these kinds of two-story jumps. I guess he's right.

It's still dark enough that I leave my killing face on until I'm in the cemetery. I stop near the row of pecan trees and peel it away, shuddering a little when the air touches my sweat-damp skin. I'm not usually bothered by taking it off—my real face is my disguise, my means of protection—but this morning, it feels strange, almost painful. Like I'm skinning myself.

I look down at it, crumpled up in my hands. My face. The thing that shows what I am.

What would Abi say if she knew I was pretending to be Rowan Hanover? She was worried about him earlier—and about me. Worried that I would kill him, I suppose out of jealousy.

I'm not sure what to make of that. It honestly makes my chest feel weird, tight and constricted like I have a cold.

I trudge forward through the dew-damp grass, heading down to the beach. This should be the greatest morning of my life. Abi let me inside her. She let me inside her while she was draped over my kill, and she came so hard that as soon as her contractions started, I came, too, spurned on by her orgasm. And that wasn't even the best part. *That* was watching her fall asleep without having to hide myself.

But I feel so out of fucking sorts. And when I stare down at my empty killing face, it just makes the feeling worse.

I reach the edge of the cemetery and heave myself over the gate.

And that's when I feel it. The inhuman presence.

It sweeps across me, thick and undeniable. I leap off the

fence and whip around to the left, catching hold of it again. Its origin is nearby. I can feel it pounding in my bloodstream.

Enough of this. I'm not leaving Abi vulnerable to a second killer. Once this presence is dead, then I *know* for certain she'll be safe.

I yank my killing face on even though the rubber blocks my sense of smell; fortunately, I can still feel the presence pulsating in the direction of the beach. I run, my arms pumping, until I come to the sand dunes. The light is grey and thin, the sun just starting to slide over the water.

And he's still close. He's on the beach. I'm sure of it.

I don't take the boardwalk; instead, I clamor over the dunes, keeping my body low against the thick, crawling dune vines. I peer over the crest of sand, scanning the beach proper.

I don't see anyone, but that presence burns hotly. Hotter than it ever has before—

Bright red movement flashes in the periphery of my vision, even with my killing face. I jump out onto the sand just as a figure cuts across the beach.

Not a man, like I assumed. A woman with long, fire-engine red hair.

I have a second of doubt—but then the wind gusts and it's undeniable that *this* was the strange, inhuman presence I've been feeling.

She disappears into the public bathroom.

"Got you," I whisper, and I take off running. I'm laser-focused on that presence. It makes the public bathroom seem to glow like a beacon. I slam up to the door of the women's restroom and find that the padlock there is shattered, the chain that the city strings through the door handle at night coiled on the ground.

I swing the door open and step inside. The light flickers, sallow and fluorescent.

I can feel her. Not just sense her, but *feel* her, the way I feel

Abi. I can hear her heart beating and count her quickened breaths.

I stomp into the corridor of stalls, moving slow and cautious. There's no way out. No windows save for a skylight, sealed shut and too small for anyone to shimmy through, regardless.

My boots stomp over the concrete floor, echoing against the walls. I shove open the first stall, the door banging against the frame. Empty.

The second. Empty.

I know she's in here. I can feel her as acutely as I can feel my own heartbeat. But what I don't feel, remotely, is fear.

I'm just about to shove open the third bathroom stall when my quarry leaps out, a blur of dark clothes and red hair. She manages to skirt around me, moving much faster than I expect. But I whip around and grab her before she can make it to the exit.

I slam her up against the cinderblock, and she looks up at me, and—

Grins. She *grins,* like this is all a fucking game.

"Hey, Rowan," she says.

My blood freezes in my veins, and her grin gets even bigger. Then she shoots her arm out, slamming her fist into my side. Pain blooms through my midsection, and I stumble back, clutching at my belly. She laughs and saunters backward, not even trying to run.

I peer up at her through my killing face, my thoughts a whirl of confusion.

"Who are you?" I rasp. "Why have you been stalking Abilene Snow?"

She shakes her head. "I haven't. I don't have any interest in your little girlfriend."

That word, *girlfriend*, blooms strangely in my chest. But then the woman says,

"I've been stalking *you*."

For the first time in a long time, I feel something like fear. *This is it,* I think. I've been caught. She's a police officer. An FBI agent. All the boogeymen Uncle Nash raised me to fear.

I take a step backward, suddenly aware that our positions are flipped, that she's blocking the entrance, and I have no way out.

The woman puts her hands on her hips and looks at me appraisingly.

"Who are you?" I ask again. "What do you want?"

A smile dances across her lips. "Don't be so nervous," she says coyly as she saunters up to me. "My name's Charlotte Careta, and I'm someone like you."

I stare at her. And I know, immediately, what she means.

She's a killer. But more than that, she's not... normal. The way I'm not normal. That's why the presence felt different.

"And you and I," she continues, "have an awful lot to talk about."

27
ABI

He's gone when I wake up. But the window's open, the sea wind making the curtains billow inward. I slide out of bed and go over to look out at the yard below, the grass damp with dew.

How did he do that? Climb down from the window? It's not like there's a lattice. The wall is smooth, with nothing to hold on to.

I drag the window shut, confusion twisting around in my belly. The truth is, I slept well last night, knowing Nameless was here, his gloved hand stroking my hair as I fell asleep.

I can still feel the ache of him between my legs, the sense memory of that crashing, overwhelming orgasm—

I wrench away from the window. I don't even know what I'm feeling at this point: guilt, fear, excitement, all three at once? It's like a hurricane is raging around inside of me.

The body, I think vaguely. Last night, Nameless shoved the drawer closed without rearranging the body. I need to clean up any evidence.

It should sicken me. It doesn't.

I get dressed quickly, brush my teeth, and go straight down

to the examination room. Everything in the house feels normal. Undisturbed. Even the front foyer, where it all started. Where he kissed me—

Where he killed for me.

The examination room also feels undisturbed, despite what happened here last night. It's as cold and sterile as it always is, and nothing is obviously out of place. There's a part of me that wonders if I made it all up. If it was just a feverish sex dream.

One way to know for sure, I think, dragging the drawer open.

And there it is. The proof. The corpse is askew, the ruin of the head practically falling off the drawer. Worse, there's an imprint on the metal from where my ass was, plus a frozen film of arousal.

There's no denying what happened. None whatsoever.

And yet, I feel nothing but a vague, buzzy happiness as I clean up the drawer—wiping down the metal with disinfectant and polishing it until it shines, then shifting the body back into place. The plastic sheeting is still on the floor where Nameless tossed it, and I pick it up and slide it over the corpse, and now it really *is* like nothing ever happened.

And that's when I get the ache of sadness in my chest.

I shove the drawer shut with a clang and take a deep breath to steady myself. I have work to do. Bodies that Nameless didn't provide for me, that he won't expect me to violate tonight.

But god, I hope he does show up again—

My office phone rings, startling me badly enough that I yelp and slam up against the drawers. "Fuck," I mutter, making my way over to my office to answer. "What now?"

At least I know it's not anything Nameless did. He was here. With me.

I pick the phone up right before it switches over to voice-mail. "Abi Snow," I say briskly, trying to keep my eyes away from the map on the wall. The map of Nameless's kills, the red pins spelling out **YOUR DARK.**

My darkness certainly came out last night.

"Abi Snow," says the voice on the other end. It sounds strange and distorted, like there's something wrong with the line. For a second, I think there's an echo. But then it says, "I know what you did."

My entire body goes cold. I swoon a little and stumble sideways, slamming my leg into the desk.

Someone saw.

Someone saw what I did with Nameless.

No, that's impossible. I'm the only one with access to the examination room. There are no cameras here.

"Did you hear me, you stupid bitch?"

The voice startles me back to the present. "Who is this?" I hiss, bracing myself against the table.

"Someone who knows what a filthy fucking liar you are." The voice buzzes and crackles. "Someone who knows you deserve to suffer, just like those other two cunts."

My panic calcifies. This isn't about Nameless.

Those other two cunts. Is this about Olivia?

"What?" I manage to get out, my head swoony.

"I'm coming for you next. And trust me: you won't get away this time."

A click and the line goes dead.

You won't get away this time.

No. No, this can't be Olivia's murderer. Nameless killed him. I *know* he was dead. I saw the fucking body twice—once in my foyer, then again on my examination slab. And he only killed Olivia, anyway.

So who's the second victim?

I wish, with a horrible tightness in my chest, that Nameless hadn't left me alone.

Suddenly, my fax machine in my computer printer kicks on,

the whir loud and mechanical in the silence. I shriek and drop the phone receiver; I'd forgotten that stupid thing was still hooked up. I'd never bothered to disconnect the number after Uncle Vic died, even though I never use it. I certainly receive faxes.

And yet I can hear the paper getting sucked into the printer, the whir of the ink. Something's coming through.

I creep forward, my heart racing. It looks like an image: blurred, smeary colors. Dark with spots of light, like fireflies. And then something else. Something brighter than the rest.

A shock of blonde hair.

I fight back nausea as the picture slowly rolls out, revealing itself inch by inch.

A blonde woman, screaming.

Naked.

Tied up.

The image drops into the tray, and I force myself to pick it up, although my hand is shaking so badly that the paper shakes, too.

There's something written underneath the photograph, a scribble in thick dark ink:

This is what she looked like before I fucked her...

The fax kicks on again, whirring and whining. I scream and stumble backward, fighting the urge to unplug it. I know evidence when I see it.

I look down at the picture again, my vision blurry with tears. The screaming woman. She looks familiar—

A split second later, the realization hits me like a punch.

It's Heather Staunton.

"No," I scream, the paper dropping to my feet. The next picture is already half in the tray, but I know what I'm going to see. I know, because I've seen it before, when I went to the gazebo in the town square.

And yet I still take slow, shaking steps over to the fax machine. I still look down at the horror sliding into the tray.

It's Heather Staunton, kneeling in the dark, her head split in half at the jaw.

And the text, scrawled out in the same cruel hand:

...And this is what she looks like now.

You're next, bitch. You and your little guard dog.

2 8

ROWAN

I stare at this woman, Charlotte, feeling as wary as a prey animal being hunted out in the open.

"What do you mean?" I finally say. "That I'm like you?"

Charlotte tilts her head. "You don't know, do you?"

I hesitate. I certainly have my suspicions about what she means, but I know better than to say it aloud.

Charlotte sighs and rakes her hands through her hair. "Fuck," she snaps. "Damn it. I figured you already knew, given all your little—activities around town." She grins up at me. "I've never known anyone who makes them look like accidents," she adds. "That's clever."

Immediately, panic tears through me like an out-of-control fire, and my blood pounds like an alarm bell. "I don't know what you're talking about."

"Yes, you do," Charlotte says affably. "I get why you don't want to say it, but trust me. I'm about as far from a cop as you can get."

I curl my hands up, dart my eyes around the bathroom. I

can't let her live, that much is clear. But I need to know who she is first.

"I know a lot of things about you." Charlotte gives me a sly, knowing look, which I don't like one bit. "So as a show of good faith, I'll answer some of your questions to even the score. What do you say?"

I stare at her through my killing face. I'm just going to have to kill her, as quickly and cleanly as I can. Then I'll figure out the story. Same as what I did with Julian Bernet

"You're thinking about trying to kill me, aren't you?"

Charlotte asks the question in a mocking sing-song, and anger seethes in my chest. This is it. Time to act.

"I won't *try*," I growl, stepping toward her.

"You will *try*," she says with a smile. "And you might even think you succeeded, if I let you. But I don't feel like dying today."

Not a single fucking thing she said makes any sense, and I suppose that's on purpose, because it stops me in my tracks.

Charlotte winks and saunters over to the bathroom door and turns the inside deadbolt. I just stare at her, my heart pounding, and hold Abi's face in my head. I have to get out of this for her. Charlotte is clearly nuts, and I know she's not capable of killing me, but she could still ruin my life. Namely, her dead body will go to Abi, and I'll have to explain to her why I murdered a random attractive woman in a fucking beachside bathroom.

Fuck. I can't kill her.

"Can we just not do this?" I blurt out.

Charlotte looks over at me. "Do what?" she asks. "Have a conversation?"

"What the fuck do you want?" I snarl, my patience wearing thin. "You said you don't want to die. Well, locking me in here isn't going to help with that, so just let me go and pretend you never saw me."

Charlotte throws back her head and laughs. "I'm not afraid of you, Rowan."

It's the second time she's said my name, and just like the first, it fills my head with a panicked rush of white noise. It's not just about this woman knowing my secrets. It's about *Abi*. Because even Abi doesn't know I'm Rowan, and so this feels like I've betrayed her.

"Rowan Hanover," Charlotte says slowly, her lips curling up even more. "Take off the mask. I know who you are. I know *what* you are. And I just want to have a conversation."

The white noise builds to a heavy, pounding static, and in that static, I hear voices. My mother calling me a monster. Uncle Nash telling me he's the only thing keeping me from death row.

And then I move without thinking, my vision banded with white. I fling myself at Charlotte, trying to grab at her neck.

She catches me by the wrists and flings me sideways.

For a second, my feet lift off the air. Then I slam into the sink, the ceramic cutting deep enough into my belly that it knocks all the air out of my lungs. I totter sideways, stunned and suddenly cold with something I think might be fear.

"You want to fight?" Charlotte says. "We can fight. Get it out of your system. Then, we'll talk."

"How did you do that?" I rasp as I turn toward her. She's not that small, and she looks strong enough, but I'm still significantly bigger than her.

And yet she threw me into that sink with real force. Not even Uncle Nash was ever able to do that to me.

"That's what I'm trying to explain to you," she says patiently. "You and I, we're not human."

I stare at her, that cold rope of fear tightening in my belly. *Not human.*

I want to protest. What else could I fucking be?

Except my mother saw it. *I gave birth to a monster*, she

screamed, and I stared at myself in the mirror as a little boy and told myself I looked human. But I knew there was something broken inside me, and so did Uncle Nash.

Bones of steel. Stronger than you have any right to be. Let's make full use of that freakishly good night vision, huh?

"Do you want to talk or do you want to fight? I'm prepared to do both."

Charlotte's voice jerks back into that damp, buzzing bathroom. I shuffle away from her, wary. My waist still aches from where I slammed into the sink.

"I wanna talk, " Charlotte says. "So that's what we're gonna do. Sound good?"

"What is there to talk about?" I growl.

Charlotte arches an eyebrow. "Seriously? I just told you you're not human. And I know you're curious about how I know your name."

The white static floods through my thoughts again. "That's not my name." A pointless lie. But it feels like the only response. I won't want to acknowledge the other thing.

"It is." Charlotte smiles. "Your mother is Maridel Hanover—"

The white static brightens until it feels like a migraine pounding behind my eye. That's her. My mother. I haven't spoken to her in ten years.

"And your father is Johnson Baldys."

That brings me up short. I never knew my father's name because my mother refused to talk about him. She told me once, right before she sent me to Uncle Nash, that he was her biggest mistake, because he had given her me. *You're just like him*, she said, staring out the window in our living room with a cigarette dangling between her fingers. *Same cold eyes.*

Uncle Nash never talked about him.

"Your mother's human," Charlotte continues. "But don't worry, I didn't do anything to her."

I don't know what to say about that.

"Your father, though. He isn't. He's like us."

I stare at her, my body shaking, and think suddenly about all those times I sensed Charlotte's presence on the wind.

Not human. Not animal.

"What are you?" I murmur, a sick, dark feeling coiling in my stomach.

Charlotte looks at me for a long time before answering. "There are a lot of names for what we are," she finally says. "But the one I learned is Hunter."

The word buzzes in the stale, warm air of the bathroom, as loud as the fluorescent lights above the salt-streaked mirror.

"And what does that mean?" My throat is dry. I don't like how this is making me feel. I don't like how it feels *right*, the way fucking Abi felt right. The way it feels like I've found something I've been searching for my entire life.

"We kill," Charlotte says. Any hint of mockery is gone. She's very serious now, and her eyes never leave my killing face. "We have to kill, in fact. You can't suppress it, or very bad things will happen."

I think of my mother refusing to look me in the eye, the cigarette smoke curling between us. *You're a monster, Rowan. And a mistake.*

I think of Uncle Nash sliding a gun into my hand when I was thirteen, one of his business associates lying bound and gagged on a cold cement floor. *Just pull the trigger, boy. Easiest thing in the world.*

It had been the easiest thing in the world.

"What kind of bad things?" I finally say.

Charlotte studies me. "You didn't know," she says carefully. "But you never tried to suppress it, did you? The killing?"

"What kind of bad things?" I snarl. My voice clangs around in the bathroom, and anyone else would have been terrified. But not Charlotte. She doesn't even flinch.

"From what I understand," she finally says. "It builds up. The need to kill. It builds and builds until it explodes out of you, and you'll slaughter anyone and anything just to feel normal again. Even someone you love."

Abi flashes through my thoughts. Standing on the porch, wreathed in light. Strolling down the beach with the wind blowing back her hair. Smiling at me from above the lavender latte I bought for her as Rowan Hanover, who, if he were real, would be the sort of man she deserves. Not an inhuman monster like me.

"But you've never suppressed it, "Charlotte says. "That's good."

We're silent for a moment, the two of us staring at each other across the bathroom. I don't know what to make of any of this.

For the first time in my life, I wish Uncle Nash were alive. If anyone could confirm what she's saying, it was him.

But if I'm honest with myself, I don't need his confirmation. I know she's right. I can feel it clicking into place.

"You can sense things," Charlotte says softly. "Emotions."

The muscles in my body tense up.

"You can tell when someone's nearby," she continues, her eyes fixed on my killing face. "If they're scared or relaxed." She pauses. "You can hear things other people can't. Like their hearts."

As soon as she says it, I'm aware of her heartbeat. Slow and steady. She's not frightened at all.

"That's how you're able to kill so well," she continues. "You're stronger than they are. Faster."

There's a slight stress to the way she says *they*, and I know, instinctively, who she means. Everyone. The whole fucking world. All those people I watch at work: the tourists and locals alike, buzzing around on the beach with all the noise of their humanity.

Abi.

And I know, instinctively, that I'm not like them. I've always known it.

"Who are you?" I ask, and my voice startles me, how much it sounds like Rowan Hanover instead of me. "Not, like your name. *Who* are you? Why are you telling me all of this?"

Charlotte smiles, and there's something sad about it. Something wistful. "I'm your half-sister," she finally says. "Johnson Baldys is my father, too."

Blood pounds in my ears. A half-sister.

"The parent who isn't human," I finally say.

"Yeah. A Hunter." Charlotte steps up to me, and I search her features through my killing face. Even in the bad, sallow light, I think I can see Rowan Hanover, a little, in the shape of her eyes, the line of her nose.

No, not Rowan Hanover. Me. Myself.

"I've been looking for you for a while," she says. "I only just found out what I am, after—" She laughs. "Well, it's a long story. But my boyfriend, Jaxon—he's like us—he thought I should know more Hunters. So I came looking for you."

I don't know what to say. The lights over the mirror pop and buzz. Through the cinderblock walls, I can hear the ocean. It reminds me of Abi's soft, steady breath as she sleeps.

"And you found me." It's the only thing I can think of. "So now what?"

Charlotte frowns a little. "I feel like I need to teach you what we are," she says. "The way Jaxon taught me."

"And how do you suggest we do that?" I can't believe I'm saying this, but at the same time, I'm curious. I've always felt detached from the world. Abi's the only thing that's ever connected me to it. And that's not going to change, of course.

But if there are others out there like me—well, I should know about that. To protect her.

Charlotte grins. "I thought maybe we could go hunting together."

It takes me a second to register what she's saying. "You mean kill someone?"

My question bounds around the bathroom. Charlotte sighs.

"Yeah," she says. "We pick a target and we hunt them down. When you do it with another Hunter, you'll feel it. It's different. And you'll understand what I'm telling you better, I think."

"Right now?" I shake my head, panic rising in my throat. "No. I can't just—I have a *process*, okay? It keeps me from getting caught. Or killed."

And I really don't want either to happen right now. Not after the night I spent with Abi.

But Charlotte just laughs. "Oh, you don't have to worry about dying. You can't. Or, I mean, you *can*, technically. But you come back. It's one of our many skillsets."

"Bullshit," I say.

"What?" She laughs. "Everything else I've told you is true. I'd give you a demonstration, but it takes a while to revive. But you'll find out eventually." She grins. "Come on, Rowan. You can live a little. I bet you never killed during the day, either."

I scowl at her, even though she can't see.

"What about without the mask?"

"It's not a mask," I say stiffly. "You wouldn't understand."

"I bet I would." Charlotte smiles in a way that makes me nervous. "Or how about this. You know that woman at the funeral home? The one you're always watching?"

My hackles go up immediately. Any wary interest I felt immediately vanishes. "Don't fucking touch her," I snarl, and I'm surprised by how vehement I am. How much I do sound like a monster.

But Charlotte is unfazed. She lifts her hands in a surrender. "I wouldn't *dream* of it," she says. "But she's human. It's hard when one of us loves a human. Two of my friends are doing it, though. So maybe I can give you some advice."

I wonder how Charlotte knows I love Abi.

"Come on." Charlotte steps up to me. "Come with me. Let me be a big sister for a day."

I ought to say no. But my curiosity is burning me up. A half-sister. Another killer.

Besides, Abi should be safe. The presence I thought was stalking her is standing in front of me now.

"Come onnnn," Charlotte says. "I'll be enlightening." Her eyes glitter. "And fun."

Although I ought to know better, excitement leaps up inside me.

"Fine," I say, hoping I'm not making a mistake. "But I need to be back before dark."

29

ABI

I lock every door in my house and double-check them. Then I triple-check them. I check each window, making sure it's sealed shut. Even the ones upstairs.

And when all of that is done, I go into the spare bedroom and pull open the closet door. Uncle Vic had a hunting rifle that he kept in a carrying case. He didn't actually like hunting, he told me once, but a rifle like that was a standard gift for a Texas boy of his generation.

After he died, I put it in this closet.

I don't know how to use a gun, but I take the case out anyway and set it on the bed.

I don't know what to do next.

Or rather, what I want to do is the one thing I *can't* do. I can't call Nameless. I don't know who he is. He slips in and out of my life like a demon. He comes to me. I don't go to him.

So I'm alone, at least until nightfall.

I leave the gun on the bed and go back downstairs, my body tight with worry. I tell myself I just need to get through the day. Once night falls, Nameless will be here, and I can show him the pictures and the messages. He won't let anything happen to me.

I don't know why, but I'm sure of it.

The line to the funeral parlor rings, filling the foyer with the shrill jangling of the downstairs phone. I shriek and nearly leap out of my skin.

It's him, I think, staring at the phone in the foyer like it's a venomous snake. It's been there for years, and I always thought of it as a decoration. But it's hooked to the same line that goes to my office.

I could let it go to voicemail. I *should* let it go to voice-mail, just like I *should* have called the police as soon as I got those pictures. But how the hell was I going to explain the part about the guard dog? Or about getting away the first time?

No, I made that decision weeks ago, when Nameless killed my attacker, and I just let him go. When I *fucked* him instead of turning him in.

Before I can talk myself out of it, I snatch up the phone and press the receiver to my ear. The line buzzes.

"Hello?" I whisper.

"Abilene? Is that you?"

It's a normal voice. Not modulated or distorted. Male, crisp, professional.

"Yes." I straighten my spine and try to calm my breathing. "Yes, it's me."

"Sorry, the line sounded weird for a second there. This is Rick Contreras, by the way."

The detective from Olivia's case. I hold my breath, waiting for him to say it.

"I'm afraid we had another murder."

Blood pounds in my ears. I don't know how to act normally about this. How to act like I didn't know it already happened. I swallow.

"Is it—" My voice wobbles. "Is it like Olivia Pearce?"

"Yes," Rick says gently. "Abilene, I need you to listen to me.

He went after Heather Staunton. We found her this morning. Set up on Pier Fourteen."

I close my eyes, my heart hammering up in my throat. Fuck. The same place Nameless left Julian Bernet. Another fucking message, as clear as the faxes I received this morning.

Nausea swirls around in my stomach, and I know Rick is waiting for my reaction.

"No," I whisper, hoping to god I sound convincing. "No, that can't be—"

"I'm afraid it is." Rick clears his throat. "Abilene, one murder is a tragedy. Two, like this, is a pattern. And I'm worried about your safety."

I stare at the empty foyer, imagining the dark lump of my attacker's body on the floor. How Nameless pulled off his stocking, and it was no one. A stranger.

I thought I was safe.

I was so, so stupid.

"Yes, I can't disagree," I say carefully.

"That being said," Rick continues, "you know this is a joint investigation. With the Magnolia department. And the Rosado Sheriff's Department."

I close my eyes.

"Kaplan wants me to bring you in. Just to talk."

I laugh, sharp and shrill. "Why? Does he think I fucking did this?"

"He's an asshole," Rick says. "That's why. As far as I'm concerned, your statement is a formality. If you don't want to come in, and I don't really blame you, I'll send someone over there to you. You need a security detail anyway."

"That's not necessary," I spit out—too quickly. The last thing I want is some bumbling police officer sitting outside my house when Nameless comes around tonight. *He's* my security detail.

Rick sighs. "Are you sure?"

"I'm sure," I say. "I'm happy to have someone come take my statement, but I don't need security."

At least not for tonight. I can tell Rick I changed my mind tomorrow.

"Very well." Rick pauses. "I also wanted to let you know I'm sending the body to Magnolia for the autopsy. You don't need to do that for us again."

"Thank you," I whisper. "I appreciate that."

"Abilene, you really need to be careful," Rick says. "It's ugly, what he's doing to them. Cruel. We're doing what we can, but we don't have any leads right now."

I bite back a surge of bile. "When do you think the officer will come by?" I ask.

"Within the next few hours. And I want you to promise me that you'll keep an eye out, okay? We don't know how this guy operates. Don't know how he's taking them or how long he's keeping them."

"I understand," I say. "Thank you, Rick."

"Stay safe."

I drop the phone in the cradle and take a stumbling step backward. Light pours in through the front door, freshly repaired from the night when I thought this nightmare was over.

"Nameless," I whisper, like I'm praying to him. "I wish I knew how to find you."

I'M a wreck the rest of the day. A nervous, pacing wreck. A Rosado police officer shows up around mid-morning, an impossibly young new recruit who smiles thinly at me from the doorway.

"Ms. Snow," he says, sounding almost apologetic. "Detective Contreras asked me to stop by. We just have a few questions."

It goes as smoothly as I might expect. We talk in the kitchen because I don't want to take him upstairs to my living room. The sun is bright and hot and reveals every trace of dust floating through the air. The entire time we're talking, I think that if the officer went into the viewing room, this glaring sunlight would show how I let a killer seduce me instead of doing the right thing.

Somehow, though, I manage to answer the questions with a calm, clear voice. They're basic things: Have I seen anything unusual. Have I gotten any threatening messages. Have I had any uncomfortable encounters in the last few days.

It should be yes to all of those questions, shouldn't it? There are the terrible pictures down in my office. There's Nameless stepping out of the shadows in his rubber mask. There's my naked body draped over a corpse while Nameless rams himself inside me and tells me I'm beautiful.

"No," I say to every question. "No, I haven't seen anything."

The whole interview takes maybe half an hour. When the officer leaves, I lock the door behind him and lean up against it and let out long, deep breaths as adrenaline ricochets through my body.

More than anything, I wish I could call Nameless. In the impossibly bright foyer, he feels like some figment of my fucked up imagination. Some trauma response I conjured up out of the hot summer night.

I try to work. Nothing gets done. I stare down at my phone, scrolling through my contacts. At one point, I stop on Rowan's name, my chest tight. It was nice meeting up with him after Olivia died. But I can't bring myself to message him.

He deserves someone normal, not someone who's fucked a killer.

Eventually, though, I do message the group chat. I don't want to put the burden of my honesty on them, but it's better than nothing.

> Y'all around? I need to talk to someone.

I set my phone down and stare up at the map of Rosado on the wall. All those red pins marking murders-that-aren't-murders. With the most recent one, the pattern seems even more clear. A message. A conversation.

What other conversations might be happening in this town?

In a burst, I grab two white pins and stick them in place. One at the gazebo on the town square, and one at Pier Fourteen.

I frown, staring at the map. I already know why the killer left Heather at the pier. But why the gazebo? Simply because it was a prominent place?

I study the twelve other white pins. Compared to the red ones, they've always seemed random to me. And they still do, if I'm looking at the design they make on the map. But two of them suddenly stand out, because they're both at town landmarks: one at the historic marker on the beach, where there's an ugly statue of some town founder. The other at the First Rosado Methodist Church, one of the oldest churches in Texas.

I grab my notebook from my desk and flip through it until I find the details of each case. The one by the statue was ruled a suicide—a gunshot. The other was ruled an accident, although there's very little information about the death. *Laceration to the neck that severed the carotid artery.*

How the hell is that an accident?

My phone chimes, and I startle, dropping the files across the desk.

PENELOPE

> What's up, girlie?

I stare down at the message, my fingers hovering over the keypad. It's a relief to hear from her, even though I don't know what to say. She's my best friend, but I can't tell her anything that's happening to me. It would make her an accomplice—

Like I'm an accomplice

And I can't do that to her. I can't. But god, I also don't want to be alone right now.

I need a video chat like rn

I got you. Usual link?

I send back a heart as an affirmative, then slide behind my desk and flip open my work laptop. I know I ought to do this on my personal laptop, but I feel safer down here. The office and the exam room are closed tight, like a cocoon.

This is also the first place I ever encountered Nameless. The first place he—

"Abi! What's up?"

Penelope grins at me through the laptop screen. Her background has changed from the blank wall of her sister's apartment; she's outside somewhere, a wall of alpine trees behind her.

"Where are you?" I ask.

"Colorado." She leans forward. "I'm here to protest that new pipeline RTI is putting in."

I have no idea what she's talking about; I haven't exactly been paying attention to environmental injustices the last few days. But I still nod, trying to act normal. "That's cool."

"I mean, it's gonna be intense. No cell service, much less Internet." Penelope frowns. "I told y'all about it? How my car broke down in Nebraska?"

Heat burns in my cheeks. She did, actually—there had been a flurry of messages over the last few days, the two of them talking to each other. "Yeah, sorry, I've been distracted."

Penelope's frown deepens. "What's wrong?"

Everything, including me. I wonder what Penelope would

say to me fucking a killer, not that I can tell her over Zoom. She's about as non-judgmental as you can get, but I don't think she'd understand that. Neither of them would.

Still, I have to tell her *something*. It's a relief, hearing her voice, not feeling so alone.

"There was another murder," I say. "Um, my lawyer from when I was a teenager—"

"Jesus Christ," Penelope says. "She was the one killed?"

"Yeah." I feel sick to my stomach, my fear twisting around tight in my guts. "Yeah, in the same way as Olivia Pearce."

"Oh my fucking god." I hear clacking through the speakers; Penelope's already diving into Google. "I found a story, but it's not really saying anything—"

"Yeah, it just happened last night."

Penelope's eyes scan across the screen. Reading the story, I guess. "Forget the protest," she says. "I'm coming down to Rosado. You can't be alone."

I stiffen. "No, that's not necessary," I say, a little too quickly. It's not that I don't want her here, her or Chloe. But I already have someone watching over me, and I don't want to put either of them in danger. "The cops are giving me a guard."

Penelope scoffs at that. Rolls her eyes. "Why the fuck would you trust the cops?"

"They have guns," I say weakly.

"Yeah, and we know who they usually shoot with those guns. The second they see this asshole is a white guy, those guns are staying right in their holsters."

"There's also Rowan," I say quickly, even though shame flushes in my chest. "We've been hanging out. I can ask him to stay with me until—until this all blows over."

Penelope leans back in her chair, arms crossed over her chest. The trees behind her sway back and forth. "I'm glad you're getting some dick, but I'd rather you not depend on some random dude."

I think of Nameless, big and strong and towering over my first attacker.

"He's not some random dude," I finally say, although I'm not talking about Rowan.

"Yeah, well, you've known us longer." Penelope pauses, wrapping a lock of her brown hair around one finger. "What if you go stay with Chloe for a while? Get out of Texas. She just inherited that big lake house from her grandparents, so she has the room."

That idea feels even worse. Then I'd have no protector, and I'd put Chloe in danger, too.

"And if the killer follows me?" I say. "I really think it's better for me to stay here."

"Abi." Penelope says my name with the air of a mom losing her patience. "I love you, but you're being stupid." She points at her screen. "I mean, these fucking deaths—it's obviously about you. What happened when you were sixteen."

"I'll be fine," I mutter.

Penelope slumps back, staring at me through the screen. "You're not telling me something," she says flatly. "Aren't you? There's something else."

A million alarm bells go off in my head. A million images flash through my thoughts.

"I just can't leave," I say, my voice shaky. "I can't risk putting either of you in danger."

"So you're just going to hang out in that big-ass house by yourself?" Penelope squawks. "And hope the police will protect you?"

"Not the police." I say it without thinking, but as soon as the words are out of my mouth, I know I fucked up.

"What?" Penelope says. "You just told me they were giving you a guard. Who else would it be? Rowan?"

"Yes," I whisper.

"Some guy who runs a hotel?"

Worse than that. A million times worse. But I nod. "I'll be fine, Penny. Really."

Penelope stares at me through the screen. "I want you to call me," she says darkly. "Every fucking night. Me and Chloe. Do you understand?"

"I thought you weren't going to have Internet access."

"Then call fucking Chloe."

I take a deep breath and look past my computer and out at the examination room. The lights have switched off, but I can still make out the gleam of metal.

"Fine," I say. "I'll call y'all every night."

"And don't trust the police." Penelope's eyes gleam. "Seriously, Abi. You're better off trusting this Rowan guy."

Hearing Rowan's name sours in my thoughts. God, I wish I could be honest with her.

But I know I can't.

ROWAN

I can not believe I'm doing this, riding shotgun in a rented Honda Civic with a woman who isn't Abilene Snow.

Charlotte hums along to the music playing softly in the background. Some mournful female singer backed by orchestral swells. I study Charlotte's profile through my killing face, looking at the family resemblance. She doesn't look anything like my mother, that's true. But she really does kind of look like me.

"You can take off your mask," she says suddenly, her eyes still on the road.

"I told you, it's not a mask."

Charlotte glances sideways at me. "Then what is it?"

I hate this. I feel like I'm under a microscope. "My face."

Charlotte doesn't say anything to that. The music plays along softly, and the scenery flashes by. Big empty fields full of short, stubby Texas corn.

"Where are we going?"

"Out to the middle of nowhere. I know what you look like, by the way."

"Obviously." I shift around in my seat and cross my arms

over my chest. "I mean, I assumed so. Since you know my real name."

I still hate that, too. I don't like this stranger knowing anything about me. Knowing my secrets. Secrets I haven't even been able to tell Abi—like what my disguise is.

"I'm just saying, you can take it off," she says. "Put it on when we do the kill, you know? That's how my boyfriend does it."

"It's different."

Charlotte chuckles a little. "How could you know that?"

"Because it is," I snap. "This is my face. This is me. The other face, Rowan—" It feels weird saying my name out loud like this, and it feels cottony in my mouth. "That's the mask. The disguise."

Charlotte goes quiet again, tilting her head a little, like she's thinking on what I just said. I hope this is the end of it. To be honest, I'm regretting coming with her. My responsibilities are in Rosado. Both the hotel—which I had to leave in Judy's capable hands—and, more importantly, Abi. I tell myself she's fine. I rarely watch her during the day, and the biggest threat to her is dead. But I still don't like it, leaving her alone.

"Has she seen it?" Charlotte asks suddenly. "Your, ah, disguise?"

I whip my gaze over to her. She's still looking at the road, hands ten and two, all very responsible. But she's wearing that smug, satisfied smile.

"Who?" I say, even though I know perfectly well.

Charlotte rolls her eyes. "The woman who lives at the funeral parlor. The one you're always following around like a lovesick puppy."

"I don't do that," I snap.

Charlotte just laughs again. "Sure. You don't sit outside her house every night instead of sleeping, right?"

"I sleep," I say, somewhat defensively.

"Not much." Charlotte leans back a little in her seat, tapping the steering wheel in time to the music. "That's another benefit of being a Hunter, by the way. You barely have to sleep."

I think of when I was younger, when Uncle Nash was still alive. How I would wander around his big mansion in the middle of the night, restless. I didn't get tired the way he did. It would be three in the morning, and I would be vibrating with a kind of weird, antsy energy. I used to try and burn it off by playing video games. Then, later, I found I could burn it off by killing for him.

After a kill, that's when I sleep.

"What else is there?" Charlotte says. "That you need to know. I told you that we come back from the dead." She keeps tapping her hands against the wheel, the rhythm pounding into my head. "We sense things, told you about that. We're stronger than humans. Kind of innately know how to fight." She glances at me again. "I should have brought Jaxon with me. He could explain this stuff better. Or Ambrose."

The names rattle oddly around in my head. "Who are they? Other—" It feels odd to say it. "Other Hunters?"

"Yeah. Jaxon's my boyfriend. Ambrose is, like, his mentor, I guess. He's super old. Oh, that's the other thing." Charlotte grins. "When I say we can't really die, I mean it. We don't die of old age. Ambrose is like two hundred. Jaxon's about sixty."

I stare at her through my killing face, and I honestly can't decide if she's making fun of me or not. "How old are you?"

"Thirty-four." She grins. "Just a baby by Hunter standards, like you."

I scowl. "I'm not a baby."

"Sure thing, lil bro." Charlotte leans forward over the steering wheel, squinting out at the landscape. We've been going west, out into the big, empty ranch lands that surround Rosado. "This should work."

"What exactly are we doing?"

Charlotte answers by yanking the car suddenly off the road, flinging me up against the door. I cry out, and suddenly, my guard's up. This is a fucking trap.

"Calm down," Charlotte says as the car plows through the scrubby field, jostling us around. "I'm not gonna do shit to you. We're both Hunters, remember?"

I brace myself against the dash, my teeth rattling around in my skull. "What'd you think I was thinking?"

The car slams to a stop. Charlotte glances over at me with dark eyes. "You thought I had just turned on you. You were bracing yourself for it. Not like a human does when they get scared. Our kind, we don't really experience fear."

"That's not true," I mutter, and I'm thinking about Abi when I say it, the absolute terror I felt when I saw that piece of shit in her upstairs hallway.

"We don't get scared for ourselves," Charlotte says softly. "But I guess we can get scared for humans."

She knows. She's looking at me with those dark eyes, so similar to mine, and she fucking knows what I was thinking.

And maybe that's why I do it. Why I say, "Her name's Abi. Abi Snow."

Charlotte smiles. "Has she seen you without the mask? You didn't answer me earlier."

"Killing face," I correct, stiffly. "And n—" I stop myself. "Yes, she has," I say, after a pause. "But she doesn't know it was me."

"Ah." Charlotte nods like a sage. Then she asks, "Does she know?"

I know exactly what she's asking. "Yes." I turn away from Charlotte to look out at the vast, sweeping field. "Everyone I kill is for her."

I'm not sure why I said that. Why I shared that with this stranger—a stranger in every sense of the word, honestly. Not just someone I don't know. Someone who's *strange*.

Strange, like I'm strange.

"And she knows that?" Charlotte sounds surprised.

"Yeah." I'm tired of talking about this. I push the door open, letting in the hot, stale wind, before turning back to Charlotte. "What are we doing here again? Are you going to kill me so I can—what? Resurrect, or whatever?"

Charlotte laughs. "I'm not going to kill you," she says. "Because that would make poor Abi sad, wouldn't it?"

I stiffen. Would it make Abi sad? I think about how she clung to me as she came, my victim wedged beneath her back. How she swallowed me whole in the graveyard.

"No, we're going to kill someone else today," Charlotte says. "Someone random. You'll feel it, I think. What it means to be a Hunter."

"I don't kill people like that." The car door's still hanging open, the hot, humid air making me sweat beneath my mask. "I have a system so I won't get caught."

"*We* won't get caught," Charlotte says. "Promise." She shuts off the engine. "Besides, if we do, just make sure the cops shoot you dead. You'll come back."

She hops out of the car with that, her laughter chiming on the air. When she slams her door shut behind her, I step out, cautious and uncertain. My killing face feels uncomfortable in the daylight, and there's already a thick layer of sweat on my skin. Charlotte bounds up to the side of the road, completely unconcerned that her face is exposed to the world.

"Follow my lead!" she calls back. "Though it'd really help if you took that mask off."

"It's not a mask!" I call back.

"Then stay back there." She looks at me, her hair blowing like a red spiderweb across her face. "Don't let them see you."

"Who?" I hate this. I'm completely exposed out here. The sun is a giant spotlight revealing all my sins, and I don't have a single fucking plan in place. "How are you planning to do this, exactly?"

"Got a knife." Charlotte hikes up the hem of her shorts, and sure enough, there's a big dark hunting knife strapped to her thigh. "How about you?"

"I don't have anything."

"So you have your hands." Charlotte crouches down in the grass and grabs it in big handfuls and then scrunches it up in her hair, making her look wild and feral. She smears dirt across her face. "Actually, you know what? I have an idea."

"What are you doing?" Maybe she has more of a plan than I realized.

Charlotte grins at me. "Laying a trap. If you don't want to take off that mask—I mean, killing face—you can be the bad guy." Then she reaches down and grabs the knife out of her holster and holds it to me, the blade pointing at her chest. I stare at it.

I could kill her. End this whole charade and get back to my life in Rosado. Get back to Abi.

But I don't *want* to. The real truth is that I'm intrigued by all this—by the idea that there are other people out there like me. That even if I am the monster my mom said I was, at least I'm not the weapon Uncle Nash shaped me into.

I take the knife, and Charlotte grins.

"I've never met our dad," she says. "I was adopted, raised by humans, and my sister and I weren't close. But I hope you and I can be, you know?"

I look down at the knife, the metal glinting in the hot, blazing sun. "We just met."

"I mean, I've been following you for weeks." Charlotte straightens up, smearing more dirt on her clothes. "And I know you felt me. You kept yelling at me like a crazy person."

"I wasn't crazy." I scowl. "You were there. I thought you were coming after Abi."

Charlotte laughs. "Fair enough." Then she stops and tilts her head to the side. "Okay, someone's coming. You hear them?"

At first, I don't hear anything, just the rush of the wind. But then, underneath it—the purr of a car engine. And something else, too. A heartbeat. The scent of human blood and gasoline.

"Yeah," I say, letting the sensations wash over me. "It's a man."

Charlotte sniffs, then lets out a bright, delighted laugh. "Oh damn, you're right, it is. That's even better. Now go hide behind the car so you can jump out when it's time."

I know it shouldn't, but excitement is brimming up in my chest, the way it always does before a kill. All that anticipation, that sense of something building. The only thing better was when I was inside Abi, her body wet and clenching as she moaned and writhed beneath me.

I clutch the knife and duck beside the car, realizing with a start that the reason Charlotte veered off suddenly was to make it look like an accident. Like she was chased off the road.

The car engine grows louder, the tires crackling against the asphalt. I crouch down, clutching the knife, my body brimming with anticipation.

"Help!" Charlotte screams, her voice whipping away on the wind. "Oh my god, help me! Please!"

I can't see her, but I can hear her—her feet pounding against the dirt, her breath quick and frantic even though her heartbeat is steady and the only emotion rippling off her is the same excitement building up in me.

"Help!" she wails, and the car shifts gears and slows down, the engine clicking as it idles. A door slam. A man's voice.

"What's wrong? Honey? Are you hurt?"

He's nervous. He's trying to sound brave, but he's nervous. Wary.

I tighten my grip on the knife. I can't remember the last time I used one. It was for Uncle Nash, not one of my kills. But it feels good in my hand. Not too heavy. Not too light. And powerful.

"He's chasing me!" Charlotte screams. "Please, you have to let me in the car! He's coming!"

Me, I realize with a start. She's fucking talking about me.

And then I act like all of this is the most natural thing in the world—and it is, I realize. I'm not some human killer.

All of Uncle Nash's warnings about getting caught fly out of my head. All I want is blood.

I leap to my feet and lunge forward, moving so fast I surprise myself. The knife blade flashes in the sun and catches the man's attention. He looks over at me, and for a split second, time kind of slows down, and I can sense everything: the pulsating, sweet scent of his fear and surprise, the pounding of his heart as it pumps the hot, thick blood I'm about to spill.

"What the fuck?" he shrieks.

Then Charlotte leaps on him, hooking her arm around his throat. I keep running until the knife sinks into his chest, sliding through the muscle and lodging into his ribcage. He screams and tries to throw her off, but she's too strong for him. Blood splatters out of his mouth and pours out of the wound I made.

I feel hot and feverish. The few times I killed like this, it was for Uncle Nash, and always in a controlled space, the victim tied down and already worn thin from Uncle Nash's information-gathering tactics. This is different. It's wild and natural. It feels like what I'm meant to be doing. What I should have been doing my whole life.

I stumble back, the knife slipping out of my blood-drenched fingers. The man slumps forward in Charlotte's arms, head lolling. His chest is ridged with all the cuts I made.

"Damn," Charlotte says. "I feel like you needed that."

She drops the body in the grass and wipes her bloody hands

on her shorts, leaving smears of crimson in their wake. And like that, the spell breaks.

"Fuck," I say, panic surging through me. "Fuck, we left all this evidence—We aren't even wearing gloves—"

"We did not leave evidence." Charlotte grabs my arms and jostles me, making me look at her. She stares through the holes in my killing face, like she's trying to see my eyes.

Abi does the same thing.

"Someone's going to drive by," I say in a panic.

"Probably," Charlotte says. "Which is why we should skedaddle. As for evidence, don't worry about it. Remember, we aren't human."

"What?" I feel dizzy. But good, too. Powerful. All that adrenaline pumping through me feels like desire, and I kind of wish Abi were here. Although if she had just seen what I did, I bet she would run screaming right to the police.

"We aren't *human*." Charlotte scoops up the bloody knife and wipes the blade on her shirt. "So whatever DNA evidence they find, it'll be inconclusive because they don't know what they're looking for."

"Don't fucking lie to me."

Charlotte ambles over to the car. "I'm not," she calls out over her shoulder. "Trust me, you would lose your mind at the kind of evidence Jaxon and I have left behind at crime scenes."

For half a second, I have no idea what she's talking about. Then I get it. I flush with second-hand embarrassment.

"Come on!" Charlotte calls out. "Before someone drives by, like you said."

I race toward the car, heart pounding, and slam into the passenger seat. Charlotte turns on the engine and peels off, and I bend over to look at the rearview mirror, to watch our victim's car recede into the distance.

"You felt it," Charlotte says suddenly. "Didn't you?"

I want to tell her no. Want to say I have no idea what she's talking about. But that would be a lie. Because I did feel it when I sank her knife into that man's chest. I can still feel it, surging through my limbs like electricity.

Power. Strength. A sense that this is my place in the world.

"Yes," I whisper, fixing my gaze on the road in front of me. My killing face feels stuck to my skin, like it couldn't come off even if I wanted it to. Like the two parts of me are finally melding together.

Charlotte laughs. "Want to do it again?"

I look at the clock on the dashboard. It's a little after noon. I have plenty of time before dark. Before I need to get back to Abi.

"Fuck, yes," I say.

The day moves too slowly. I manage to get some paperwork done, but I don't even bother performing the autopsy I have on the docket. I tell myself I'll do it tomorrow, that when Nameless comes by tonight, I'll ask him to stay even after the sun comes up. I think he will.

I hope he will.

The promise of nightfall is both terrifying and reassuring. Reassuring because Nameless has only ever come to the funeral parlor at night, and he's the only person I want to see right now. The only person I trust to protect me.

But it's terrifying, too. Because I don't know who else will be looking at me in the dark.

Fortunately, my fax machine stays quiet. No more photographs. No more messages. No one calls my work phone. Penelope and Chloe text me a few times, checking in on me. I tell them I'm fine. Lies.

Sunset is around eight o'clock this time of year. When it arrives, I sit on top of the dais in the viewing room so I can watch the yard slowly draping itself in shadow. Eventually, the streetlights come on, all at once, like someone flicked a switch. Hatch Street is empty.

"Are you out there?" I whisper, sliding off the dais so I can press my hands against the window and peer outside. It doesn't help. I don't see much of anything.

My chest twists around. It's true that I don't necessarily see him every night, but after last night—

He has to come. Doesn't he?

My breath fogs the glass. The wind moves through the yard, but all it does is push the shadows around. And I think about the last two times I saw him, including last night. He didn't just announce himself. I went out on the front porch, and then he made himself known.

Of course, tonight is not last night, and the idea of going outside makes me feel dizzy and sick.

Uncle Vic's gun, I think.

I peel away from the window and go upstairs, my breath tight and shallow. The gun case is still resting on the bed where I left it, and my hands shake as I flip the latch. The gun looks like a toy. Mostly because I've never seen a real gun before.

I take it out, and it's heavier than I expect. There's a box of bullets, but I leave those. I don't know how to load the thing. I just want to hold it, like armor.

Then I carry it back downstairs, cradling it awkwardly against my chest. My footsteps creak on the stairs, on the floorboards in the entranceway, and I turn the lights on as I go from room to room, flooding the house with light. As if light can protect me.

I check the video feed from my doorbell camera before I unlock the door. Nothing. Just darkness. Then I turn the deadbolt and nudge the door open and step out onto the porch.

The wind is up, damp and salty, and I can taste the sea in the back of my throat.

"Hello?" I step cautiously out onto the porch. The wind

answers, blowing low and mournful across the cemetery. "Are you there?"

I don't get an answer, and my body tightens with anxiety. I clutch the gun a little closer to my chest.

"I need to talk to you," I call out, louder this time. The last time I called out to Nameless in the dark, he showed up. And then he destroyed me.

But no one steps out of the shadows tonight. The wind lifts and makes the trees rattle around, and I swallow back that sick feeling in the pit of my stomach.

He's not here.

I'm sure of it. If he were here, he would make himself known. I would hear his footsteps, soft and rustling through the grass. But all I hear is the wind.

"Please?" I add, but it comes out as little more than a whisper.

Something bangs around in the back of the house, as loud as a gunshot. I jump and whirl around, holding my own gun out awkwardly. "Nameless?" I say, then immediately feel stupid. I doubt he remembers me calling him that the night in the viewing room.

Silence.

I can't stand being out here. The night feels like it's closing in on me, thick and constricting. I duck back inside and slam the door shut and lock it. Then I breathe, still holding the gun, staring at my pale reflection in the door's new window.

God, how stupid am I to think a murderer actually wants to protect me? How stupid am I to think I can trust him at all? Just because he was with me when Olivia and Heather died doesn't mean he isn't involved. Every dark, beautiful word he said to me could have been a lie.

Maybe he killed the first attacker to throw me off the trail.

Maybe that's why he won't show me his face, because if I see it, I'll recognize him. One of Blake's friends, maybe. A man I used to know as a boy.

My face is hot. My eyes burn with unfallen tears. I squeeze the gun close to my chest and try to decide what to do, now that the one person I thought would be here for me didn't show up.

Penelope was right. I should get out of town. Go stay with Chloe. Maybe this nightmare won't follow me that far north, and I can come to terms with what I let happen. I can shove my darkness back down inside me where it belongs.

Another bang echoes in the back of the house.

I whip around, gun up, staring into the darkened hallway leading toward the back of the funeral parlor. Back toward the examination room.

Nameless? It's a weak, fluttering sense of hope, but the examination room was the first place I ever saw him. The first place he kissed me, pushing his mask up so his lips would brush chastely over mine.

"Is that you?" I call out, taking slow, cautious steps forward. I readjust the gun, cradling it awkwardly in my arms. "I wish you wouldn't play this game right now. I, um, I need to tell you some—"

The floor creaks. Not where I am, in the bright-lit foyer. But from deep in the darkness up ahead.

"Please don't do this," I call out. "Just say something. Let me know it's you."

Another creak, long and low. Someone is in the hallway leading to the examination room. I just pray that it's Nameless.

"Please," I whimper, and one of my hot tears falls in a straight line over my cheek.

I'm at the edge of the hallway, and I can feel someone in the darkness, watching me. I reach over and flip the switch.

The light reveals a figure dressed all in black. But any relief I feel is momentary, because this figure isn't tall enough. He's too thin.

And he's wearing a stocking over his face, not a twisted rubber mask.

"Not who you were expecting?" he asks in a cruel, taunting voice, and I have the quick, fleeting thought that it's a voice I've heard before. But then it disappears when I press the gun's trigger on instinct, and all I hear is a useless click.

"Stupid bitch," the man says. "Women never know how to use guns."

Then he launches himself at me, barreling down the hallway at a full run. For a second, I'm a prey animal trapped in headlights. But then, just as he's about to grab me, I swing the gun like a baseball bat and slam into the side of his head. It makes a terrible thumping sound, like tapping a watermelon. The man stumbles sideways and howls, his hand going up to his temple.

Spots of red drop across the floor.

"You *whore*!" he shrieks, looking at his bloody fingers. "You think you can hurt me?"

I whirl around and run. The gun gets in my way, and I throw it into the viewing room as I pass, then pump my arms and legs toward the door. The killer is behind me, his steps heavy and loud.

"You can't escape me," he calls out. "I got the other two cunts. What makes you think you're so special?"

I slam into the front door and undo the lock and throw it open, letting in a sweep of damp, howling sea wind. Then I spill out onto the porch and race across the yard. "Help!" I scream. "Nameless! Please!"

I don't know why I called out to him. I know he's not here. Not when I need him most.

"Shut the fuck up!" An elbow hooks around my neck and drags me backward. Panic surges through me, and I kick out and try to scratch at his arm. But he heaves me around and throws me into the damp grass, then slams his heavy booted foot hard on my chest.

All the air slams out of me. I gasp and choke and try to wriggle my way free. But his weight is too much. I'm pinned down like a butterfly.

"Finally," he says, looking down at me. It's too dark for me to see anything but shadows. All I can make out is the silhouette of my attacker. My would-be murderer. "I've been waiting ten fucking years for this."

I scream again and try to grab his ankle. He responds by bearing more of his weight down on me, angling his boot so it goes into the soft part of my belly and not my ribs.

"Don't want you puncturing a lung," he says. "I got plans for you that require you to be alive for a little while longer."

I squirm and sob, writhing around in the grass. I keep imagining Nameless coming out of the shadows. Snapping this man's neck. Saving me like he did last time.

But nothing happens. He's not here.

"Time to go," my attacker says.

He grabs my hair and yanks me sideways, dragging me across the grass. Burning pain tears through my scalp. I try to fight, but it just seems to make the pain worse.

"Enough of that," he snarls, yanking me up to my knees. Tears stream over my cheeks, blurring the familiar expanse of my yard. We're in front of the big oak tree that grows next to my living room window, and I lift my gaze to the branches stretching thick and sturdy toward the glass.

"Say nighty-night," the killer says, and then he slams my head against the trunk.

For a moment, there's nothing but pain.

Then there's nothing.

ROWAN

The sun is low against the horizon, turning the sky into a wall of flames. I feel full and sated. Charlotte and I have just shared three kills between us, much more than I've ever done in such a short amount of time. The blood is all over my clothes, and I know I ought to change before I go to Abi's house. But it's already getting dark, and we're nearly forty minutes outside of Rosado.

Charlotte says something, although I'm not focused on her right now. Everything feels more heightened after the mayhem of this afternoon. The buzz of the car's engine as it vibrates up through my seat. The sound of insects outside, the rustle of wind. The thick scent of humanity in the distance.

I can't wait to go to Abi like this. To smell her. Touch her. Taste her. *Devour* her.

"Rowan?"

Charlotte's voice snaps me back, and I jerk my gaze over to her. "What?"

"I asked if you were okay."

"I'm fine." Fine doesn't even begin to cover it. When Charlotte told me I'm some kind of killer monster that can't die, I thought she was crazy. But now, I can feel it, this dark magic surging through me. I'm powerful and inhuman and I can do anything I fucking want. "I'm just anxious to get back to Abi."

Charlotte smirks. "Yeah, I bet you are."

I know immediately what she's implying, especially when she gives me a knowing little wink. Heat floods into my cheeks. "I need to watch over her at night," I say stiffly.

That earns a full-throated laugh from Charlotte. "Look, I'm not judging. If Jaxon were here, we'd be fucking already."

My face burns even hotter. "You're my sister, right? I don't want to hear about you fucking your boyfriend."

"Half-sister. *Estranged* half-sister. I'm just saying, I get it." She laughs and guns down the highway, flying toward the sunset. "It's part of being a Hunter, I think. Killing gets your blood up."

She's not wrong. I can feel all that energy coursing inside me.

"Just hurry," I mutter.

"She okay seeing you like that?" Charlotte asks.

I shift in my seat, not sure how to answer, even though the blood feels good on my skin. "She's seen me kill someone before."

"Oh, really?" Charlotte glances over at me. "Did you fuck her afterward?"

"No," I snap, irritated. I just wish we were *there* already. "I had to dispose of the body."

"Would she have fucked you?"

I squeeze my hands up into fists. "Maybe."

It's the wrong thing to say, because it makes Charlotte whoop out. The car veers around on the road.

"Jesus fuck," I snap, bracing myself against the dashboard. "Watch out."

"I'm just excited for you, lil bro. That's all."

"Stop calling me that."

"What? Lil bro? You are. You think I didn't find out how old you were before I came out here?"

"Yeah, but we don't— we don't really know each other." That doesn't feel true, though. Not anymore. Not after an afternoon of killing together.

"Yeah, well, we can change that, right?" Something changes in her emotions, like she's becoming more serious. When I look over at her, she's staring at the road, and her expression is thoughtful. "I mean, you don't have to go through the world by yourself anymore. You're a Hunter."

"I'm not by myself," I say softly. "I have Abi."

As soon as the words leave my mouth, I don't know if they're true. I mean, yes, she didn't run after I killed her attacker, but that was about saving her life. And as for last night—

Well, I haven't seen her since then, have I? Maybe the daylight changed how she saw what we did. Maybe it turned it into a sin.

"But she hasn't even seen your face," Charlotte says suddenly. "Or, excuse me, she doesn't *realize* she's seen your face."

I freeze. Charlotte keeps her eyes on the road.

"I told you," I say darkly. "*This* is my face. This is who I am."

But the words feel ashy on my tongue. For the first time, they feel—untrue. I've worn this mask since I killed Uncle Nash, since I started killing for myself instead of for him. Rowan was his weapon. Then Rowan became my secret identity. And now—

After today, after seeing all that bright red blood in the gleaming sunlight, the whole arrangement feels hollow.

"Rowan," Charlotte says. "Can I give you some sisterly advice?"

I want to say *no*. Or rather, I feel like I should say no. But the word just doesn't come out. So I don't say anything.

And that's enough permission for Charlotte, apparently. "You need to take that fucking mask off. Not right now." She glances at me, and her features are getting hard to see. The sun is already half hidden by the horizon. I should be with Abi right now. Instead, I'm in this car, covered in blood and feeling alive while a stranger-who-doesn't-feel-like-a-stranger gives me unsolicited advice. Yet I don't protest.

"I mean, you should take the mask off in front of Abi," Charlotte continues.

My skin prickles with something like electricity.

"If you want to be with her," Charlotte says, fixing her gaze on the road. "She has to see all of you. She has to see you covered in blood. Has to know what you're truly capable of doing."

I shift, my chest tight. "What does that have to do with my killing face?"

"That's my whole fucking point," Charlotte says. "That's not your face. It's a mask. You wear it when you kill people, fine. We've all got our thing. Like I said, Jaxon does it. My friend Sawyer, he wears a mask, too. But you aren't going to kill Abi, are you?"

"No!" I shout, horrified by the thought. I would kill every person in this world before I would harm Abilene Snow. Other people—

other humans

—Are for killing. But Abi is for protecting.

"Then why are you wearing your killing face to be around her?" Charlotte asks.

The question stuns me. Brings me up short. I fumble around for an answer, my tongue dry. "Because," I say. "Because this is who I am."

"Of course it is," Charlotte says. "But you're also Rowan Hanover. Rowan and—" She flaps her hand toward me. "This guy. The guy in the mask? They're the same."

I open my mouth to protest, but Charlotte surges on.

"You told me you've been killing people to talk to her," Charlotte says, and I cringe, regretting ever sharing that with her earlier. "Well, maybe you should stop murdering randos because you want to talk to the woman you love. Just fucking talk to her and murder the randos because you like it." She looks over at me, and in the encroaching darkness, just for a second, her eyes seem to gleam like a cat's. "That's what we did this afternoon. That's what you're meant to do."

I turn away from her. My killing face feels thick and restrictive, like it has all day. And I think about those times I've lifted it just enough to kiss Abi. To taste her lips and her cunt.

What would it be like to feel her hands on my skin? Or her mouth? To bury myself between her breasts and breathe in the sweetness of her flesh?

Heat surges through me, hot and sparking from all the death earlier. Violent, bloody, pointless death. Not clean. Not coordinated. Charlotte and I left a trail of destruction that can't be anything but what it is.

And it felt right. It did. Just like it felt right the first time I looked into Abi's eyes, certain she was the one person in the universe who would accept me. She had smiled at me that day at the funeral. A bright, genuine smile. The same smile she gives me when I'm with her as Rowan Hanover.

Would you still smile like that at Rowan, at me, if she knew?

"Just think about it," Charlotte says. "Like I said, it's just a bit of sisterly advice."

"Fine," I mutter, looking out at the dark highway. I can just make out the lights of Rosado up ahead. It's full dark, but at least it's not late.

"Now." Charlotte presses down on the gas, and the car surges forward. "Are you going to want to clean up first? Or go straight to Abi's house?"

I don't have to think about it. "Go straight there. And hurry."

Charlotte smiles. I can feel the wickedness seeping off her, and I think it's the same as my wickedness. "Good boy. Seems like you can listen after all."

I feel it as soon as Charlotte pulls up in front of the funeral parlor. The night is *wrong*. There's a scent that permeates the air, overly sweet like rotting roses.

Abi's fear. But it's faint. It's *old*.

"Fuck." I scramble for the door handle in a panic. "Fuck, someone was here. "

"I feel it, too." Charlotte's voice is as cold as steel. She cuts the car engine and puts her hand on my bicep. "Rowan, stop. We need to take this slowly so you—"

"Fuck that! I need to make sure Abi's okay." I kick the door open, letting in more of that scent. It reminds me of the first night Abi saw me—saw the *real* me, with my killing face.

She'd already seen the real you.

I shove the thought aside and tear across the lawn, sniffing at the air. I feel like I can't get at anything, though. My killing face is in the way, making everything smell like rubber. There's the trace of Abi's scent on the air, but the face—the mask—is like a barrier between me and her.

So I yank it off and breathe deep, the air shuddering into my lungs. I take it all in: Abi's fear, the salt of the ocean behind me, the dry dusty scent of the cemetery. And something else. A tang of adrenaline.

Footsteps patter behind me. "There's no one here," Charlotte says.

I whirl around on her, and her eyes widen when she sees me without my face. But she doesn't say anything.

"I *told* you I needed to be back before dark."

"We can find her," Charlotte says. "Don't worry."

I scoff at that—right now, I'm nothing but worry. I bound across the yard and up to the front porch and stop, my heart slamming around in my chest.

The door is hanging open, letting out a sliver of inside light like a knife blade.

"No," I whisper, pushing the door in with the toe of my shoe. Light floods the foyer of the funeral parlor, as if Abi were trying to keep the darkness at bay. My chest knots up, tight and choking. *Fuck,* I should have been here.

For a moment, I just stand in the entranceway, hating myself. The scent of Abi's fear is stronger inside, although it still feels faded, like a lingering cloud of perfume. That other scent is stronger in here, too. Human, I can tell that much. It doesn't have the wildness that Charlotte's does.

"Rowan!" Charlotte's voice rings in from outside. "I've got something!"

Terror lances through me, and I race back out into the yard, my thoughts all in a panic. There's no sign of Charlotte, and for a second, I think this is all some terrible trick. But then I feel her. She's around the side of the house.

I jump off the porch and move into the shadows to find her standing beside the big oak tree where I spent so many nights watching Abi through the window. The light is on in her living room window, and for a moment, I can almost pretend that she's in there, the TV turned low, and I'm nestled in the branches and she's safe. Everyone's safe.

But no. Charlotte is kneeling at the base of the tree, holding something.

"I found a gun," she says.

I stalk toward her, my throat dry with fear. She stands up

and shows me a basic hunting rifle. I snatch it out of her hands and check the chamber. Empty.

"It hasn't been fired," she says. "You would smell the gunpowder. But there's something else."

I jerk my gaze up to her, my blood pounding in my ears. This is her fault. Her fault for talking me into that third kill, even though I was already antsy to be back here with Abi.

"What?" I bark. Anyone else would have flinched away from me. But Charlotte doesn't even blink.

"You don't smell it?" she asks.

I want to strangle her. I'm about to, in fact, when the scent hits me. Coppery. Sweet.

Blood.

Abi's blood.

"No," I gasp out, throwing the useless gun aside. As dark as it is out here, I've always been able to see at night. Just like Charlotte, I suppose.

And I see it now: a smear against the tree trunk. I press my fingers into it, and they come away wet. I can both see the red of Abi's blood and smell the fear in it. The air buzzes around me, hot and unforgiving. My eyes are wet like my fingers. I blink, and a tear falls.

I wipe it away before Charlotte can see.

"Rowan," she says softly, putting her hand on my shoulder.

"Get the fuck off me!" I whirl around on her, throwing out my arm to hit her. She catches me by the wrist, unbothered, and wrenches me away. "This is your fucking fault! I told you I needed to be here before dark, and you—"

"I know," she says, which brings me up short. "I'm sorry. Truly. I should have brought you back earlier, okay? But we can find her." She swallows. "*You* can find her. That blood is fresh, which means they can't be far."

My heart races. The wind blows through the oak tree and stirs around Abi's scent.

A trail, I think suddenly. How many times have I tracked prey through the night, waiting for them to step into my trap?

Charlotte's staring at me, grim and determined. I think she knows what I'm thinking.

"How do I do it?" I say. "Show me how to fucking do it."

"You already know how to do it," she says. "Rowan, we're called Hunters for a reason."

I take a deep breath, desperately trying to latch onto Abi's scent.

"It's time for us to go hunting."

33
ABI

All I can feel is a constant, throbbing pain in my head.

I blink my eyes open, trying to make sense of my surroundings. They're a dark blur. Everything's dark. The last thing I remember—

The oak tree. Wet grass. Sea wind.

A man with a familiar voice, his face covered by a stocking.

I shriek and try to sit up, but I'm stopped short by my wrists, which are pinned in place above my head. No, not pinned. I'm tied down by thick, rough ropes, one around each wrist.

I slump down. I'm on a mattress, I think. A thin, lumpy mattress. I'm inside. I can tell that much. There's a window across from me that's covered in a thick but transparent plastic tarp, enough to let in some yellow light from outside. It's bright enough that I can make out the edges of the room. The surrounding walls seem unfinished. I can see bare beams, the occasional tangle of wiring.

I twist against my bindings, trying to push myself up by shoving my feet against the mattress for leverage. It works, although I bang my head against the wall behind me. A finished wall, I think, and I manage to twist around to look at it.

It *is* finished. It's also covered in overlapping sheets of cheap printer paper, each with a photograph on it. For a moment, I can't make out what I'm looking at. Just blobs of light and darkness. But then one of the images comes into focus—

It's a blonde woman, stretched out naked on a pale mattress, her arms tied to hooks in the wall above her, her face twisted in fear.

Ms. Staunton.

I scream and jerk on the ropes, scraping them against the printed photographs. One of them comes detached and floats down and lands beside me. It's a close-up of a woman's face, her eyes red from crying, her lips smeared with a pale, creamy liquid. I can't tell who it is, if it's Heather Staunton or Olivia Pearce or someone else. All I know is I can't look at it, and I flop my body around until the picture crumples beneath me.

I slump down, my chest heaving. Panic courses through me like a riptide.

I think of Olivia Pearce lying on my examination slab, her head split open. I think of the photograph of Ms. Staunton that came through my fax machine.

"No," I whisper, tugging on my constraints, my hands twisted up into fists. The rope burns against my skin, and that pain burns into me the whole, terrifying truth of my situation:

I'm going to die.

"No!" It comes out louder, a wet, miserable scream. My vision blurs with tears, and the printed picture crumples beneath me, a reminder of what I know is going to happen.

I arch my back, trying to leverage against the ropes. I can almost feel them slipping against my wrist. Almost. But then I flop back down. Defeated.

Nameless's mask flashes into my thoughts, and I bite back a

swell of tears. It's my fault for trusting him. For assuming he was always out there, watching me in the dark.

But despite his betrayal, my memories of him keep washing over me. The way he would step into the light like he was announcing himself. Or the sensation of his gloved hand running up my bare thigh as he pressed his mouth to my cunt. His breath on my throat as he filled me, over and over. His lips dry and chaste against mine.

May I touch you?

I know it's pathetic, but all those memories calm me. I can feel my breath steadying as I focus on him. He asked if he could touch me, and I said yes. Everything he did to me, I let him.

The last man who touched me without permission is dead. I shoved him down a flight of stairs and never once did I feel guilty about it.

I shift on the mattress, pushing myself up to sitting, the printed pictures sticking to my sweat-damp skin. I don't have to look at any more of them to know what they are:

A glimpse of my future if I don't fucking do something.

I'm afraid, but I was also afraid when Nameless broke into my examination room. When he kissed me. When he fucked me. But that fear just spurned me on and let me take what I wanted, as dark as it was. Nameless forced me to face the truth of what happened ten years ago—

That I can kill when I need to.

Now, another killer has me trapped in this room. But why the fuck should I be afraid of him when I know how fucked up I am, even if I buried it deep down inside myself? Fucked up enough that I let a serial killer fuck me on top of a corpse? That I dream of a murderer's soft touch when I go to sleep at night?

Maybe Nameless did abandon me. But he also showed me I'm not afraid of monsters.

That I can be a monster myself when I have to.

I twist my body around, this time not to look at the picture but to look at the ropes around my wrists. They aren't that tight, and they're only looped around once, then knotted into a metal ring fixed into the wall. I brace my legs against the mattress, shoving myself up until I'm crouched on the bed. The ropes won't let me go any further.

So I can't stand all the way up. But I can still twist around and grab at the knot with my teeth.

It tastes like salt, like the sea. I bite back a gag and gnaw at it, trying to work the knot loose with my teeth. Rope fibers flood into my mouth, and I spit them out, then try again.

At first, I don't think it's doing anything. Part of me expects the killer to come in, and I do listen for him. But all I hear is the wind outside. The wind and the ocean. I think this place is on the beach.

But then I'm able to hook my teeth around one of the loops of the knot and drag it backward. And when I do, the knot loosens.

Excitement flares inside me. I attack the knot with more fervor, sliding my tongue into the rope to drag it upward. It already feels looser, and I wriggle my wrist around.

And then, like petals dropping off a flower, the rope unravels.

I yank my wrist away and stare down at it, slightly stunned. There's a red mark from the rope. But otherwise, my wrist is fine. I'm free.

Immediately, I grab at the other rope, tugging and plucking until that rope comes undone, too. It's easier work than the first, and as soon as both of my hands are untied, I scramble off the bed. Sheets of paper stick to my sweat-drenched skin, and I rip them away. Terrified eyes stare up at me. Olivia's eyes. Heather's eyes. Two women who helped me when I needed it.

I couldn't be there to help them. But I can save myself. And

I can make sure that the monster in this house gets what he deserves.

I try the window first, ripping the plastic away. But the window is welded shut; I can see where the metal frame has melted into itself. I crane my head, trying to get a view of what's outside. I can't see much in the darkness. Rippling seagrass, mostly. I was right. I'm near the ocean.

I dart over to the door. Locked.

"Fuck," I whisper, and the triumph of earlier starts to fizzle. I'm not going to give up, though. I spin around in the room, peering through the yellow-tinged darkness for something I can use as a weapon. There isn't much. The mattress is on the floor, and it's mottled with dark stains I don't want to think about. I could maybe pry off one of the loose beams—

Or the ropes. Maybe I could use the ropes.

But then I hear something, out in the hallway. A heavy, decisive thud. Another.

Footsteps.

Hot panic surges through me, and I leap back onto the mattress and frantically wind the rope around my wrists so that I look as if I'm still tied up. I squeeze the end of the rope in my fist, though. It's not much of a weapon, but it's something.

The footsteps stop outside the door. I hold my breath, staring through the darkness at the glimmering doorknob.

It turns.

"Wakey, wakey," says that rough, masculine voice. The door swings open, and I brace myself against the wall, my heart hammering so hard in my chest that I can barely hear anything else.

My kidnapper steps into the doorway and turns his gaze toward me—

And my stomach falls out from beneath me.

Because my attacker isn't wearing his stocking anymore.

And I realize why his voice is familiar. Because I've heard it thousands of times over the last two years. Chiding me. Criticizing me. Telling me I'm not good enough.

"There she is," says Sheriff Kaplan. "Are you ready to play?"

ROWAN

"First step," Charlotte says. "Look for clues."

I glare at her. "Are you fucking kidding me?" I shout. "This isn't a goddamn game. We aren't playing Sherlock Holmes."

"Keep your voice down." Charlotte pushes past me, grabs my wrist, and drags me along after her. "A human did this. He left signs." She looks at me, her eyes flashing in the dark. "Like scent. You picked up on it, didn't you? That sour, spiky smell?"

I jerk my arm away from her. "Yes," I say stiffly. "It's adrenaline, isn't it?"

Charlotte smiles. "Yeah, it is. Slow down. Breathe it in. Focus on it. See if you can pick up a trail."

I stare at her, panic surging through my veins. I don't want to focus on anything. I sure as hell don't want to slow down.

"This is how you're going to find her, " Charlotte says gently. "It took me a while to learn how to do it, but I think you've got desperation on your side."

"What I don't have is time," I growl.

"Which is why you need to stop arguing with me."

I hate that she's right about that. I whip away from Charlotte and look out at the graveyard. At the road.

He would have driven here. He took her away, and Abi wouldn't have gone willingly. It's not like he could have carried her out in the open without drawing attention to himself.

I step through the grass, past the sunflowers, heading to the road. As I walk, I breathe in, trying to separate all the scents billowing around me. I've done this before, even if I didn't realize it—even if I thought it was something everyone could do. It was how I would track down men for Uncle Vic. Business partners who didn't pay their bills on time. Double-crossing mob guys. That sort of thing. I used to resent it. Now, it feels like it was practice, preparing me for this moment.

There are a lot of scents in the Rosado night. There's the beach and the ocean and the animals that live in the sand. There's the metallic tang of the roads, the dieselly scent of car exhaust. A dry, papery scent that I think might be the dead lying in the ground.

But there's also Charlotte's fear and her kidnapper's disgusting adrenaline.

I catch a thread of that adrenaline, starting at the tree and winding down to the road. There's something else layered underneath it, though, and when I come to the curb, I see it:

A few splatters of blood.

"He drove her away from here," I say numbly.

"That doesn't matter." Charlotte comes up behind me and crouches down in the grass, her nose wrinkling up. "We can track him. You smell that?" She looks over at me. "The exhaust. He was in a pickup truck."

All I can smell is Abi's blood. Her terror. How could something that smelled so sweet when we were in her office together fill me with such a sick, terrible worry right now?

"Rowan," Charlotte says sharply. "You've got to focus."

"I smell her," I whisper, blinking back tears. God, I don't

want Charlotte to see me cry. I can only imagine she'll react the way Uncle Nash did: mock me, beat me. I'm supposed to be a killer, after all. I'm supposed to be a Hunter.

"I know you do." Charlotte stands and moves toward me. "But the exhaust will be easier."

I wipe the back of my hand over my eyes before I look over her. If she notices, she doesn't acknowledge it. Instead, she says, "Focus. I want both of us to have the scent in case the other loses it."

"Why are you helping me?" I say darkly.

"Because this is my fault." Charlotte's face is shadowed in the darkness. "And you're my little brother. I was hoping we could be friends. But I need you to fucking focus right now, okay?"

I believe her, mostly because I have to. There's only one thing that matters right now, and that's finding Abi. So I close my eyes, and I breathe in deep, sifting through the scents—

And I catch it. The exhaust. It's pungent and sharper than the other mechanical scents on the air, and it seems to take off on a trail heading toward the shoreline.

"It's going that way," I say, opening my eyes. I point to the right. "I think it's heading toward the beach."

"I think you're right." Charlotte beeps the lock on her car, making the headlights flash. "Get in. I'll drive, you track."

It feels a little like what we did earlier, tracking our victims along the highway. Two predators working in tandem. But this time, our prey is precious.

Charlotte rolls down the windows as we drive along the dark road and into the little park that runs up alongside the grave-yard. I stick my head out the window like a dog, breathing in the air. Following the trail.

It's bright. As bright as the moon hanging heavy and full in the sky, casting everything in thin, silvery light.

"Turn left," I say. "Toward the beach."

Charlotte's already turning, though, like she sensed it, too. She takes us down a narrow residential street, and my skin prickles, because there's too much conflicting noise out here. Not just the scents of all the people in the houses, but other things. Their voices. Their presence. Their humanity.

"Fuck, I lost it," Charlotte says, her eyes fixed on the road, her hands gripping the wheel tight. "Tell me you didn't."

She sounds genuinely concerned, which I appreciate. It's the least she could do.

"No," I say, although the trail is definitely fainter now. Drowned out by all the fucking humans that aren't Abi. "Keep going. Toward the beach. They went to the beach."

I don't like that, them being on the beach. Images keep flashing through my head: Abi's blood turning black on the moonlit sand. Abi's pale body drifting in the waves, her lungs flooded with seawater. Abi's screams being torn away by the wind.

We drive until we come to the road that runs parallel to the strand, although this is the empty part, away from hotels and tourist spots. Beach houses rise against the horizon, although they're dark. They look empty.

The trail seems to strengthen.

"Got it again," Charlotte says, pressing down hard on the gas. The car's engine roars as we fly down the road. "Seems stronger. I think we're close."

I don't say anything, though, because I've got something else. A faint whiff of Abi's fear, like a distant shout. I push my head further out the window, trying to listen past the rush of the sea wind.

I swear, just for a second, I hear her scream. Maybe it's my imagination, but terror burns hot in my chest anyway.

"Hurry," I murmur, clutching at the car door. "Before she—"

And then it all hits me at once: a racing heartbeat, a rush of blood. A music I've been memorizing since I was eighteen years old.

"Here! Here!" I scream, dragging myself back in the car. "Turn left!"

Charlotte jerks the steering wheel, making the tires squeal. We slam into a narrow side street marked by a big painted sign: FUTURE SITE OF THE LA PLAYA DEL SOL SUBDIVISION! Half-built beach houses rise out of the sand like storks.

"Which one?" Charlotte breathes out. "I can't narrow it down."

I can. Abi's heartbeat is like a beacon screaming into the night. For a moment, I swear I can see it, like a lighthouse marking danger in the dark.

"That one there." I point to a dark house on the corner, illuminated by a yellow streetlamp. It's half-built, the walls nothing but plaster. But she's in there. And she's still alive.

Charlotte's barely slowed down before I fling the door open and throw myself out onto the street.

"What the fu—" That's all I hear before she slams on the brakes, flooding the street with red light. I take off running toward the house, my blood pumping hot in my veins. It's like when we killed people earlier, but so much more focused. I have a single purpose: to destroy whoever took Abi from me.

But then Charlotte jumps in front of me, stopping me in my tracks.

"Get the fuck out of my way," I snarl, moving to shove her aside. She stops me, of course, her grip on my wrist almost painful.

"You need to think this through," Charlotte says in a sharp whisper. "She's still alive in there. I can feel her."

So can I. It's all I can feel, actually, and I look past Charlotte at the beach house, my blood surging.

"She's not alone."

I jerk my gaze over to Charlotte's face. "I'll kill him," I say.

"Not if he kills you first." Charlotte lets go of my hand and steps back. "We technically do die, remember? We come back, but not right away. It could take months. Maybe even years. And that's time Abi can't afford."

I take deep, choking breaths. I don't care about dying. I only care about Abi living.

But I also know that Charlotte is right. There's someone else in there. Someone human. Someone male.

And his blood is up, too.

Anger twists in my chest. "I have to get to her," I snarl.

"I'm not trying to stop you," Charlotte says. "I'm telling you to be fucking careful and to go in there with a plan. This isn't like—"

"I've been killing men since I was thirteen years old," I say. "I know what I'm fucking doing."

Charlotte's eyes flash. "I'm sure you do. But you're not exactly in the best frame of mi—"

A scream tears through the night.

Charlotte freezes, and I shove her aside just as a swell of Abi's terror comes rushing over me with the sea wind.

Her terror—

And the fresh, sharp scent of her blood.

35

ABI

I stare at Kaplan, certain that I must be wrong. That I'm hallucinating.

He grins at me, baring his teeth. "Surprised to see me?" he asks as he saunters into the room. I press my back against the wall and squeeze my hand tighter around the rope.

He kicks the door shut, making the walls rattle. "Answer me, bitch."

Blood rushes into my ears. "Yes," I finally croak out, dizzy with fear.

He nods at that and saunters up to the mattress. I curl away from him on instinct as he towers over me. I'm used to seeing him in his sheriff's uniform, but he's dressed in dark tactical clothes now.

"I do think we need to have a little chat before we get started, though." He ambles around the mattress, and my heart feels like it's going to erupt out of my chest. But he doesn't touch me. He just bends down and picks up one of the photograph print-outs I knocked off the wall earlier. "I always hated that bitch," he mutters. "Ms. Staunton, *esquire*." He rolls his eyes as he says the final word, then throws the photograph over his shoulder. "She sucked my cock good, though. I think she thought it would save her life."

Nausea rises in my stomach, but I know I have to focus. I squeeze the rope. *You're free*, I tell myself. *You're free, and he doesn't know it.*

Kaplan crouches down beside me, his arms draped over his knees. For a long time, he doesn't say anything. Just stares at me, his face cruel in the shadows. Then he licks his lips.

"I know you've got questions for me," he says. "The other ones did. But you're keeping your mouth shut."

He reaches over to me like he's going to cup my face. I jerk my head away, and he immediately slaps me. Pain blooms on my cheek.

"Look at me," he orders. "There aren't any fucking stairs for you to push me down now, are there?" He grabs my chin and jerks my gaze over to him. "That's your M.O., isn't it? You did it to Blake. You did it to Julian, too. I don't give a fuck where they found his body."

Another surge of nausea. There were two of them. Julian Bernet, a stranger, and Sheriff Kaplan. All his disrespect over the last two years suddenly feels far more sinister. A sign I should have seen coming.

"Is that what you did to Julian?" Kaplan asks, leaning forward. "Shove him down the stairs?"

I shake my head, and Kaplan slaps me again. Harder this time. Tears brim along my lashes.

"Don't play stupid with me," he snarls. "You and I both know Julian didn't drink himself into a stupor out on Pier Fourteen. You killed him and then got that pathetic fucking simp to dispose of the body. Didn't you?"

I look up at Kaplan through the glimmer of my tears, and I realize, with a jolt, that he's talking about Nameless.

Kaplan doesn't know he's a killer, too.

"I always knew you were a danger to this community,"

Kaplan continues. "A little lying murderess. My nephew was your first, wasn't he?" Kaplan grabs my chin again, and anxiety spikes hard through my chest.

Blake Fletcher was Kaplan's nephew. How did I not know that? No wonder he tried to oppose my appointment.

And no wonder he killed Olivia Pearce and Heather Staunton.

"I can't believe you got off for that shit." Kaplan leans in close to me, his breath blowing hot over my face. I shudder, trying to squirm away from him. "And those two cunts helped you. Accomplices, as far as I'm concerned."

He shoves my head back, and it slams hard against the wall. The room spins as he stands up, his eyes still fixed on me. "Well," he says. "They're finally dead. And soon you will be, too." He smiles. Then, with a slow, deliberate movement, he adjusts his crotch.

I stare up at him, my fist tight around the rope. "Julian attacked me," I finally say. "Just like Blake did."

Kaplan freezes, rage crawling over his face. I know it makes my situation worse, pissing him off, but there's also something satisfying about it. Knowing how easily I can get under his skin.

"Blake never hurt anyone," Kaplan snarls. "Blake was a fucking All-Star offensive lineman."

"Blake was an asshole," I shoot back. "A bully. And a rapist." Heat floods through my face. "Just like you."

Kaplan hits me again, and it's not a slap, either. His fist connects with my cheek, and my head slams hard against the wall. Pain blooms in my temple, and the room blinks in and out of focus. All I hear is a kind of fuzzy static. Then—

"—a lying cunt."

I blink up at Kaplan, who sneers down at me, his face twisted and ugly. For a moment, it reminds me of Nameless's mask, and I feel a twist of sorrow inside me. A simp, Kaplan called him, but Nameless isn't here to protect me. He didn't come to me when I needed him most.

Now, I'm trapped in this terrible room, and it's like when I was sixteen. Blake had leered down at me, too. Smirked as he flung me up against the wall and shoved himself inside me.

And I was alone. No one came to save me. So I had to save myself.

I squeeze the rope in my fist. It's not much, but it's all I have. Just like I had the stairs when I was sixteen.

"I'm going to enjoy this so much," Kaplan says, running his hands down his dark jeans. "You have no idea how hard it was to hold off until the time was right."

There's too much space between us. I have a rope, and I need to get it around Kaplan's throat. I need him *on* me, a thought that fills me with a sick, squirmy disgust.

"How long have you been planning this?" I ask, the first thing I can think to say. He's already shown that he'll attack me if I piss him off enough. I just need to rile him up enough, then make my move before he can hurt me too much.

Kaplan smirks. "Since you showed back up with your fucking fancy degrees. I've been taking the trash out of this county for years."

My map flashes in my head. The deaths I marked with white.

The "accident" at the church. Lacerations to the throat.

Kaplan covered it up. He didn't have to make it look like an accident because he's the sheriff. He just had to say it was one. He might have done the same with the suicide on the beach. With any of the other white pin deaths in this town.

"How many people have you killed?" I rasp out.

"Not people," Kaplan says. "Subhumans. Like you."

I squeeze the rope tighter. He's not angry enough. He keeps leering at me, his eyes hungry, but he's savoring it. Savoring my fear.

Nameless's leering mask flashes through my head. *You're the focus of everything I do, Abi.* And yet I trusted him, a killer of nine people that I know of.

Of course I did. I'm a killer, too. A killer of one.

If I'm lucky, a killer of two.

We're all killers, all three of us. We all have that darkness burning like a black flame in our chests.

I pull on my rope, my breath tight. "Who was Julian?" I ask. Maybe that'll get him upset.

But Kaplan just scoffs. "He was another good man that you killed. That's all that you need to know."

I don't take my eyes off Kaplan's face. "He said that *he* killed Olivia Pearce."

Kaplan's eyes narrow at that, and I sense a thrum of anger. "He didn't do shit," Kaplan snaps. "Julian was a pussy. Couldn't handle the killing. He collected you whores for me. Happy to do it as long as he could have his way with 'em first." Kaplan's mouth splits into something like a smile. "Did you fuck him before you killed him?" he asks. "Just like you did with Blake?"

Rage surges inside me, a hot column of fire, and it takes all my willpower not to fling myself at him. My muscles quake with the force of not moving.

Kaplan laughs. "Oh, you don't like that, do you?" He reaches down and unzips his fly. Nausea surges into my throat, and I shift against the wall, holding onto the rope like a life preserver. *This is it*, I think, as Kaplan pulls out his half-limp cock and strokes it, watching me with a grin.

"I'm tired of talking," he says. "It's time to get started."

Kaplan throws himself on the mattress, jostling me backward. Then he reaches down and extracts a big hunting knife from his side. I hadn't noticed it before, but it must have been in a sheath on his thigh, blending into his black clothes.

I stare at it in horror now, the blade big and silver in the sallow light. All I have is a fucking rope.

"Let's get these clothes off you." Kaplan slides the blade up into my shorts. "Give me something to work with."

I can't stand the feel of his hands on me, wet and warm from perspiration. I can't stand the cold blade of the knife. I can't stand *him*, this monster who made my life hell in more ways than one.

So I act. I move in one frantic motion, knowing I only have one chance. I drag my arms forward and fling the rope out so that it slaps across Kaplan's face. He howls, more in surprise than anything else, and I scramble forward. That's not what I meant to do. I was trying to wrap it around his throat.

"You fucking *bitch*," he shouts, stumbling backward. "How the hell did you—"

I roll off the mattress and run for the door. Kaplan roars behind me, and I throw the door open and scramble out into the hallway. It's windowless. Dark. But there's a thin sliver of light up ahead, and I run toward it, arms pumping, keeping my eyes fixed on my escape—

A sudden, freezing coldness explodes in my upper back. I scream in agony and slam face-first onto the dusty floor. The pain brightens, and something hot and sticky flows down my back. I try to reach out, and I feel it, the handle of the knife, sticking out of the muscle of my upper back.

I also hear the footsteps behind me. Slow. Heavy. Mocking.

"You didn't really think you could get away from me that easily, did you, bitch?" More pain, in my scalp this time. Kaplan has me by the hair, and he wrenches me around so I can no longer see the exit. I sob, grabbing at his arm as he heaves me backward down the hallway. This is it. I lost my weapon. There are no stairs for me to shove him down, and the killer I told myself I could trust wasn't there when I needed him.

Kaplan wrenches the knife out of my back, and I scream again, feeling the blood pulse thick and hot out of the wound.

He shoves me against the wall and straddles me, pinning me down against the floor. Pain tears up from my wound.

Then he slices at my clothes, not caring if he cuts me, either. Blood splatters across my chest and my face and my arms in hot drops. I push against him, screaming and fighting him and trying to cover up my breasts all at once. And that only seems to excite him more. His breath blows hot across my face in sharp rasps, and he laughs like he's delighted.

"This is going to be so much fucking fun," he cackles as he rips my clothes away. "You have no idea what you're—"

He freezes. I stare at him, blinking through my pain and terror. I don't understand what made him stop.

"What the fuck was that?" he hisses, shoving his arm up under my chin to hold me in place. I squirm against him, choking down small gulps of air. He doesn't have his full weight on my trachea, but it's enough.

Kaplan looks away from me, squinting into the darkness.

That's when I hear it, too. Soft, heavy thuds.

Footsteps. The same footsteps that followed me into my examination room weeks ago.

And although it shouldn't, hope blooms in my chest. Because Nameless came for me after all.

"What the fuck are you doing here?" Kaplan snarls.

I manage to twist my head around, hope and fear warring inside myself. A figure steps toward us: tall and broad, big enough that he almost seems to fill the hallway.

It's him. Nameless.

"Let her go," he says, taking another step forward. And that's when I realize it. He's not wearing his mask. For the first time, I can see him.

Rowan Hanover has come to save me.

36

ROWAN

I've never wanted to kill someone more than I do in this moment. Abi, *my* Abi, is bleeding and half naked, her clothes hanging in tatters. And the man who did it to her is standing over her with his cock out.

It's Sheriff Kaplan. I've seen his face on re-election billboards, watched him on the news as he gave updates on a few of my kills.

And right now, he's looking over at me in confusion.

"You're Nash Deegan's son," he says, dumbfounded. "What are you—"

The idea that anyone, even this piece of shit, would think Nash Deegan is my father sets another dynamite explosion of rage off inside me. And this time, I let it propel me forward. I launch myself at Kaplan, moving on instinct and adrenaline. He shouts and swings his knife at me, but I catch it by the blade and wrench it out of his hand and throw it aside with a clatter. Then I fall upon him. I slam his head up against the wall, hard enough that white plaster rains around us. Then I throw him against the floor and leap down to slam my fists into his face, over and over.

I never kill like this. I never kill like a wild animal. It's always planned, calculated. But this afternoon with Charlotte loosened something inside me, and my terror at almost losing Abi set it free completely. I don't even care that it's the sheriff, a man I've always known could ruin my life. All I know, right now, is that he's human, that he hurt Abi, and that I am going to beat him until he's no longer breathing.

Kaplan squirms beneath me, trying to get away. I grab his shoulders and slam his head back. He grunts; blood splatters across the floor. Then I punch him again, over and over and over, my fist sinking deeper and deeper into the mess of his face. Some of his teeth scatter across the floor. Hot blood sprays across my face—*my face,* and not my killing face. For the first time, I feel it on my skin, as warm and sweet as one of Abi's kisses.

Kaplan twitches beneath me, and I hit him harder. You wouldn't know it's him anymore. His face is nothing but blood and bone and swollen muscle. But I keep going.

Because he was going to take Abi away from me. He was going to torture her. Brutalize her. Rape her. Kill her. And he deserves to be punished.

The blood flows thicker, pooling across the floor. There are other things mixed in with it, too. Brain. Bits of bone. My fist sinks through his face, and I yank it out, dripping with gore.

And then I feel Abi's eyes on me.

All my bloodlust evaporates in an instant. The world goes from red to black. I freeze and look over at her, suddenly aware of what I look like: Blood-covered. Feral.

Faceless.

"Rowan," she whispers in a ragged voice. Her eyes are two bright spots in the dark. "Rowan?"

She repeats my name like a question, and I can hear a tearfulness in the way she says it that makes me slump backward.

"All this time?" she asks. "At the hotel—when we went for

coffee—and the golf course—" Her eyes widen, and her mouth drops open. "Oh my god, that's how you knew. I thought you were spying on us—I'm so fucking stupid—"

"You're not stupid," I say immediately. "I didn't want you to know."

She stares at me over the mangled corpse between us. Kaplan's dead, of course. He was dead a long time ago, but I kept going. If Abi weren't here, I think I'd still be going, grinding him down into hamburger for thinking he could hurt her.

"R-Rowan," she whispers, and the truth is, I like it, hearing her say that name. *My* name. I shift toward her, moving slow and cautious. I don't want to frighten her away. When I step over the body, and she doesn't run, I take that as a sign to keep going.

"Why didn't you—" She shakes her head, eyes tracking my movements. "Why didn't you tell me? I thought—I thought I wasn't good enough for you—for Rowan—"

My heart twists as I kneel beside her. Her breasts are bare, gleaming in the soft moonlight from the open door at the end of the hallway, but she doesn't try to cover them up. Not from me.

"You're perfect for me." I cup her face with thinking, and her cheek darkens with blood. But she doesn't pull away. In fact, she does the opposite. She leans into my touch, her eyes still fixed on mine. On my face. "So you're perfect for Rowan, too."

Abi takes in a sharp, shuddery breath.

"Rowan was my disguise," I say, because I feel like she deserves an explanation. "I thought he wasn't the real me. That's why I wore my—my killing face. To show who I really am."

Abi wraps her hand around my wrist. She's shaking with fear, and I pull her into me, pressing her body against my chest.

"That's how I wanted you to see me," I whisper. "The true me. I realize now that Rowan is me, too. But this—"

Abi kisses me.

It startles me, the forcefulness in how she moves, the sudden warmth of her lips against mine. But my blood is boiling from all the day's killing, and I return that forcefulness, dragging my fingers up into her hair to hold her in place as I explore her mouth with my tongue.

Then, just as abruptly, Abi jerks away, her eyes blazing. "Where were you tonight?" she spits out. "I thought you abandoned me."

"I will never fucking abandon you." I hold her in place, never taking my eyes off her. "I'm so sorry, Abi. I should have been there. I know that. I'm never letting you out of my sight again."

Then I pull into another kiss, rough and violent, and she moans against my mouth. I kiss along her jaw until I find her pulse point. "I'm so sorry," I murmur. "I'm so fucking sorry. "

"How'd you find me?" she gasps.

I nip at her neck, making her moan and roll her hips. "That's complicated, too," I say. "And I'll tell you later. But right now—"

I pull away and stare down at her, beautiful with her swollen lips and my bloody handprint across her cheek.

"Right now I really want to fuck you," I say.

I still expect her to scream. To run. To call me a monster, the way my mother did. Instead, she shivers and wraps her hand around the back of my head.

"I want to fuck you, too," she says breathlessly.

It's all I need to hear. It's all I've ever wanted to hear. I drag her into me for another long, devouring kiss, and I run my bloody hands over her body to pull away the last tatters of her clothes. She makes a sharp hissing sound as I pull her shirt over her head.

"Careful," she says. "He stabbed me."

"He *what?*" Panic nearly overtakes my lust, but Abi pulls me in close to her.

"I'm fine," she breathes. "Now fuck me, Rowan."

And then she pulls me in for a kiss, and I lay her down, gently, onto the floor. I lay her down in Kaplan's blood.

Abi moans when it touches her skin, and I'm afraid I'm hurting her. But then she gasps, "It feels good," and I know she's horrified because I can feel it. But I can also feel how turned on she is, too. "It's so warm."

"Good," I growl, kissing down the valley between her breasts. "Because this is where I want to make you come."

Abi moans at that. She moans when I pull her nipple into my mouth. Moans when I lick away the blood from the tiny cuts Kaplan made in her skin. As I kiss her, I touch her between her legs, running my fingers through the hot wetness already gathering there and mixing it with the warm, thick blood.

"Rowan," she gasps, grabbing at my arms. Hearing my name sends shudders through my body, all of them rippling toward my heavy, swollen cock. "It shouldn't feel this is good."

"But it does." I slide one finger inside her, rubbing against her inner wall. Abi groans—a dark, throaty sound that makes me feel like the feral creature that I am. "No one's ever going to hurt you again, Abi. I swear it."

Abi's eyes shift toward mine, her gaze unfocused from lust.

"I swear it," I say again, right before I spread her legs wide, revealing her glistening, blood-covered pussy.

I shift between her legs and pull my cock out and press it against her entrance. It's agony—every cell in my body wants to shove inside her—but I take my time. Teasing her. Brushing my cockhead against her clit. Abi moans and grabs at me. "Please," she pants. "Please just fuck me, Rowan."

"I love when you do that." I slide myself halfway inside her and rub her clit, making her writhe around in the blood.

"Do what?" She gazes up at me through her fluttering eyelashes.

"Say my name," I growl.

"Rowan," she gasps.

I shove in to the hilt, and Abi's hot, slick pussy clenches around me. I brace my arms on either side of her body as I roll my hips up to the seam of her legs. Abi groans and jerks up toward me, faster and harder than I'm currently fucking her.

"You want it like that?" I murmur, running my hands through Kaplan's blood so I can smear it up around Abi's waist and over her tits, painting her in crimson. "You want it rough?"

"Yes," she growls back at me.

"You said you were hurt—"

"Rowan," she says, her eyes glittering. "I want you to fuck me like you killed him."

Her words go straight to my cock. So does the fire in her eyes, searing and hot, and I realize that Abi's showing me her real self, too. She may be human. She may not be a killer, not really. But she craves all this depravity, and I know I'm the one who's going to give to her for the rest of her life.

I rise onto my knees so I can slam into her, over and over, hard enough that her body jostles and slides through the blood. And with every violent thrust, I can taste her pleasure as it drifts through the air. It tastes like blood and wine.

I fuck her as hard as I can, plowing into her perfect, dripping cunt. And Abi unravels for me, moaning and grinding against my hips, the blood drying on our skin until we're stuck together. I wrap my fingers around her throat, pinning her down, and when she looks up at me, her eyes brim with heat and lust.

"You're mine," I whisper, matching the words to the rhythm of our fucking. "I'm yours. Do you understand?"

"Yes," Abi pants out. Her body quakes with small, rippling contractions.

"You're about to come, aren't you?" I lean close, still plowing into her, not daring to change my rhythm.

Abi nods, her lips glossy.

"Good. I want you to come in Kaplan's blood." I hunch over her, still thrusting into her. "And I want you looking at my face while I do."

I tighten my grip around her throat—not to cut off her air, but to hold her head in place. Already her orgasm's starting. I can feel it, the way her muscles clamp down around my cock. But I can hear it, too: her frantic breaths. Her pounding heart, beating as fast as Kaplan's when I killed him.

"Rowan," she whimpers, her eyes boring into mine, drinking in my face—my real face, my killing face. They're the same, under her gaze. "Rowan, I'm going to—"

She cuts herself off with a wail, and I press my weight down on her lower body as her pussy ripples and contracts around me because I don't want her arching her gaze away from me. And she doesn't, my sweet human girl. She keeps her eyes fixed on mine as the pleasure makes her whole body shake.

"Perfect," I breathe, dragging my hand away so I can fuck her through the quivering aftershocks. And so I can look at her, too: spread out on the floor and drenched in the blood of a man who hated her. Who thought he could harm her.

If anyone ever tries to harm her again, I'll do the same to them.

I dig my hands into her hips, rutting hard against her. Abi moans, her eyes rolled back, the blood beautiful on her pale skin. My own orgasm is building, a tension deep in my balls, and I give one impossibly deep thrust and then it spills out in her pussy in hot, pulsing bursts.

Then I slump on top of her, breathing hard. For a moment, I'm afraid she's going to push me away. But she doesn't. Instead, she nuzzles against me and wraps her arms around my shoulders, drawing me in close.

"Thank you," she whispers, over and over. "Thank you. Thank you."

I pull away just enough to catch her gratitude with my mouth, and then I kiss it out of her. I keep kissing her, there in Kaplan's blood, in the place he thought he could take her from me.

But he couldn't. He didn't.

I may be a killer, but I saved her life. And that's a treasure no one can ever take from me.

37

ABI

Two days later, I'm on a rented catamaran at sunrise. It jostles over the waves as we ride out on the Gulf, toward the horizon where the sun is just starting to come up. The sky is pink and grey and gauzy, like an old silk dress.

I sit at the bow, the wind blowing my hair back from my face, and think I should be traumatized by everything that's happened. But I'm on a boat in the soft light of dawn, and all I feel is calm and happy. When Rowan led me out of that half-built beach house, his shirt draped over my shoulders to hide my nudity, I wasn't sobbing the way I was when I left Blake Fletcher's house that night ten years ago.

I was content. And I was safe.

Just like I'm content now.

"Charlotte says we're almost to the spot."

I twist around to find Rowan standing on the deck behind me, looking shy and handsome with his floppy dark curls and pretty dark eyes. I don't know how I managed to look into those eyes so many times in the funeral parlor and not connect them to the Rowan Hanover—the man I thought was too good for me. The man I thought didn't *deserve* me.

All that time, he was watching me behind the mask of a monster.

"Do you need my help?" I ask.

"If you want." Rowan slides into the plastic bench beside me and winds his hands through mine. "But me and Charlotte can take care of it."

Charlotte. She had been waiting beside a rental car when Rowan led me out of the beach house. She smiled and held out her hand and said, "I'm Rowan's half-sister. Let's get you home."

It's been two days since then, and they've passed by in a blur.

They didn't actually take me home, but to Rowan's house, a tidy little bungalow set into the dunes. There, he washed me off in his bathtub, his touch shocking gently compared to his earlier brutality. Afterward, he pressed butterfly stitches from a First Aid kit into the knife wound and washed the other cuts with stinging witch hazel. Then he tucked me into his bed.

I slept.

When I woke up, he was still there, and he brushed my hair out of my eyes and said I didn't need to worry about Kaplan, that Charlotte knew what she was doing, and it was all going to be taken care of.

And that's what we're doing now. Taking care of it.

Rowan squeezes my hand a little tighter and smiles at me, that shy, nervous smile I first saw when I went to the Palm Breeze Hotel. When I was investigating him, following the breadcrumbs he left to draw us together.

I'm still not sure what it says about me. But I'm not so confused that I didn't get on this boat, or that I'm not going to sit beside him as the sea wind blows across my face, our hands intertwined.

"What are you thinking?" he asks suddenly.

I look over at him, the waves spraying us with a fine mist of seawater. "I was thinking about my investigation," I say. "The letters."

"Your dark whisperer," he says.

"What?" I laugh a little, shifting toward him as the boat careens over the wave.

Rowan's cheeks turn a soft red. "That's what I was spelling out," he says. "I was introducing myself."

I stare at him, the dawn light softening his features. I like it, being able to look at him. To see his big, expressive eyes more clearly. The dimple in his left cheek. The crook in his smile.

"I thought it was about me," I finally say. "*Your darkness*, maybe." I fold my hand on top of his. "I thought you'd seen it. My darkness."

He studies me. "You only have a little," he finally says.

"Just enough." I smile.

He looks like he's about to say something else when Charlotte steps onto the deck, her red hair in a big knot on the top of her head. "Sorry to interrupt," she says. "But we're at the spot. I'm about to kill the engine."

Rowan nods. "Be there in a sec."

She flashes a grin at us and ducks into the pilothouse. Rowan sighs.

"You looked like you were going to say something," I say softly, my heart fluttering.

"Let me take care of this first," he says. "You don't have to help."

He means it. I can see it in his eyes. But the truth is, I want to. Kaplan never made my life easy, and then he tried to end it. He ended the lives of two women who helped me when I was a scared, terrified teenager.

He deserves it, to be chopped up and thrown overboard into a Gulf stream that will take him out into the Atlantic Ocean, hundreds of miles from here.

"I'll help," I say.

We stand up just as the boat's engine cuts out, stilling us in the soft, rolling waves. The light is still gauzy from the sunrise, and it casts everything in a sort of pinkish wash that makes this much more beautiful, much more idyllic, than I suppose it technically is.

But then, I've never been one for the idyllic, have I?

Rowan and I walk around to the stern of the boat, where two big coolers sit waiting. I know what's in them.

Charlotte's already there, her hands in black gloves. She tosses a pair to Rowan, then raises her eyebrows at me.

I nod, and she tosses me my own pair.

When Rowan opens the first ice chest, it's a tangle of limbs. I stare at it, trying to comprehend that this flesh was the source of all my terror for the last month. This meat destroyed Olivia Pearce and Heather Staunton. Others, too.

He's nothing, now. Fish food.

Charlotte grabs an arm and tosses it overboard, and then Rowan does the same with a foot. I step forward, memories running jagged through my thoughts. The blood-stained mattress. The photographs on the wall. Kaplan's hot, sour breath on my skin.

Rowan, stepping into the hallway, just as I knew I was about to die.

I pick up a chunk of Kaplan's torso. Charlotte and Rowan cut him up while I was recovering, and the work is choppy and amateurish. My coroner's brain is already filling out the report, even though I don't need to. As far as Rosado is concerned, Kaplan disappeared.

I throw the meat overboard and listen to the satisfying *thunk* as it hits the water.

We work in silence, the three of us. It's not hard. I'm used to dead bodies and blood. So are they.

When we finish, when the last of him is on his way south,

Charlotte announces, "I'll finish the rest of the cleanup. I know —" She looks at Rowan. "I know you need to, uh, talk."

My anxiety flares suddenly, and I look between them. I'm still not sure what I think of Charlotte. She's been kind to me, but there's something dangerous about her, something that goes beyond the fact that she's a killer, too.

"Talk about what?" I say, trying to break the silence.

"It's nothing bad," Rowan says. "Not as bad as that, anyway." He tilts his head toward the ice chests. "I mean, you already know the worst thing about me."

I look at him, vaguely aware that Charlotte has turned away, like she's giving us privacy.

"Let's go back to the viewing bench," he says sheepishly. Then he peels off his gloves and drops them next to the ice chests. A beat later, I do the same, still quaking with uncertainty. Not fear, though. It's crazy, but I'm not scared of him.

How could I be, after Rowan saved my life?

The wind blows across the deck, washing away any lingering scent of death. All I smell is the salt of the sea. Rowan guides me over to the bench and sits me down, and I can sense how nervous he is—shaking his leg, twisting his hands up together, letting his hair flop into his eyes.

"You're kinda freaking me out."

I mean it as a joke, but Rowan jerks his gaze up to me with something like alarm. "You don't seem scared," he says.

I blink in surprise. "I'm not scared. As confusing as all this is—" I gesture out at the boat, at the water, at Kaplan floating away. "I'm not scared. Not of you."

Rowan studies me with those dark, serious eyes.

"I like this," I say softly. "Seeing you. Without the mask."

A startled smile flickers across his lips. "I—I like it, too. It's —different. But I'm getting used to it. I'm getting used to a lot of things."

I frown. Sea spray blows up between us, bright and

sparkling, and for a second, I think I see a rainbow shimmering in the air.

"That's what I wanted to—" Rowan moves closer to me and takes my hand and then looks down at it. So do I, our fingers braided together. Coroner and killer. And yet I don't want to let him go.

"Charlotte told me some things about myself," he says, and I look up at his face again. He tilts his head away from me, toward the ocean. The wind blusters, bringing more sea spray. "This is going to sound crazy."

"Crazier than everything else about you?"

"Yes." He's serious, and his hand tightens around mine. "She says I'm something—not quite human."

The confession hangs on the air between us. I feel a flash of panic that I'm out on this boat with him and Charlotte, miles from the shore. It flares and fades, like a guttering candle, but Rowan still jerks his gaze up to meet mine and says, "Don't be afraid of me."

"I'm no—" I cut myself off under the intensity of his eyes. There he is, my Nameless. "I'm not," I finish weakly.

"You are a little." Rowan's gaze never leaves mine. "This is what I mean. I can sense things, Abi. I can tell when you're afraid or when you're happy. I can track scents, like a dog. *That's* how I was able to find you."

I stare at him, a kind of hollowness in my chest. Of course I had wondered about that when I was tucked away in Rowan's bed, still trying to process what exactly had happened. But then, he was Nameless. And Nameless always knew how to appear when I needed him most.

But now, out here on the ocean, the waves lapping against the side of the catamaran with a soft, rhythmic slapping, I feel it—that sense that I'm looking at a predator. I felt it before, and I assumed it was because he's a killer. Now, though...

Now, I'm not so sure.

"I know it sounds insane." He moves closer so that our knees bump. "And I honestly don't know what it means, really. Just that—I've always known, my whole life, there's something different about me. I thought it was because I—you know." He gives me a sheepish grin, and I ought to feel that panic again, but I don't. Because I know, more than anything, that he'll never *you know* me. "And Charlotte's gonna help me figure things out. There are others, like me."

Rowan's grip tightens. His eyes gleam.

"I just hope," he says softly. "That you'll be with me as I figure things out. I really like—" He hesitates, shakes his head. "No, I love you, Abi. I've loved you from the moment you first came to Rosado, and I haven't stopped."

My breath catches in my throat. I stare at him as the sea wind blows his hair across his eyes, as he watches me. A killer. And maybe something else—some inhuman monster that can move out of the shadows and track me down when I'm in danger.

And he loves me.

The thing is, I can feel it, too, that love. I feel it pumping like blood through my body. It's almost indistinguishable from madness—the madness that makes my body heat at death and darkness. The madness I've always tucked away, and only let loose when Nameless came into my home and drew it out of me with his touch.

Not Nameless. Rowan.

I pull my hand away from his to cup his face. His *actual* face. I want to feel the skin and muscle and bone there, not rubber.

He's showing himself to me. And I've shown myself to him.

I lean forward and kiss him, as gently as the first time he kissed me. My heart pounds. I suspect I'm condemning myself to some kind of hell, but I don't care. Not with Rowan at my side.

"I think I love you, too," I whisper against his mouth. "No matter what you are."

He smiles. I feel it more than I see it.

And then he's kissing me in earnest, drawing me into his chest, and I know I will happily fall into whatever darkness he lays out for me.

EPILOGUE

ABI

SIX MONTHS LATER

I hum along to the music spilling out of the speakers, some old pop song that was popular when I was in college. Penelope, Chloe, and I used to dance to it during late nights when we smuggled wine and weed into the dorm, and it always makes me think of them.

They know about Rowan now. Well, most of it. There are some things you can't share over Zoom calls, but the next time we're together in person—maybe. I don't like keeping secrets from them.

I move around the body on the examination table. A woman named Mildred Morris from the nearby retirement home, dead from a stroke. I already found the clot that blocked the blood flowing to her brain, and I'm moving through the rest of the autopsy on autopilot. I've got a bit of a backlog, although things are settling down now that Rosado has finally elected a new sheriff. A woman, surprisingly, one of Kaplan's captains who came forward with evidence that he had covered up at least three murders. She'd been investigating him, it seems.

I like her enough that I told Rowan he has to take his kills out of the county, so I don't have to cover for him. And of course he agreed.

After all, he doesn't need them to speak to me anymore, does he?

My phone's timer goes off, startling me out of my thoughts. It's 6:30 P.M., and although I need to catch up on my backlog, that timer is sacrosanct. It tells me when to stop for the day.

Nervous excitement flutters around in my belly.

I turn it off and clean up my work as quickly as I can, then slide Mildred back into her refrigeration unit. I wash my hands, scrubbing them with soap until they feel tight and antiseptic. The whole time, my excitement builds up. I've always liked winter—the empty beaches, the cooler weather. But now, I like the early dark, too.

As soon as I'm done, I do a once-over to check that everything is in its place. Then I go out and lock up the examination room and head outside by way of the back door.

The night is chilly and windswept, and I wish I had thrown on a sweater before coming out here. Not that it matters. I'll be plenty warm in no time.

I switch on my phone's flashlight and shine it out into the surrounding trees, flashing it over the dark, bare branches. "Here I am," I murmur, knowing he can hear me. It's shocking, the things Rowan knows and senses. But exciting, too.

I walk around the side of the house, my heart beating fast. All I can hear is the wind, howling as it blows through the trees. By the time I get to my flower garden—dead for the winter, full of old, dried-up stems that I leave out for the insects—I'm shivering, my arms wrapped tight around my chest. But I don't go inside.

Something crackles behind me, and I whip around, shining my flashlight. My fear blooms a little, although it's not real fear. It's horror movie fear. Haunted house fear. The kind of thrilling fear you experience when you know you aren't really in danger.

"Hello?" I call out, my voice catching on the wind. "Is someone out there?"

I already know the answer, but it's still fun to pretend.

More rustling footsteps. I whip around again, bringing the flashlight with me. And this time, I'm rewarded with a brief glimpse of a dark figure in a twisted mask.

My excitement surges. So does an anticipatory heat between my legs.

Then I take off running.

I bound across the front yard, pumping my arms and legs through the cold, gusting wind. Footsteps fall into a rhythm behind me. He's going slow. Giving me time to try and get away from him.

I have *never* gotten away from him, and I don't ever want to.

I slam up against the gate of the cemetery and drop my phone into the grass, face down so the flashlight shoots a column of light up around the fence. I fumble with the unlocked latch and swing the gate open, feeling his presence behind me, nameless and faceless. I risk one glance over my shoulder and find him standing on the curb, watching me in the dark.

I duck through the gate and run into the cemetery.

Rowan follows.

This time, he isn't going slow. I run as fast as I can, my body stiff from the cold, but he's always faster. His heavy boots pound against the dirt, and I weave through the tombstones, zig-zagging my way toward the row of pecan trees.

I don't make it. Strong arms grab my waist and pull me backward, my feet lifting off the grass. I shriek in surprise, but a gloved hand slaps across my mouth, muffling me. I moan into the familiar leather and slump back against his sturdy body, already squirming with need.

"Where do you think you're going?" Rowan rasps into my ear.

It's funny, how different he sounds when he's wearing the mask—his killing face, he still calls it sometimes, although that's rare. And getting rarer, the longer we're together.

"Let me go," I say into the glove, my words muffled. Lies, and we both know it.

Rowan chuckles. "I don't think so."

He whirls me around and tosses me into the cold grass. I cry out and make a half-hearted attempt to crawl away. He's too quick for me, though. He throws himself on top of me, pinning my arms overhead. His mask leers, and my clit pulses at the sight of those ugly features.

"You kept me waiting," Rowan purrs, wedging his hips between my legs. I can feel his erection straining against his pants. "You know I don't like to wait."

I whimper softly, rolling my hips up against him. "I'm sorry, baby," I mutter. "You know how busy I've been."

"You work too much." Rowan pins down both of my arms with one hand while he slides the other between my legs to gently cup my pussy, his palm grinding up against his clit.

I moan softly, bucking into his touch. "Well," I pant out, "Not all of us have—oh, fuck! Seasonal jobs—"

Rowan yanks my yoga pants down and grunts in appreciation when he sees I'm wearing nothing underneath. I squirm against the cold ground, aching with need. Rowan just slides his fingers along my slit, teasing me.

"I work all year long," Rowan growls. "Someone's got to keep you coroners busy."

He slides one finger inside my pussy, and I groan at the intrusion. No matter how many different ways he touches me— out here in the cold graveyard, up in my warm bed, in the big sunny suite on the top floor of the Palm Breeze Hotel, which is always unbooked this time of year—nothing compares to that first touch of his leather-covered finger pushing up into my cunt.

"Fuck," I gasp. "More."

He pushes another finger inside me, stretching me wide to the cold. "Like that?"

"Yes," I gasp, shoving my hips toward his hand. For a few minutes, he fucks me with his hand, sliding his two fingers and out of me with his slow, careful precision. I shudder, legs quaking, on the verge of orgasm—

And he pulls his hand away.

"Not yet." He slides his hand up under my shirt, then under my bra, so he can squeeze and massage my breasts. I stare up at his mask. At his eyes, burning behind the mask. Burning straight into me.

"Take it off," I say huskily. "I want to see you."

He leans back on his heels, taking his hands with him. "Touch yourself," he orders, and I do, snaking one hand between my legs and grabbing at my breast with the other. For a moment, he just watches me, silent and dark like the killer he is.

Then he pulls the mask away.

It's still a surprise, seeing Rowan beneath that twisted face. Sweet, shy Rowan, who curls up on the couch with me to watch horror movies. Who helps me make dinner and holds my hand whenever we walk along the beach, just out of reach of the cold, foamy waves.

But Rowan isn't what he seems to be. And neither, I know, am I.

"Better?" he asks, still in his rough, gravelly killer's voice.

"Fuck me," I pant. "Please."

Rowan grins. Then he unzips his jeans and pulls his cock out. I can barely see it in the dark. He bats it against my pussy, against my clit. More teasing. I moan.

"You're so fucking mean," I whine.

"I'm a killer," he says. "Be grateful this is all I'm doing."

I smack him for that. Or try to. He catches my hand before I can make impact.

"I do the spanking around here," he says.

Then he rolls me over, pressing me face down into the grass. I groan and lift my ass for him. The first strike of his leather-covered hand rings out into the cold, windy night and makes my flesh sting.

"Again," I pant.

He hits the other side of my ass, a little harder. Heat sparks in my clit. The third strike makes me groan and shudder, and Rowan rewards me by sliding his fingers down into my slit again.

"I can feel how wet you are even through my gloves." He draws his hand away and climbs on top of me, his cock pressing up against my pussy. He pulls my hair to the side and nuzzles my neck, his mouth leaving blooming spots of warmth on my skin. "Are you ready for me, little detective? Ready for your killer's cock?"

"Yes," I cry. "Please. I can't fucking stand it anymore."

"I love when you beg like that." Rowan shifts around behind me, arranging his cock at my entrance. I spread my legs and lift my ass in anticipation.

He shoves in with one thrust, and I cry out again, digging my hands into the dirt.

"Fuck, I'll never get tired of that," he gasps. It doesn't sound like he's talking to me but to the dark, sweeping night. The night that brought us together.

He braces his arms on the ground beside me as he starts to rock into my cunt, slow and teasing. I push up on my elbows so I can rock back into him, matching his rhythm. The old, mossy gravestones rise around us, shielding us from anyone driving by on Hatch Street. And I don't care that it's cold and damp and windy. This is exactly where I want my killer to fuck me—in the dark, surrounded by the dead.

His thrusts quicken. So does his breath, hot against the top of my back. I bite my lip, trying to stop my moans and failing. They fall out of my mouth like flower petals, small and inconsequential. But his thick cock is striking against my G-spot, pulling the pleasure out of my body.

"You're going to come for me," he pants, lowering himself down on top of me so he can kiss the back of my neck between words. "I can feel it."

"Tell me," I pant out.

"Your heart's already racing," he purrs. "All the blood is going to your cunt."

I fuck back on him harder.

"I can smell your arousal," he continues, brushing his lips over my upper back. "Sweet as orchids. It changes right before you come."

I squeeze the dirt and clench my pussy around his cock. I'm right on the edge, all my muscles squeezing up tight.

"That scent," he purrs. "The scent of you coming? It's my favorite fucking smell in the whole world. It's like lemon and lilies and death all wrapped up together."

I groan, loud enough that someone could hear. I don't care. Rowan thrusts harder.

"I can smell it now," he whispers into my ear. "You're on your way, little detective."

My orgasm hits me in waves. I scream into the grass, bucking up against Rowan as pleasure surges through me like a rip tide, threatening to drag me away. But Rowan pins me to the ground, still fucking me, dragging the orgasm out until I think it won't ever end.

"Perfect," he sighs, riding me harder. He squeezes my waist, holding me down. "You're so fucking perfect, Abi."

Then his hips shudder and still, and I whimper as I feel a surge of hot seed inside me. He slumps down on top of me and kisses his way until he finds my mouth. It's awkward, twisting around like this, but I like it, too. I like his weight on top of me, pressing me into the ground. It makes me feel safe.

"Thank you," I whisper into his kiss.

Rowan rolls me over, then presses himself on top of my body, still pinning me down. His eyes search mine. They always seem bright in the dark. Predator's eyes.

"You don't ever have to thank me for that," he says.

Then he kisses me, his hand tangling up in my hair. I wrap my legs around his hips, holding him against me.

The wind blows through the cemetery. The night drapes over us like a blanket. And this is the only place I ever want to be.

THE END

Thank you for reading *Half the Summer's Night!* I hope you enjoyed it.

The series continues with Chloe's story in Under the Killing Moon. And if you'd like to learn more about Charlotte and the other Hunters, be sure to check out the other books in the series, starting with Bird on a Blade.

You can also read a spicy extended epilogue that takes place on Rowan and Abi's first anniversary by signing up for my newsletter here: rosebitterly.com/newsletter.

UNDER THE KILLING MOON

4.17.2026

I thought it was my dream house. Then he turned it into a nightmare.

CHLOE

When I inherit a gorgeous lake house from my grandparents, I'm thrilled at the prospect of home ownership, even if it is in the middle of nowhere.

But I find out quickly enough that the lake outside my back door has a history, and it's not a pretty one: Drownings. Disappearances. And a ghost story that goes back sixty years.

The locals say an undead killer haunts the woods around the lake, taking out trespassers. I figure they're just trying to scare me back to the city.

That is, until I notice him: a dark figure watching from the shadows.

And it turns out I might have to believe in ghost stories after all.

THEO

All I want is to be left alone.

But the developers came and built houses on my land anyway. I tell myself that as long as the strangers stay on their side of the lake, I'll let them live. But if they cross the water, they'll meet my blade.

Until *she* does it.

Chloe Monroe is the first trespasser in sixty years that I don't want to kill. And I think, at first, it'll be fine. That I don't *have* to hurt anyone.

I just hope I can keep the urges quiet.

I just hope I don't feel the pull of the killing moon—

Right to her back door.

Read Here

ABOUT THE AUTHOR

Rose Bitterly is a hopeless romantic who has been reading and writing scary stories since elementary school—imagine her excitement when she learned you could blend the two! Today, she writes dark, immersive horror romances featuring slashers and other monsters, all shot through with a hint of the occult. Visit her online at rosebitterly.com.

Never miss a new book! Sign up for Rose's mailing list and receive free bonus stories: https://www.rosebitterly.com/news letter.

ALSO BY ROSE BITTERLY

HUNTER'S HEART

Bird on a Blade

The Fire Went Wild

Turn That River Red

Half the Summer's Night

Under the Killing Moon

THE DEVIL'S COURTS

A Dream of the Forest

A Nightmare in Her Heart